CHAOS

OF THE

SENSES

CHAOS

OF THE

SENSES

AHLEM MOSTEGHANEMI

Translated from the Arabic by Nancy Roberts

B L O O M S B U R Y

LONDON · NEW DELHI · NEW YORK · SYDNEY

First published in Great Britain 2015

First published in English in 2007 by The American
University in Cairo Press

Copyright © 2007, 2015 by Ahlem Mosteghanemi
English translation copyright © 2015 by Nancy Roberts

The moral right of the author has been asserted

Every reasonable effort has been made to trace copyright holders of
material reproduced in this book, but if any have been inadvertently
overlooked the publishers would be glad to hear from them

Bloomsbury Publishing Plc
50 Bedford Square
London
WC1B 3DP

www.bloomsbury.com

Bloomsbury is a trademark of Bloomsbury Publishing Plc

Bloomsbury Publishing, London, New Delhi, New York and Sydney

A CIP catalogue record for this book is available from the British Library

ISBN 978 1 4088 5728 1

10 9 8 7 6 5 4 3 2 1

Typeset by Integra Software Services Pvt. Ltd.
Printed and bound in Great Britain by CPI Group (UK) Ltd, Croydon CR0 4YY

Sometimes we have to write an entire novel in order to answer a one-word question: 'Why?'

Then we discover that the answer is found in other small words. It's the cycle of life with its never-ending circles, from 'Beginning' to 'Inevitably'. However, we lend no weight to the smallest words, even though it is precisely these that determine our fates. Nor are we wary of men of silence, because we are only suspicious of what is said. And herein lies women's folly.

To the men of silence, and to the chaos within us that they leave in their wake.

Contents

Chapter One

Beginning

As he hadn't with other people, he wanted to put sincerity to the test with her. He wanted to experience with her the satisfaction of loyalty born of hunger. He wanted to nurture love amid the mines of the senses.

As for her, she didn't know how she had found her way to him.

With a single glance, he could strip away her reason and clothe her in his lips. What confidence she needed to resist that glance!

And what silence he needed to prevent the flames from betraying his secret!

He was a man who knew how to touch both a woman and words with the same hidden blaze.

With a kind of mock lethargy, he would embrace her from behind the way he might embrace a fleeing sentence.

His lips would pass over her with deliberate slowness, and at a studied distance, in order to produce the maximum arousal. They would graze her mouth without quite kissing it, slide down towards her neck without actually touching it, then ascend again with the same deliberate slowness as though he were kissing her with nothing but his breath.

This man who determined her fate with his lips, writing her and erasing her without kissing her – how could she forget everything that hadn't happened between the two of them?

At a late hour of longing, his love would take her unawares.

He would come at a late hour of the night, surprising her between one oblivion and another, set her ablaze with desire, and leave.

She would gasp as untamed steeds of longing took her to him. His love would be as a luminous state in the darkness of the senses. He would send electricity into the recesses of her soul, awaken her inner madness, then be on his way.

She sat in the seat across from his absence – there, where he had once sat across from her – recalling how smitten she had been with him in the beginning.

What would she do with all those mornings without the ghost of his fragrance? He had violated a truce with love; he had left a vacant seat belonging to memory; he had left doors ajar in anticipation; he had left a woman. Until he came, she would love him as though he weren't going to come, so that he would come.

If he did come – the man of time in yearning – she feared that her unexpected elation would expose his presence after nothing but ink had exposed his absence.

For him to come, if he should come . . .

How many lies would she need in order to go on living as though he had never come? And how much honesty would she need in order to convince him that she had really waited for him?

If . . .

As usual, he had skirted love. So she wouldn't ask him what road he had taken to reminiscence, or who had led him to a woman who had waited for him so long that she'd stopped waiting.

If . . .

Yearning had swept him towards her mid-flight. Hence, she wouldn't ask him the reasons for his forced landing.

She knew, as a sailor's wife knows, that the sea would steal him away from her, and that he was the man of inevitable departures.

Until he came.

He was a master of time, a master of impossibilities, a voice that traversed continents, a sorrow that traversed long evenings, and an eternally dazzling first night.

Until he became hers again, until she became his again, she would go on wondering at every late hour of the night: What is he doing now?

Then one day he came back.

He was a man who embodied the words of Oscar Wilde: 'Human beings created language in order to hide their feelings.' Whenever he spoke, he was clothed with language, but the silences in between stripped him naked.

As for her, she was still a woman of repercussions, who hurriedly, restlessly, who took words off and put them on again.

3

Here she was, her voice naked, shrouding the words of their encounter in a vacillation between two questions. As usual, she tried to hide how cold she felt in his presence by keeping up a constant chatter.

She nearly asked him why, on this day in particular, after two months of absence, he had put on his smile like a coat.

Then she thought of another question: Is love over when we start to laugh at the things that used to make us cry?

It seemed to her that all he cared about was her silence in response to his laughter, and only then did she notice that he wasn't wearing a coat.

Sorrow – our ceaseless, secret downpour – doesn't require a coat.

Nevertheless, today she was resisting her habit of talking and trying, with him, to be silent, just as he was trying, with her, to smile.

Yet it was an absent, wordless smile: that other language in which he seemed to be talking to himself more than to others, and which he used to poke fun at things known only to himself.

His concealment had often aroused her anguish. However, when he abandoned her one day between two sentences, it was her curiosity that was aroused. She recalled how, on that day, he had closed in on the anguish with a laugh, and left, without her knowing exactly what he'd been intending to say.

She didn't want to believe that he'd abandoned her because she'd refused to go with him to a certain film he'd been anxious to see.

She'd asked him if it was a schmaltzy film. 'No,' he replied.
She'd asked him if it was a comedy. 'No,' he replied.
'Why do you want to see it, then?'
'Because I like things that make me cry.'
At the time she'd laughed. She'd concluded that he was an eccentric who didn't know how to deal with love.

She didn't believe him when he'd told her that the tragedy of every great love is that it dies young on account of something we least expect.

Was it conceivable that her love had died for the simple reason that she hadn't felt like crying with him in the darkness of a cinema?

She would have preferred that he invite her to some safe place, far from others' inquisitive eyes, where they could dive into each others' flames.

She suspected that he'd wanted to humiliate her as a way of ensuring that he really possessed her. Perhaps he'd thought that if a man wants to hold on to a woman, he has to keep her under the illusion that he might leave her at any moment.

As for her, she'd always thought that a woman should be willing to give up anything to keep the man she loves.

And that was how it came about that, one day, she'd given up everything and gone to him. But she hadn't found him.

She remembered sitting alone in the left-hand corner of that café that knew so much about the two of them, and which from that day onward had mistakenly borne the name 'The Date'.

Sometimes places need to change their names to fit what we've become since being there, so as not to provoke us with counter-memory.

Maybe this was why, when she'd called him the day before, he had said, 'Wait for me there,' and then, as an afterthought, added, 'Find us another table that isn't in the left-hand corner,' and, after a brief silence, ' "Left" isn't the place for us any more.'

Had wars and political disputes invaded everything now, even lovers' tables and beds?

Or was it that, because he didn't want to humiliate memory, he'd wanted a table where love wouldn't recognize them, so that they could laugh where they'd never been able to cry?

In any case, here they were, sitting at the table across from memory.

They were sitting in the place where, one day, he'd put out his last cigarette on words' body. Then, since he didn't have any cigarettes left, he'd smoked up what was left of all her dreams and said . . .

She didn't remember exactly what he'd said before turning her heart into an ashtray and leaving.

Be that as it may, since that day she'd resisted her longing, which he had booby-trapped with a challenge. She would distract herself from her love for him by hating him until she could find some respectable excuse to call him: some occasion that would give her a pretext to say, 'Hi, how are you?' without being entirely defeated.

In an attempt to camouflage love's failures, one day she proposed that they become friends.

Laughing, he replied, 'I don't know how to be friends with a body I crave!'

She would have felt happier if he hadn't added, 'You're more delectable when you go away. There are women who are more beautiful when they aren't around.'

She hadn't understood what he meant. However, it had mattered to her to listen to him.

So, he hadn't changed. He still had a penchant for things that can only be said with the eyes, while all she could do was keep quiet so that they could listen together to the clamour of silence between two ex-lovers.

Between one glance and another, love continued its playful dodging, and passion's memory was in confusion.

With some other lover she could have stirred up a commotion and feigned laughter. She could have contrived a voice to cover up her silence. She could have invented answers to every question. With him, however, she either kept the questions to herself or posed them to him all at once, not with a voice but, rather, with the vibrations of a silence that he alone would recognize.

And he, without putting out his cigarette completely, without saying anything in particular – without saying anything at all – would confess to her that he had changed a lot since they'd been together last.

He was a man whose sudden silences between one word and the next gave him away. Consequently, he was someone for whom silence had become a kind of atmospheric condition brought on by a sudden cloud of memory.

He undoubtedly had a bit of the sadist in him.

At that moment, too, she saw him, at once seductive and hurtful, but didn't ask him why he was the way he was. After all, is it possible for seduction – the seduction that awakens in us the ferocity of dreams – to be kind?

All she'd wanted had been to ask him how he was. But before she said anything, he stole from her that very question, the question that would be both his first and his last. 'How are you?' he asked.

After a couple of smiles, he wrapped the question around his neck like a cravat crafted from elegant duplicity, and reverted to his silence.

Was he afraid the words would get cold? Or was he afraid that questions might hurt her?

Questions are generally a ruse: a polite untruth by means of which you draw others into stating a greater untruth.

He himself had said as much one day long before, before . . .

She remembered his saying, 'Avoid asking questions when you're with me. That way, you won't force me to lie. Lying starts when we're forced to give an answer. But everything I say to you of my own accord will be the truth.'

She'd learned the lesson well, and from then on had striven to create a new language tailor-made for him, a language devoid of question marks.

She would wait for the answers to come, and only then would she place them under her questions, remembering to follow them with exclamation marks, and often with admiration marks.

Over time she'd found some wisdom, and perhaps a blessing as well, in his philosophy of dialogue – dialogue devoid of questions and answers.

She appreciated the fact that he exempted her from the consequences of the lies, big or small, that she would tell without thinking, and she began to enjoy the game of carrying on a so-called conversation in which there were neither questions nor answers.

Now here he was, himself faced with a question. He was probably wondering whether to pose it or to answer it, though in either case he would be lying.

A question is a ruse: a way of taking somebody by surprise in his or her private space. As in war, then, surprise becomes the decisive element. Maybe this was why the man in the coat had decided to steal her question from her and abandon his usual exotic way of engaging in conversation.

It was a way of conversing that had long unsettled her, causing her to choose her words carefully, and forcing her to explore all sorts of linguistic turns in the road in an attempt to avoid the interrogative form. It reminded her of a radio game that requires players to answer questions without saying either 'yes' or 'no'. However, that game had suited her perfectly, since she was a woman who, standing poised on the edge of doubt, liked to reply with 'maybe' even when she meant 'yes', and 'might not' when she meant 'won't'.

She liked vague formulations and statements that sounded promising even when they really weren't: sentences that ended not with a full stop, but with ellipses.

As for him, he was a man of categorical language. His sentences consisted of words that put all doubt to rest, from 'of course', to 'definitely', to 'always', to 'absolutely'.

Their relationship had begun a year before with one of these words, just as, with one of these words, it had ended two months earlier. She remembered how, on that day, he had suddenly cut the conversation short with one of these guillotine words, and for a few moments she had remained suspended from the telephone cord, not understanding what had happened.

She discovered later that she couldn't have changed a thing, since those words weren't only his language; they were his philosophy of life. She realized that things happen in a fixed, predetermined sequence, just as they do in the life cycles of organisms. We go 'voluntarily' to our destinies to repeat 'inevitably', with an enormous degree of stupidity or feigned intelligence, what 'most decidedly' had to happen, since it has 'always' happened from time immemorial, believing, 'of course', that we're the ones who create our destinies!

How are we to know, amid the dualities of life that tug us back and forth between birth and death, joy and sorrow, victories and defeats, hopes and disappointments, love and hate, loyalty and betrayal, that we choose any of the things that happen to us? And that in our ebbs and our flows, our ascents and our descents, we're governed by a recurring sequence of Fate from whose grand cycles and vicissitudes we're separated by nothing but a hair's breadth?

How can we escape the power of that intricate cosmic law whose huge back-and-forth swings govern details as minute as the tiniest words in a language, including the little words that change the course of a life?

The day she heard him talking this way, she hadn't tried to understand him very deeply, since it had been during a sweet time known as 'the beginning'. How long had it taken her to realize that the two of them had completed the cycle of love, and that on account of some trifling matter that she couldn't yet name, they'd entered the final chapter of a story that had 'most definitely' reached its conclusion?

When love's flames go out, we always lose a part of ourselves, but we refuse to acknowledge it. So it was obvious that, in order to alleviate the pain of loss, he deliberately avoided practising the art of breaking with a lover.

She thought back on the day when she'd said to him, 'I want us to have a pleasant parting,' to which he had replied with veiled sarcasm, 'And is there any such thing as a pleasant parting?'

There were times when he seemed to her like a despot who amuses himself with the guillotine of language. He was a man infatuated with incisive words and decisive positions, whereas she was a woman seated on the swing of 'maybe'.

How then could language accommodate both of them at once?

All he had said was, 'How are you?'

Until that day, she hadn't expected to be flustered by such a question. To her surprise, she discovered that she was daunted by routine questions, the kinds of questions we answer unthinkingly every day when speaking to strangers who don't care about us in the end, and without caring whether they believe an answer that's no less hypocritical.

Yet, it takes no little astuteness to conceal our wounds with language.

Some questions lead to gloating, and the question mark with which they end, though it comes clothed in a warm voice that was once the voice of someone we loved, is a titter designed to incapacitate.

*

'How are you?'

It was a devious way of formulating another question, so one would have to be careful not to parse it incorrectly.

It contained an unstated pronoun with a challenge attached, the underlying meaning being, 'How are you without *me*?'

As for the unstated assumption behind it, all schools of love would agree on it. After all, we find it easier to accept the death of someone we love than to accept the idea of losing him, then discovering that he can carry on with his life in all its details without us. That's because in death, a loss takes place on both sides, a fact in which we find some solace.

She was weighing two possible replies when she noticed that their session had suddenly turned into a silent emotional battle, and that it was being fought with linguistic weapons chosen with the greatest of care.

The square table that separated them had become a chess board and, in preparation for the showdown, each player had chosen his colour and his position, arraying before him an army of knights and castles amid the mines of silence.

Intending to surprise him, she said, '*Al-hamdulillah* – Praise God!'

The very religions that urge us to be truthful provide us with expressions so loose that we can invest them with any number of meanings. After all, isn't language a tool of distrust?

Then, with gleeful pride, as though she'd scored her first victory, she added, 'And you?'

She was moving toward his region of uncertainty and stripping him of his first knight. He wasn't accustomed to seeing her drape confidence over her shoulders like a burnoose.

She eyed him steadily. Would he finally take off his coat and tell her he missed her and that he'd never forgotten her? Or would he turn up his collar and give her a reply that would make her feel even colder?

Which chess piece would he play, he who seemed suddenly engrossed in thought as though he were about to deal his own fate with a word?

As she sat pondering him, she remembered the words of Garry Kasparov, the man who had defeated everyone who ever sat across a chess board from him: 'The moves we make in our minds during play, then decide against, form as much a part of the game as the moves we carry out on the board.'

She wished she could discern which two answers he was debating in his mind, since the things he decided not to say would form part of his reply. However, all he did was shift in his seat and pick up a piece she hadn't expected him to. Without putting down his cigarette, he said, 'I'm the same as you are.'

Then, after a brief silence, he added, 'Precisely.'

He hadn't said a thing. All he had done was use one of his 'categorical' words in a new way this time, and the challenge between them had been aborted.

She truly didn't understand. She didn't understand how a silence between two words could have such an impact on her, or how he had managed, with little more than an indolent glance, to infect her with a desire that climbed up her black dress, lighting passion's fuse as it went.

With a word, his hand was restoring the memory to its place. It was as though, with the back of a word, he had sent everything before them crashing to the floor and cleared the table of all the petty disagreements that had driven them apart.

She knew that love isn't a good thinker, and, what's worse, that it has no memory. It doesn't benefit from the foolish mistakes of its past, or from the little disappointments that once left it with a gaping wound.

Nevertheless, she'd forgiven him everything.

She was 'most definitely' happy with this defeat of hers, which had taken on the flavour of victory after the fact.

As for him, he was 'inevitably' happy with a quick triumph in an extemporaneous duel he had fought without 'exactly' taking off his coat!

* * *

I liked this story, which I'd written without knowing exactly what I'd written. I'd never written a short story before, and I wasn't entirely confident that the term 'short story' even applied to such a text. All that mattered to me at the time was to write something – anything – that would enable me to break two years of silence.

I don't know how the story was born. I know how my silence was born, but that's another story.

Some time ago I surprised myself by going back to writing: just like that, without forethought, and without there having happened anything in particular that would have inspired me to put pen to paper. Maybe it was nothing other than the fact that a few days before that, I'd bought a notebook the look of which enticed me into writing.

I'd gone to a stationery shop to buy some envelopes and postage stamps, and I happened to see a notebook along with a number of others the shop owner was unpacking. As I watched, he began setting them out neatly in preparation for the approaching school year. As my glance might be arrested by a man, it was arrested by that notebook. It was as though I'd stumbled upon something I wouldn't have expected to find in that dreary place to which I went only rarely.

Isn't writing like love: a gift you find when you're least expecting it?

There are houses where you can't write a single line, no matter how long you live there and no matter how beautiful they are. It's something that defies logical explanation.

There are pens which, from the moment you buy them and from the first word you jot down with them, you'll never use to write anything worth mentioning. You know that their lazy temperament and spasmodic breathing will keep you from reaching words' secret passageways.

Similarly, there are notebooks that you buy out of habit and that sit in your drawers for months without ever awakening in you that irresistible urge to write or provoking you to scribble even a few lines.

I find that the longer I write, the better I get at making on-the-spot judgments about such things.

So, prompted by a feeling that went beyond me, I paused before that notebook. I was captivated by this 'thing', which was set apart from the other things in the shop by nothing but my conviction – or illusion – that it would bring me back to writing again.

From the moment I saw that black spiral notebook with its glossy, plain cover, I sensed a rapport between us, and I knew somehow that I was going to write something lovely on its smooth blank pages.

I ran home with it and hid it as though I were hiding evidence of a crime, and didn't get it out until several days later to write that short story, which might be called 'The Man With the Coat'.

As I usually do when I finish writing something at night, I reread it as soon as I woke up the next morning. I was anxious to see whether the story was really as nice as it had seemed when I first wrote it. Maybe I just wanted to make sure I'd actually written something.

I read it several times, and each time I read it I felt more exhilarated than I had the time before. At long last I'd written something good. Even better was the fact that it was outside of me: everything in it had originated in my imagination. I'd created everything in it. I'd decided not to interfere with it in any way or introduce into it anything from my own life.

This alone was an achievement that amazed me, since I'd never known anyone like this man, with his alluring remoteness and his unsettling presence: a man veiled behind the mysteriousness and ambiguity of silence, a man with the ability to create a state of sweet discomfiture whenever he speaks, even when he happens to be uttering one of those unequivocal words that he relishes in choosing according to the occasion.

Nor is the woman in the story anything like me. She says the very opposite of what I'd say myself, and does the opposite of what I would do. With the fatuousness of a young girl, she believes that those we love were made to share pleasure with us, but not pain, and that the man who loves her should cry alone, then come to enjoy her, or find enjoyment with her.

In fact, she's so naïve that she sees his words as evidence of his love for her. She fails to see that when he replies to her 'How are you?' with 'I'm the same as you are . . . precisely,' all this means is that he's decided not to tell her anything!

And whereas what I liked about this story was the fact that it bore little resemblance to my life, the fact that it did bear *some* resemblance to it reminded me of how I resent the strange logic of Fate, which requires that in every relationship between a man and a woman, one of the two doesn't deserve the other. Maybe, in my heart of hearts, I wished this man were mine. After all, he was well suited to both my silence and my way of speaking, and he resembled me in my anguish and my passion.

However, this wasn't my problem, and this story wasn't my story – or, rather, it wasn't my story yet.

So I gave it a title, which I didn't have much trouble deciding on, and went back to my daily preoccupations.

Nothing had prepared me to become a party to this story or to enter into some protracted literary adventure.

I'd wanted the story to be as short as possible and as distant from me as possible. I'd wanted it to be hard-hitting and to move rapidly towards its conclusion. But, like the seaweed that clings to your feet when you swim in the ocean, its final sentences clung to my mind. Its theme haunted me, and something inside me rejected the way it had ended.

It didn't matter to me why these two lovers had parted, whether they would be reunited, or which of them had lost the challenge. Their story, which I'd entered by coincidence like someone who, surprised to find a window open across from her balcony, begins stealing glances at the people in the house next door, didn't pique my curiosity.

All that mattered to me was that man. I was curious to understand him. I'd also made a bet with myself over whether I could get him to take that coat off. It was a challenge for me, nothing more.

Before this experience I'd never realized that a novel can be a linguistic usurpation of sorts in which the novelist compels her characters to say what she wants them to, extracting by force all the confessions and statements she wants them to make for ill-defined, selfish reasons of which even she is unaware, then flinging them on to paper, weary and maimed, without stopping to wonder whether they really would have said those things if she'd given them the opportunity to live outside the pages of her book.

However, this realization didn't dissuade me from my intention to force this man to speak. He was the only thing that mattered to me. His proud silence unnerved me. His thick coat irritated me. His razor-sharp words had become a guillotine that spelled death for any future text in the making, and it was clear to me that I wouldn't be able to write a thing until this man had spoken.

So I sat down with my notebook and continued the story as though I hadn't stopped writing it the day before.

* * *

One rainy day his voice came across the telephone line. Despite the cold, he seemed to have taken off his coat as he asked her, 'How are you? Are you still fond of the rain the way you used to be?'

18

She didn't know whether she should conclude from his questions that he loved her again, or whether it was simply the rain that had brought him back to her.

She hadn't forgotten how he'd once said, 'Questions are a kind of romantic involvement.' She also remembered the time they'd been together in his car in the middle of a downpour.

On that day she'd discovered the beauty of being lovers whose only address is a transitory abode with the intimate atmosphere of a car on a rainy day.

She'd felt that at long last they were alone, concealed from everyone, shielded by a curtain of rain trickling down the windowpanes.

She had wanted to say things that can only be said at such a moment. But then he pulled over to the kerb.

Lighting a cigarette, he said, 'It's no use taking refuge under the umbrella of words. When it's raining, it's better to be quiet.'

She hadn't argued with him. She'd contented herself with the illusion of possessing him, her rainy-day captive inside a car, where she could share his breaths, the aroma of his tobacco, and the jingling of the keys in his pocket as he looked for a lighter. In the warmth of the car she sat watching him, mesmerised by all the details of his manhood as he fidgeted next to her, and his calm, unsettling presence.

She'd long been dizzied by the fine points of a man's makeup: the self-important suggestiveness, the unspoken, intimate provocation whose vibrations have nothing to do with virility but which a female picks up on and to which she falls slave.

The bliss she had experienced with him that day led her to realize that rain doesn't treat us all as equals. When the beloved takes leave of us and we find ourselves facing the rain alone, we have to ignore its painful invitation to romance and its sadistic provocation lest it exacerbate our suffering, since we know full well that, at that very same moment, it is creating happiness for others whom love hasn't abandoned.

In fact, there are times when nothing is more unfair than the rain!

She was still wondering which weather forecast he was preparing her for.

Had he come back because he wanted her? Or had he come in anticipation of the smell of the earth after it rains?

The only thing he liked about sunny weather was the damp soil left by the rain. He would breathe in its fragrance with senses ablaze as though he were taking in his partner's scent after making love.

'Can I see you tomorrow?' he asked. 'I thought it would be nice for us to see that film together on a rainy day.'

Before she could ask him which film he was talking about, he added, 'Did you know it's been showing in the same cinema for the last two months? That's how long it's been since we saw each other last.'

This time she didn't try to make up excuses. She just asked, 'Where shall we meet?'

'At the Olympic Cinema before the four o'clock matinee.'

Then, as an afterthought, he said, 'Or, if you'd like, you could wait for me at the university entrance. I'll pick you up there at 3:30. That would be better.'

Without giving her time to say another word, he hung up in farewell, leaving her once more to her questions.

* * *

I was happy with this ending, which I'd thought up without much effort. In fact, I'd written it down just like that, the way it had occurred to me, without debating between it and some other version and without crossing out a single line or rereading it more than once the way I usually do. It was as if I wanted to convince myself that I wasn't the person who had written it.

But isn't there always something that words conceal, even when they come this spontaneously? In fact, when they come pouring out so naturally, in one way or another, this itself should arouse one's suspicion.

Language can be more beautiful than we are. In fact, we beautify ourselves with words. We choose them the way we choose our clothes, in keeping with our moods and our intentions.

There are also words that have no colour, that are scandalously transparent, like a woman who's just come out of the sea wearing a diaphanous dress that clings to her body. Yet transparent words are decidedly more dangerous, since they cling to us to the point where they pass into our very beings.

This man who insisted on remaining silent while I insisted on getting him to speak, who insisted on keeping his coat on while I insisted on taking it off him, unnerved me in all of his states, even when he took off his silence and put on my voice and my sodden words.

But at last I'd got him to talk. I'd made him say something that I wanted him to. So perhaps I'd actually defeated him.

But, I confess, he surprised me, not because he'd invited this woman for the second time to go and see that film, which was out of character for him, but because he'd given her the name of a cinema I'd never heard of before. I didn't know whether it existed or not, since I'd never been to cinemas in this city before or taken note of the films playing there.

Then suddenly it occurred to me to look in the newspaper to see whether there really was a cinema by that name. I began searching on the entertainment page where television programmes and film screenings are listed. I pored over the names of cinemas until, lo and behold, I came across an 'Olympic Cinema' where an American film by the name of *Dead Poets Society* was showing. I guessed it must be dubbed into French, since no one around here knows English, and I tried to find a translation of the film title in hopes that this might solve some of the mystery.

I found it hard to believe that it would be the same film the man in my story had been talking about. So I went searching through the old newspapers piled on the floor of my husband's office, the ones he would bring home every day as part of his job, then leave on the floor until he threw them out.

I looked at the entertainment pages in all the issues I came to, and every time, I found that same film playing at the same cinema.

The last newspaper I looked at took me back a month and a half. On this basis I concluded that the film might have been playing for the last two months, just as the man had said. This surprised me; in fact, it bowled me over, since I hadn't been familiar with this particular cinema, and had never heard of this film. How could I have known that it had been playing there for the last two months and that, as the newspaper also confirmed, one of its showings was at four o'clock in the afternoon?

The shock of this discovery left me nonplussed. Had I received some sort of revelation telling me to write things I knew nothing about? Should I be wary of this story I'd written, whose details had turned frightening? Or should I view it as a sign from the Beyond and a promise of some future encounter?

All my questions revolved around that man. Why did he matter so much to me? Why did he raise so many questions in my mind? Were questions really, as he said, 'a romantic involvement'? And was he the one who had said this, or had I said it myself?

He'd only asked one question: 'Can I see you tomorrow?'

It was a question that he'd posed to her in particular. But how could I, the writer, fail to show up for the date they'd made? Wasn't I the one who had wanted it, who'd set the day and time? If so, then wouldn't I need to be there in order to invent more conversations, dates, arguments, happy encounters, disappointments, amusement, astonishment . . . and endings?

This is the exclusive privilege of the novelist, who, mistakenly imagining that she owns the world by proxy, toys with the fates of creatures of ink before closing her notebook and becoming, for her part as well, a puppet suspended from invisible strings or moved, like others on life's vast stage, by the hand of Fate! And once this happens, it's useless for her to preface her plans with 'God willing' as though she were bribing Fate to fulfil her dreams.

I remember once telling someone, 'Learn to say, "God willing".' Then one day I asked him, 'When shall we meet?' At the time he'd been hurriedly packing a suitcase of sorrow, and he answered me, in typical fashion, with a line from a poem by Mahmud Darwish – something like, 'We'll meet in a while . . . a year . . . a generation.'

But we never met again. Both of us had forgotten that day to say, 'God willing'! Is that why he didn't come back? Or maybe it was because he went to bury his father in that country that kills poets while hosting all manner of poetry festivals, and ended up being buried, a maimed corpse, next to the one he had gone to bury.

Before that he used to say he was going to stop writing poetry and try his hand at a novel!

Do you suppose those two lovers would really have met again if I'd given her the freedom to reply as she'd wanted to? And what would she have said?

I think she would have replied with one of those nebulous expressions of hers. She would have said, for example, 'Maybe we'll meet,' knowing full well that she meant 'of course'. And to be even more circuitous, she could have said, 'It might not happen,' to give him the false impression that it wasn't going to happen.

In that case, he would have upped the ante and replied, 'Absolutely. It doesn't matter anyway.' Then he would have put down the receiver and buttoned up his coat again.

Silence in and of itself doesn't bother me. But I hate men who withdraw into an absolute silence like someone who buttons his shirt up to the very top, like a door with myriad locks and keys, in order to convince you of his importance.

That kind of armoured door doesn't inspire my confidence. The possessions such a person keeps hidden behind it don't so much impress me as they expose their owner as some nouveau-riche obsessed with his newly acquired fortune. After all, truly rich people always forget to close a window or a wardrobe in their mansion.

Keys are the obsession of the poor, or of those who are afraid that if they open their mouths they'll lose other people's illusions about them.

The nice thing about this man was that, like all people who dream of being wealthy, he would leave one button undone at the top of his heavy coat of silence for the sake of illusion, like a door that's left ajar. This may have been the most seductive thing about him. He wasn't entirely silent, nor did he say any more than necessary in order to crack open the silence.

He was a character ready to be set in a novel, who granted himself to you in instalments.

And is a novel anything but the distance between the top button that's been left undone and the bottom button, which may have been left undone as well?

Did this man really exist only in my imagination? If so, then what was to explain all the factual details I'd included in that story without ever having heard of them before? Although I'm doubtful of authors who claim that there is some supernatural force that dictates what they write, I also doubt that such details, taken together, are nothing but a coincidence.

Had I fallen prey so thoroughly to writing's seductive allure that I thought this man had dictated to me an appointment I'd thought up myself?

I love that moment when I'm surprised by a man, even when, after the moment of surprise, he no longer resembles my illusion of him.

Every story with a man lands you on the shore of surprise. If he's a husband, the story is bound to usher you into a series of surprises. In the beginning, we know who it was that we married. But the longer we're married, the less certain we are who it is we're living with!

The most mysterious and surprising men are the ones who've been through protracted wars that swallowed up their childhoods and youths without mercy and turned them into men who are at once violent and fragile, sentimental and superhuman.

A man of this type always has another man hidden inside him who might wake up when you least expect him to. He also conceals a little boy who grew up at a time before they'd invented Legos so that, like boys of the younger generation, he could practise putting their pieces together and taking them apart again according to the dictates of his childlike imagination.

I suspect that my husband was born with a military mindset, and that the first thing he ever held was a weapon. So what wonder is it that he breaks me without meaning just as, years ago, he allured me without trying? Doesn't power, like wealth, make us seem more beautiful and appealing?

Don't women, like the peoples of the world, always fall prey to the charm and prestige of a military uniform before noticing that, by allowing themselves to be dazzled by it, they've given it its power?

It's true, of course, that he did it gradually, with a good deal of tact and, quite possibly, with a good deal of planning. It's true also that I entered into slavery of my own free will, though probably without noticing. I was content in my meek surrender to him, leaving to him the more enjoyable role: the role of manliness that commands, decides, demands, protects, pushes, and goes to extremes.

In his demeanour I found something of the authoritative, fatherly nurture I'd been deprived of, while he found in his dominion over me an extension of the professional tasks he was used to performing away from home.

* * *

Our relationship began with a mutual infatuation, and with the violent passion of an unspoken challenge.

I should have realized that violently passionate connections are short-lived by virtue of their very ferocity, and that we can't invest everything in a single relationship. We can't be spouses, friends, parents, sweethearts and symbols to each other all at the same time.

As for him, it seems most likely that, in the area of relationships, he thought with the logic of a military officer who, when he comes to power, insists on occupying every major government post and receiving every ministerial portfolio of any importance in the belief that no one else would be competent to do so, and that the mere presence of someone else in any of these posts would constitute a threat to his regime.

Consequently, he'd given me no freedom, nor had he left any space in my life into which anyone could steal. He'd taken all the seats, yet without occupying any of them worthily.

I noticed later that it was my husband's fatherly role that meant the most to me. His political duties and military rank didn't matter to me because of their prestige but, rather, because they were an extension of the patriotic nostalgia I'd been raised on, because they hearkened back to the glory days of an Algeria of which I'd always dreamed.

In his stature I saw the homeland with its strength and pride, and in his body, which had endured hunger, fear and cold during the years of liberation, I saw justification for my craving and admiration for him in honour of memory.

It took me a long time to discover how foolish I'd been to confuse my 'past complex' with the counter-reality of the present. But now I'd fallen prey to a similar confusion between the illusion of writing and real life. Consequently, I insisted on going on the date that I'd tried in vain to convince myself I had nothing to do with. I'd tried to convince myself that it concerned nothing but creatures of ink that would never leave the world of paper.

Even so, I decided to go, not realizing that the writing process in which I'd sought refuge from life would take me, albeit obliquely, back towards life itself, thrusting me into a story that would, one page after another, become my own.

Chapter Two

Always

MY FATE LAY SOMEWHERE between torrential, incessant desires and their opposing forces.

Love was stealing into me through a half-open door and a half-closed heart.

Had I been waiting for it casually, leaving the door ajar for it while I amused myself closing the windows of logic?

Not long before love struck, its symptoms started to appear and I recognized them, subtle though they were. Of course, dwelling as I do in a heart with cracked walls, I've never been panic-stricken over a passion that sweeps in like a hurricane. Rather, I capitulate to the storms, each of them with a name of its own, that turn everything in me topsy-turvy and leave a lovely swath of destruction in their wake.

I've always had an affinity for lovers who cram themselves into love's narrow passageways and, after insinuating themselves into that cramped space between the possible and the impossible, stumble into whatever love story life has placed in their path. They live inside a tempest of love that never abates, swept away by storms of passion and mesmerized by flames which, in return for lighting up their lives for a few days, devour everything around them. They live fully prepared for those luminous moments, which come by stealth and which, when they go out – as go out they must – leave their souls strewn with ashes.

I've always loved them, and maybe I'm like them.

This time, though, I thought I was too smart to stumble into some love story that literature had placed in my path, not to test my ability to write but, rather, to see whether I had the audacity to treat writing as a lived reality.

I'd been taken by André Gide's statement that 'the nicest things are the ones that are suggested by madness, and written by sanity'. I was so taken by it, in fact, that when madness proposed that I go on a date that a character in my story had made with another woman, I took it, and decided to go on the pretext that it would give me something interesting to write about.

I was nervous for several hours before the date, the way you get before an encounter in which you don't know what to expect, but which you're determined to go through with anyway. I was curious, of course, to meet this man and anxious to see the film. After all, it might be the quickest way to understand him, and to figure out why he was so insistent on seeing it himself.

At the same time, I knew that by going alone to see a film in a city like Constantine, where women don't frequent cinemas, I was embarking on a foolhardy adventure with entirely unpredictable outcomes. How much more foolhardy, then, would such a venture be if the woman concerned was the wife of one of the city's senior military officers, and if she arrived in an official car to be greeted by an army of men whose sole preoccupation in life was to harass any female who was sufficiently free (or out of her mind) to sit by herself in a cinema?

Consequently, I made a point of arriving fifteen minutes late so that I wouldn't have to wait in line or be seen as I went in. I also asked the driver to come back fifteen minutes before the film was over, since this way I could avoid the lights that come on at the end of the showing and allow people to look each other over in a way that had unnerved me so many times before.

Since I got there some time after the film had begun, I could sit wherever I wanted. It also gave me the chance to stand there for a few moments and gauge the atmosphere in the place, which appeared to be half-empty. As I'd expected, the audience was all men and, most probably, young men who had come to kill time inside a cinema rather than killing it leaning against a wall somewhere.

I only saw one couple, a man and a woman, sitting in the back, who appeared to have come for some purpose other than watching the film.

Concluding that they were 'the ones', I took a seat right behind them, as though I were either hiding behind them or spying on them. I suspect that my being there annoyed them. However, the fact that I was female seemed to make me sufficiently unthreatening, since they made no objection.

Lovers must be miserable in a city like this, where love has to spend every minute holding its breath, cowering in the darkness on seats that have been knifed to shreds by hands that have never touched a woman's body!

I distracted myself from the couple in front of me by watching the film. When I arrived, the star of the film was arriving in class at the beginning of the school year.

He was a forty-something secondary-school teacher who'd had his share of disappointments in life. With a ready and wry sense of humour, a touch of romanticism and, possibly, some secret sorrow, he'd come back more than a generation later to teach English literature in the same institution where he'd once studied. It became clear as the movie proceeded that he'd come to save the students from the fallacies he'd learned while sitting in the very seats they now occupied, or the convictions he'd been raised on but had later proved to be baseless.

With a kind of provocative hilarity, he came into class whistling. This amazed the students, who weren't accustomed to this kind of behaviour in a staid academic institution known for its adherence to long-standing tradition. He headed straightaway for a wall covered with black-and-white photographs of students who had occupied these same academic seats, one graduating class after another, one generation after another, over the course of an entire century.

Then he gestured to the students to come and stand with him. He asked them to ponder these group photos that had never given them pause before, and to study the faces they saw there.

Bewildered, the students came up to join him, and he began to talk to them as though he were continuing a previous conversation, or as though he were introducing himself to them as one of the people whose pictures they'd walked past without a thought.

He said, 'All the people you see in these pictures – athletic-looking just like you, young like you, with their big grins and their great ambitions, their projects, their dreams, their absolute confidence in life – they're all nothing but bones now in fancy tombs. They're dead, just the way you're going to be some day!'

As the students were still processing the strange things they were hearing from this teacher they were meeting for the first time, he continued, 'For every one of you standing here, some day everything inside him is going to stop. His body will grow cold, he'll be eaten by maggots, and it will be as though he never existed.

'Look at them. They're looking at you! They're telling you something you need to hear. Come on. Lean in. Try to hear them whisper their legacy . . .'

Stunned, the students approached the photo-lined wall as the teacher's voice followed them from behind, entreating them to hear it: *Carpe, carpe diem*. Seize the day. He whispered to them that they should make their lives extraordinary, since one of these days they would stop being anything. They would be gone as though they'd never come.

He concluded by telling them that this was their first lesson, then instructed them to go back to their seats and open their books.

My absorption in the movie didn't prevent me from thinking about the man and woman in front of me. After all, it was on their account that I'd come in the first place.

They were silent. I don't know whether they were actually busy watching the movie, but they weren't saying anything to each other. At the same time, I had a feeling the teacher's remarks and advice had made an impact on them somehow. I thought I saw the woman's right hand moving slowly and determinedly in the man's direction. This encouraged me to believe that she was 'the one', since she seemed less interested in the film than she was in getting a reaction out of her companion.

It was obvious that she'd been anxious to be with him. After all, what, other than love, could have brought her to a place like this, where she was bound to be the sole female, to watch a movie like this?

I sort of pitied her, and myself, too, knowing that both of us had come for the sake of the same man.

From behind, the man looked around forty. His hair was neatly combed and he looked quite respectable compared with the other men there, who gave me the creeps. So I figured he was probably 'him'. He was wearing a coat, and had just stood up to take it off and spread it over his knees in such a way that it covered both his lap and that of the woman beside him. So it wasn't difficult to imagine what would come next!

Just then a man came along and sat down in the seat next to mine. This irritated me all the more, and I regretted being stupid enough to come to a cinema and make myself look so suspicious. After all, nobody in the entire place would have believed that I was a writer who'd been drawn there by mere curiosity, and nobody would have understood that I considered myself entitled to spy on a certain couple and even come between them since they were my creations!

By this time they were exchanging suspicious-looking touches in plain sight of me. I was trying to convince myself that I was a writer, just a writer, and that the only reason I was interested in what was happening in front of me was that it would help me understand the characters in my novel.

I knew, of course, that I was lying to myself, and that what I was concerned about was this man, the man with the coat, who for all I knew might have brought me to this place just to torment me by flirting with another woman while I looked on. After all, he'd already seduced me as a woman with something unstated and unnamed and had deceived me, as a writer, into believing that under his coat of silence he concealed some secret that would justify the risk I'd taken.

And here he was taking his coat off, not for me, or because of me, but, rather, to use it as a screen behind which he could run his hands over a woman sitting next to him!

So, then, he was scum, the type of man who conceals all the world's hang-ups and filth behind a façade of staid decorum, who sits beside his wife without a word, looking dignified and prestigious, while his feet carry on a vulgar conversation under the table with another woman!

However, what shocked me most wasn't this discovery but, rather, the realization that from the very beginning of this story I'd been acting like a perfect fool. I'd invented situations, dialogues and trysts for no other reason than that I wanted to experience a kind of make-believe romance.

I'd even convinced myself that a man could leave the page and make a date for me in the world outside my notebooks.

But it was obvious now that this had been a stroke of madness.

Deflated, I nearly got up to leave, to get away from the poisoned atmosphere I'd placed myself in. But then I remembered that the driver wouldn't be back for another hour, not to mention the fact that I'd miss seeing a film that, according to the placards at the cinema entrance, had won a number of prestigious awards.

So I went back to watching the movie, trying to ignore what was going on in front of me.

The teacher was giving his students a lesson on how to understand poetry based on a method presented in the introduction to their poetry textbook, which had been written by renowned literary critic J. Evans Pritchard. According to Pritchard, one could rate the quality of a poem and compare it to other poems through the use of a mathematical formula that could be plotted on a graph, where the y-axis was used to quantify the meaning and the x-axis was used to quantify the structure. In this way, one could determine how weak or strong a given poet or poem was in relation to others based on precise mathematical criteria.

As the students sat engrossed in drawing vertical and horizontal lines in their notebooks and copying what the teacher had written on the blackboard, he suddenly stopped and erased everything he had written. He exclaimed that Mr J. Evans Pritchard's method was excrement, and that this was poetry, not the laying of pipes.

Rather, he explained to them, the true measure of poetry is our astonishment, our dazzlement, our emotional response. In response to a poem, women faint, gods are born, and poets bawl like babies. After all, who can measure our tears, our joy, or anything else a poem does to us? The reason we read and write poetry is that we're human beings. But how could we possibly measure our humanity with mathematical formulas? He told them to tear up everything they'd written in their notebooks. Then, after a brief silence, he added that they could rip out the introduction too, while they were at it.

The students looked at him questioningly, not knowing whether to take him seriously or not. However, in the face of his insistence, they had no choice in the end but to rip out the first pages of the book, which now contained nothing but poetry.

Meanwhile, the teacher made the rounds of the class with the wastebasket, gathering the ripped-out papers into the receptacle with a gleefulness for which he alone knew the reason.

He hadn't given them a lesson in understanding poetry, but in understanding life. He'd given them a lesson in having the courage to question everything, even the things they saw written in textbooks on the authority of some big-name scholar, and the audacity to tear up everything they believed to be wrong and throw it in the dustbin!

I don't know how responsive the audience was to this wonderful scene, or if there were some there who saw it as still more justification for ripping the seats to shreds.

In any case, the man sitting in front of me was busily looking for a pen and paper. As soon as he found them, he began writing something, which I assumed to be some thought that had occurred to him.

Dying to take a peek at what he'd written, I edged forward a bit as if I were trying to see the screen better. Maybe he was writing something he wanted me to see. After all, he knew I was there, and that I'd been spying on him.

But before I could see what he'd written, I sensed that I'd dropped something. I felt my ear, and sure enough, one of my earrings had fallen out. I bent down to look for it, relying on the light coming from the screen, and before I knew it the man beside me had bent down with his cigarette lighter to help me see.

His presence took me by surprise, as I'd nearly forgotten he was sitting next to me. What surprised me even more, I think, was his cologne or the smell of his tobacco. I felt as though he was deliberately catching me unawares, his masculinity taking me by storm in that dark place. There he was, just a few breaths away from me, watching me search for something without saying a word, and without even asking me what I was looking for. It was as though the flame he held in his hand was there not to help me find what I had lost, but simply to illuminate my face.

I looked up from the floor, unhurriedly climbing his chest with my eyes. But when I reached his face, his eyes took me completely off guard. It was as though the darkness had imbued them with a depth that was as unsettling as it was seductive.

I couldn't see exactly what colour they were. What I could see, though, was that I couldn't go on looking into them.

Then suddenly I decided to give up the search. The earring didn't matter to me, and I wasn't bothered by losing it. All I cared about was the looks I was receiving from this man or, more precisely, his disquieting presence.

Before settling back into my seat, I murmured out of politeness, 'Sorry for troubling you.'

'Not at all,' he replied as he put out his lighter and slipped it into his pocket. Then he went back to watching the movie.

His terse response jarred me. It made me freeze. He'd uttered it as though he were uttering a password that was known to no one but us, or as though he were tossing me his calling card. The brevity of his response had an urbane provocativeness about it, or a subtle sarcasm.

Had he fallen silent in order to convince me, with an irrefutable argument, that he was the man of categorical language? I didn't know.

But from that moment on, I couldn't concentrate on anything going on around me.

Love always sits in a seat other than the one we were expecting it to, right alongside the place where we expected love to be.

38

This is something I've long known to be true, something I've experienced firsthand. So how could I have sat for more than an hour next to such a man without attaching any importance to his presence, distracted from him by another man in front of me who, unbeknownst to him, had come disguised in the garb of love for the simple reason that he was wearing a coat and sitting with a woman!

On the other hand, what if this man who had said, 'Not at all,' and then fallen silent wasn't 'him'? What if he'd said what he said without thinking? What if he'd only taken the seat next to mine because it was closest to the exit? What if life wanted to mock me as a writer, not just once, but twice?

I've often wondered what kind of a distance it is that separates us from the things we long for. Is it measurable in terms of space? In terms of time? In terms of the impossible?

And what kind of logic is the logic of desire? Is it a linguistic logic? A temporal logic? Or is it the logic of a circumstance in which life places you?

This man who, by virtue of three small words, had gone from being a stranger to being the man I longed for – how had he managed to ascend in rank so quickly, and with such ease? Had he colluded with language? With the darkness? With this ambiguous place that lay somewhere between falsehood and fact, day and night, dream and reality, literature and life?

If he'd spoken, he would have helped me somewhat to under-stand what was happening. As it was, however, he hadn't left any room for further exchange. Instead, he'd gone on watching the film, seemingly paying no attention to me while, at the same time, emitting the vibrations of a silent conversation in the dark-ness of the senses.

I myself couldn't think of anything to say to him. Rather, speech had been extinguished, giving way to a conflagration in the silent intervals.

I don't know how long we went on this way, with him watching the movie and me either watching him or stealing occasional glances at the lovers who didn't matter to me any more, since, from the moment this man had uttered his three little words and fallen silent, nothing they said had been of any more use to me!

Now that I was so preoccupied with him, I couldn't focus on the film any more, and a number of scenes and events passed me by. One of them, however, grabbed my attention:

As the teacher gave a lesson one day he began explaining to the students how our perspective on something changes depending on our location and the angle from which we look at it. Then he asked them, one by one, to come to the front of the class and stand on top of his desk so that they could see how the classroom looked from there. He wanted them to see that the proper way to understand the world is to break out of the tiny spot we occupy in it, to dare to change our orientation even if it means standing on top of a table rather than sitting at it and leaning on it.

As he spoke, the students took turns standing on top of his desk. Sometimes he would have one of them stay there a bit longer, encouraging him to take a little more time to look at the things in the room from his new vantage point, and to observe how his desk looked without him sitting at it. Then they came down, dazzled.

But suddenly, after this light-hearted phase of the story, things took a tragic turn with the suicide of a student who had decided to try out for a theatrical production without his father's permission. The student's involvement with theatre had involved rebellion against his father, who had sent him to this prestigious, upmarket academy in order to become a doctor, and nothing else. After the student delivered a marvellous theatrical performance for which he received a standing ovation, his father, having somehow got wind of events, came to the school and angrily drove him home. His father informed him that as punishment for his defiance he would transfer him forcibly to a military academy. Faced with this prospect, the boy took his life.

The boy's father held the teacher responsible for his son's suicide. The teacher was fired for having corrupted his students' thinking and, through his unconventional teaching methods, having encouraged them to rebel. The academy's headmaster then prepared a document condemning the teacher for having flouted his authority, and threatened to expel any student who refused to sign it.

I wanted to see how the film ended. I wanted to know whether the students would desert this teacher who'd taught them everything, including the importance of defending what they believed to be the truth. Would they be defeated in the face of the first challenge life sent their way?

But then I noticed that I was nearly out of time, and that if I stayed, the lights would come on and blow my cover. Like a modern-day Cinderella, I'd be turned from the mistress of the impossible into an ordinary woman sitting in a shabby cinema next to a man who might not be worthy of all the lovely feelings he'd created inside her.

I'd given up on the hope that this man might surprise me with a word that would confirm or deny my suspicions. So, having decided to surprise *him* by leaving, I got up and, trying to sound as natural as possible, said to him, 'Excuse me. Could you let me pass, please?'

'Of course,' he replied.

He stood up and, pressing himself against his seat, left just enough space between us for his body to brush mine from behind. I don't know whether I traversed that space in a moment, or in hours. In any case, it was the kind of space that's as vast as it is infinitesimal, the kind that, when you cross it, you feel as though you've passed from the world of dreams into the world of reality.

Was the time it took me to traverse it long enough for his cologne to cling to me, to penetrate my senses to the point where, for months thereafter, I knew I'd encountered a man I'd only be able to recognize again by his scent?

I suspect that his gaze escorted me all the way out of the cinema. He made no attempt to make me stay. Even so, I could feel his eyes bidding me a silent farewell.

I suspect, too, that he was engrossed in the film's ending. As I left, the teacher was collecting some papers from the classroom as the elderly headmaster taught the day's English lesson in his stead. Anxious to fix everything this wayward teacher had broken and to make certain that the students were taught the entire curriculum from the very beginning, the stern and unyielding headmaster had them open their books to the introduction on literary criticism, only to discover to his surprise that the introduction had been torn out.

It thus became apparent that although this teacher was leaving, he was only doing so after having discarded everything he believed to be untrue, and that from now on, no one would be able to convince the students of something they'd chosen to tear out and throw away.

Papers in hand, the teacher was about to leave the classroom when, without a word, one of the students suddenly climbed up on his desk and stood facing him in an emotion-laden farewell salute. The boy's act of courage inspired a number of the other students who, one after another, climbed on to their desks to bid a silent farewell to their former teacher, who had taught them to defy senseless prohibitions and to look at the world in a new way. As one would expect, there were a few students who, kowtowing to the headmaster, remained in their seats. In their cowardly surrender, however, it wasn't these students that captured the audience's attention, since they'd been dwarfed by all the other students who were standing on top of their desks!

As the teacher left the classroom, I was leaving the cinema, confident that this nameless man and I had shared both a tearful moment, and several moments of unspoken desire. By this time it didn't matter whether the woman sitting next to the man in front of me had been 'her' or 'me', since things had happened between us as he himself had wanted them to, in the darkness of a cinema.

* * *

When I saw the driver waiting for me at the entrance, I flung myself hurriedly into the car, wanting to keep those sweet sensations in a safe, closed place. I was afraid that the lovely thing I'd experienced in silence next to a strange man might fade away inside me, or be destroyed or scattered by the street with its bright lights, its noisy bustle, its curious passersby, and the misery that lived there.

It reminded me of the experience we have when we sit for a while next to or across from a stranger in the metro or on a train. We know nothing about the other person, and during those shared moments we exchange nothing but an occasional collusive glance. Then we get off, contenting ourselves with the pleasure of silence and a few transparent moments which, having brushed by like a shawl of passion-scented lace, leave in their wake a lovely inward chaos, as well as the peculiar realization that we might never see that face again and that just a bit of courage, or a few words, might have been enough to give that face a name and an address.

Yet in that case, how would we experience the enjoyment of the unknown?

That evening as I was cleaning out my handbag, I came across the earring I thought I'd lost. It had fallen inside one of the compartments.

And I wondered: Could something this small change the course of a story? If it hadn't been for that tiny incident, would I have noticed the man beside me rather than the one in front of me? I would probably have come home from the cinema convinced of the stupidity of having banked on illusions!

Indeed. Aren't our lives just a series of coincidences and details so small that we wouldn't think of them as important enough to alter our fates or our convictions? Details the size of those five little words which, small as they were, caused me to believe that the craziest dreams can come true, and that there are no boundaries between writing and life?

From the beginning I'd been enraptured by the beauty of the bizarre, hypothetical, nay, impossible love relationship that might join a man of ink with a woman of paper, who meet in the hazy realm between writing and life and set about together to write a book that both emerges from life and rebels against it.

Intrigued as I was by this man's persona and its shadowy areas, I was still more intrigued by the possibility of our meeting between the darkness of ink and the darkness of the senses.

The more I let this idea sink in, the more fervently I believed, and the more involved I became in the words of André Gide, confident that I was capable of writing the most beautiful love story madness had ever inspired!

Madness begins with a dream, and my dream now was to take up residence inside the body of the woman in whose place I'd gone to see a film that afternoon. I wished I could borrow her body for the duration of a book, the way women borrow jewellery or a dress to wear to a wedding.

In this city where women borrow virtually everything from each other and trade everything imaginable, what if I, who'd lent everything in my wardrobe at one time or another, borrowed the one thing I could never truly possess: the body of some other woman – her face, her features, her memories of romance, her story with a man that mattered so much to me?

Yet it mattered even more to make sure I hadn't been dreaming, that I hadn't lost my mind, and that I'd actually sat beside him for a whole two hours in the course of which he'd spoken five words to me!

I wished I could disguise myself in her clothes so that I could see him in the light rather than in the dark.

. . . so that we could have a normal conversation rather than just clipped phrases.

. . . so that we could sit across from each other, not side by side, in the left or right corner of whichever café it might be.

But how? And where?

These details led me one by one to another crazy thought, and before I knew it I was scurrying to my desk and grabbing the black notebook. I began rereading the story I'd written, my eyes leaping breathlessly over the pages in search of a particular thing. When I found it, I stopped reading with the excitement of someone who's found something he'd lost at the bottom of the sea.

Heaving a sigh of relief, I shut the notebook. I'd found the name of the café where the two of them used to meet.

And as with the cinema, it was a place I'd never heard of before.

When I asked the taxi driver to take me to 'The Date' café, the bewildered expression on his face made me wonder whether the place actually existed.

When he saw me laden with notebooks and newspapers which I'd brought with me as a sort of camouflage, he asked me if I meant the café near Faubourg Lamy. Hoping to avoid more questions, I answered in the affirmative.

But then he started talking about the security situation. He told me about a policeman who'd been thrown off a bridge the night before, and about a couple of girls who'd been kidnapped on their way home from school and who'd been found later with their throats slit.

I sat there listening to him as he told me stories about relatives, neighbours and clients and all the tragedies he'd ever heard about. I didn't know whether it was better to engage him in conversation so as to keep him from being too curious about me, or to be quiet so that he wouldn't ruin my mood. I knew very well how bad the security situation was. In fact, it was one of the reasons my husband was visiting the capital. So the last thing I needed, on this morning in particular, was more details about this sort of thing.

I was aware that I was committing another act of folly by going somewhere I knew nothing about when I didn't even know whether I'd find the man I was looking for. The only precaution I'd taken was to go in the morning at an hour when it wouldn't be very crowded, since this was the time, it seemed to me, when a couple would be most likely to meet in such a place.

As for the notebooks and newspapers I'd brought with me as a smokescreen, it appeared now that they might do more harm than good and that, rather than protect me, they might actually invite suspicion.

In the end, the only thing I could take refuge in that morning was the words of Irish poet Seamus Heaney, who spoke of treading air when the line runs out, and the fishers, 'who don't know and never try', pursuing the work at hand as their destiny.

So it was that I, against all logic, went treading towards my destiny.

The café was quieter than I'd expected it to be. Even so, I was visibly flustered when I walked in. I didn't know who I was looking for, where to sit, what to order, or whether to hide my papers or spread them out on the table as though I'd come there to write.

I didn't know which corner I should head for either, and I was afraid that if I chose the wrong one, I'd miss my mark.

He'd said to find a table anywhere but in the left-hand corner, adding, 'Left isn't the place for us any more.' So, did this mean I should sit in the right-hand corner of the café and wait there? Or should I sit in the left-hand corner with the expectation that somebody would come and sit to my right?

The place seemed huge to me. In one left-hand corner sat a young couple absorbed in a lively discussion. In its right-hand corner sat a man wearing a white shirt without a necktie who was busily engaged in some sort of writing project. He had papers and newspapers spread all over the table, and his ashtray was full of cigarette butts.

I sat in the corner across from him, leaving a distance of three tables between us to be on the safe side.

He turned his head in curiosity. He cast a brief glance at me and the newspapers I'd set down on the table. Then he went back to his writing.

I've never understood how some people can write in a café or on a train, as if they didn't have any sense of what an intimate activity writing is.

How could you just sit down and start writing in a public place? Wouldn't it be like making love on a bed with creaky metal springs so that everybody could follow your psychological states and your mood shifts, if even from a distance?

I tried to distract myself from the man, but I kept thinking about him. I was amazed by the way he absented himself from everything around him the minute he started to write. Even more amazing to me was the fact that he seemed to write everything down in its final form: without hesitation, without thought, and without erasing or scratching anything out.

Every now and then he'd stop, take a drag on his cigarette, and go on writing again.

At one point he seemed about to say something to me. He stopped between sentences and began looking at me without a word. I expected him to make some gesture that would tell me more about him. But instead, it was as if he were looking at something that only he could see. I couldn't find any way to flee from that look of his except to open a newspaper I had with me and start reading wherever my eyes happened to fall.

Just then he gave a smile that I didn't know how to interpret. Was it a greeting? Was he pitying me because I was by myself? Was he laughing to himself at what I was reading? Or was it just a way of telling me that he recognized me?

This may have been the first time I'd taken a good look at his features. He was rather handsome, and I felt a sort of vague affection for the countenance I saw, as well as a weakness in the face of a silent manly presence that bore no resemblance to that of the typical male in this city.

Something told me that at some time or other I'd loved a man like him, or that he was like a man I'd love at some point in the future. Even so, I didn't dare conclude that he was 'the one' until he made some gesture that revealed his identity more clearly.

Was he really too busy to pay attention to me? Or was he just trying to get a rise out of me with that silence of his, sitting across from me a destiny away and waiting for a question that would escort us into some other realm?

Cowardly woman that I was, I'd never initiated a conversation with a man before. So how was I supposed to make a move? How was I going to press the buttons that would get him to stop writing and say something to me?

I was dying for him to speak. But instead, he was working on me with words that could only be uttered in silence, and that had ushered me into a state of sweet discomfiture.

As I sat there thinking, the waiter came and asked me for my order. Without knowing why, I said, 'Coffee,' even though I hardly ever drink it. Maybe I said it just to make him forget I was a woman, since coffee is what men usually order.

In any case, he left and didn't come back.

I was less concerned about the waiter's disappearance than I was about the arrival of a distinguished-looking man wearing a black shirt and dark sunglasses. Looking to be in his thirties, he had a confident gait and exuded an effortless manly elegance.

It seems that this man knew me, and that he was surprised to see me there. After casting me a look of astonishment, he greeted me warmly with a nod of his head and went to sit down with the man at the table across from me, who at last stopped writing, and the two of them launched into a conversation I couldn't make out a word of.

The longer they talked and the longer I went on waiting for something that didn't come, the more mortified and insignificant I felt.

When you're waiting for someone, you don't see or focus on anything in particular, since your gaze is as scattered as your mood. However, the person you're waiting for might come out of nowhere and take you by surprise, jolting you out of your stupor and your jumble of thoughts and questions.

Who was this man? Had he recognized me? And how was I supposed to recognize him? Further, this woman whose identity I'd stolen: What did she look like? What colour was her hair? What was her customary way of greeting others? What sorts of mannerisms did she have? What kinds of things did she do or say when she was waiting for something or someone?

And this man who'd greeted me and gone his way: Did he know me? Did he know my brother? Or my husband? Do you suppose he knew 'her'? And why was he looking at me the way he was? Did I look like her? Had he been waiting for me, or for her? Or had he come just to talk to this friend of his? And what if he was 'him'?

I searched his eyes for something: a memory, a deferred longing, the remains of a secret sorrow, a love that had died in this place.

But his eyes, which scrutinized me from across the room from behind dark glasses, gave me no clues.

Of course, for him to steal glances at me during a conversation with someone else meant nothing in and of itself. Any other man would have done the same, if not out of curiosity, then as a way of silently harassing a woman who dared to sit alone in a café in a city like this.

But what if his friend were the man I'd come for? What if he was pretending to ignore me the way he had in the cinema? After all, that would have been just like him. However, he'd been betrayed by his silence, and by the right-hand corner he'd chosen to sit in, across from memory.

At long last the waiter brought the cup of coffee, set it down in front of me – or, rather, flung it down – and left. Noticing that he hadn't brought any sugar, I raised my hand and was about to call out to him. But then I thought better of it, since he was across the room by this time, and I didn't want to raise my voice just to say something trivial like, 'Excuse me, please, could you bring me some sugar?'

I felt as though my silence was too sweet to break by saying something to a waiter, especially in view of the fact that, based on what I knew about men with beards, the consequences of speaking might not be pleasant. He might refuse to bring it to me. He might tell me that if I want coffee, I should go home and drink it there, with sugar, tar, or whatever else. That is, if he didn't throw it in my face first!

After all, from time immemorial Algeria has been a country where, with a waiter, anything can happen!

It reminds me of an incident from the 1970s that a journalist friend of mine once related to me. She'd been staying in a swanky hotel in the capital with a delegation of foreign journalists on the occasion of the twentieth anniversary of the outbreak of the revolution. She was in the hotel restaurant and had waited so long that she'd nearly given up on getting her order. So, in true Oriental fashion, she summoned the waiter and said, 'We've been waiting for half an hour. But we're guests of the president, so you should be giving us special treatment!'

In reply, he quipped, as only an Algerian could, 'Since you're a guest of the president, why don't you ask Bendjedid to serve you?'

Then he walked away, leaving her with her mouth hanging open.

Of course, when she went back to Syria and told the story there, nobody believed her. After all, only in Algeria would a waiter tell the President of the Republic to come serve his guests himself!

Given all the stories I'd heard, I'd decided not to ask that waiter for anything, especially since, as far as he was concerned, I was an object of suspicion.

In fact, I ended up not even wanting that coffee.

Then all of a sudden, the man wearing the black shirt got up and came towards me carrying a bowl of sugar.

Given how busy he'd been talking to his friend, I don't know how he'd noticed that I needed some.

In any case, a hard-to-describe feeling came over me as he approached and handed me that bowl. Penetrating my senses, his cologne took me back to the scent I'd picked up in the cinema when that man had bent down with his cigarette lighter to help me look for my earring, and I was gripped by a mixture of fear and surprise.

All that was missing to complete the scene was a look from him. Yet even without removing his shades, he aroused in me the same feelings I'd experienced before, since that cologne was now associated with a memory that identified him for me in the darkness of the senses.

I couldn't resist the urge to recreate the scene with him by using the same words I'd used before.

'Sorry for troubling you,' I said.

'Not at all,' came the response, astounding in its perfect correspondence.

And, as he had the first time, he spoke the words and went his way without adding anything further.

I was so stunned, I just sat there for a few moments, watching him as he went back to his table and sat down with the same spontaneity with which he'd got up and come over to me.

I'd wanted so badly to hear those words that it took them a while to sink in, since I suspected that I'd just been imagining things.

It wasn't my earring that fell this time – it was my heart, which swooned every time love started to play hide-and-seek with me: presenting me with one man, then another, and making me tell which was which on the basis of nothing but a few tiny words!

I was still under the spell of those words when I saw the two of them get up. The man wearing the white shirt nodded as if to bid me farewell. His nod was accompanied by an absent look that promised something. And then he was gone.

I noticed that he'd been wearing white trousers, too. Meanwhile, I was approached by the other man, who was holding a newspaper that he hadn't had with him when he came in.

He stood in front of me for a moment. Then he asked, 'Might I sit down?'

I was supposed to say, 'No,' or, in another scenario, 'Be my guest.' Instead, I said, 'Of course.'

However, he didn't sit down. Still on his feet, he said, 'Actually, I hate this place. So I'd prefer that we go and have something at some other café. Would you mind?'

'Not at all,' I replied.

I was supposed to say the opposite, of course. However, his dislike for the place served as further evidence that he was 'him', and I found that the only language I possessed any more was his.

He took a coin out of his pocket and left it on the table to pay for the coffee. Then, with a gentility that took me by surprise, he pulled my chair out for me as I got up to leave.

All I could do was follow him – or rather, Seamus Heaney – and, against my better judgment, keep on 'treading air' now that the line had run out!

After flagging down a taxi in front of the café, he got in the front seat. I got in the back, and found myself sitting behind a young driver who was surprisingly well-mannered. He was so kind, in fact, that I forgave him for his cramped, deathly-hot cab.

I was about to open the window, but decided not to for fear that people would see me. Then I sat waiting for the man in black to say something so that we could be on our way.

'Do you know somewhere we could go?' he asked the driver.

The driver gave him a bewildered look, since it was the first time a passenger had ever asked him such a question.

The driver's expression then turned to one of amusement, which seemed to mean either that he felt sorry for us, or that he commiserated with our madness.

'Where do you want to go?' he asked us.

The man in black replied, 'Anywhere we won't be bothered. Are there any quiet cafés or tea shops around here?'

The driver smiled sardonically at his request and, having apparently concluded that we were from out of town, started the engine and took off at top speed.

It was a fairly long drive, and all the way there I had an overwhelming desire to sit with this man at last, to be next to him or across from him, not behind him. As the smell of his cologne wafted back in my direction, borne on the breezes of a speeding car, the two of us shared the same current of air, and countless unuttered questions.

The first question was: Why had he sat beside the driver? Was it to put some distance between us for one reason or another? Or was it simply because every taxi driver in Algeria insists that his male passengers sit in the front seat rather than the back, and if one of them should happen to do otherwise, he might scream in his face, 'Listen here, brother, I'm no servant of yours!'

However, the most important question wasn't why I was sitting behind him, but, rather (of course), why I was with him at all.

How had I ended up where I was? Had my literary curiosity led me into this bizarre adventure? Or was I running after love on a literary pretext?

How could a man who'd only spoken a few words to me bring me all this way without my even asking him who he was? It was

55

as though all my mental faculties had been suspended and replaced by my senses, which had stored up this man's fragrance and made me follow him wherever he went.

At one point I nearly asked him, 'What kind of cologne are you wearing, sir?' Then I hesitated. It would have been madness to ask a man what cologne he used before asking him what his name was! As for asking him his name now, it would have been an affront to the dream, since a dream has no name.

And he, did he know my name? If so, which name did he know: my name, or hers? Who had he been sitting with in the cinema: with me, or with her? And with whom was he going to some unknown destination: with me, or with her?

The taxi stopped in front of the Sayyidat al-Salam Café, which lay nestled in an idyllic, elevated spot overlooking deep, deep valleys.

The driver took off, richly laden with our verbal and monetary thanks, and leaving us in the face of innumerable questions.

When the waiter came to take our order, our joint reply was, 'We want Coke!' or, in other words, 'We want to be left alone!'

Then we fell silent, clearing the way for bigger questions.

I'd been expecting him to say quite a bit. However, he didn't say anything. He just lit a cigarette and began scrutinizing me between one train of thought and another. Then, as he poured me my drink with the same hand that held the cigarette, he said, 'Here you are at last!'

His tone conveyed a yearning or pleasant surprise that was so intense, it was as if it had to be condensed into those five words.

He seemed to be continuing a previous conversation with some other woman. Maybe it was that woman to whom he'd given nothing but his silence, and maybe it was someone else.

It perplexed me to arrive at this sort of conclusion. After all, would it make any sense for him to mistake me for her?

However, as he continued to speak, he confirmed my suspicion. He said, 'How strange that I should have run into you in that café. If it hadn't been for my friend, I wouldn't have gone there!'

After a brief pause, he went on, 'Something about you has changed since the last time I saw you. Maybe it's your hairstyle. I like you in long hair. You know, if it weren't for that black dress you're wearing, I wouldn't have recognized you.'

'And do you know this dress?' I asked, surprised.

'No,' he replied with a laugh, 'but I know your way of wearing black, which turns it into a colour that's glamorous rather than plain and sober.'

I didn't know how to respond to flirtation that I didn't think of as being intended for me.

However, going along with him in his confusion, I said, 'As for me, I've got to admit: you surprised me. You're the first man I've ever seen wearing black in this city, even in mourning. It's as if men hate this colour, or are afraid of it.'

'So what colour did you expect me to wear?'

'I don't know, but people around here tend to wear clothes that don't have any colour.'

Then, after a bit of thought, I went on, 'Your friend doesn't seem to be from around here either.'

'Why?' he asked, laughing. 'Because he wears a white shirt and white trousers?'

'No, because he wears white with a kind of happy flamboyance, whereas everybody else in this city wears it to show how pious they are.'

He smiled and said, 'My friend isn't really happy. He just has an extravagant way of showing his sadness, that's all. White, for him, is actually the equivalent of black!'

Seeing my confusion, he continued, 'The colour white is a kind of optical illusion. Didn't you know that?'

'No,' I said apologetically, 'I didn't.'

I sank into a moment of silence.

How was I supposed to carry on a conversation with a man who appeared to be as insincere in his show of happiness as his friend was extravagant in his show of sadness?

And I, who'd turned up by coincidence in a black dress, how could I justify my appearance when I'd never connected with the colours of things?

Trying to get off the subject of colours lest I expose my ignorance in this area, I said, 'Isn't it amazing the way our relationship started in the dark? Ever since that day I've wanted to shine some light on this story!'

'But we didn't meet in the dark,' he replied with a smile.

I nearly asked him, 'So where *did* we meet?' However, it would have seemed strange to ask a question like this, and it would have exposed me in the event that he thought I was 'her'.

So I tried to lure him into a confession of sorts. I said, 'I love stories about people coming together. In every meeting between a man and woman there's a miracle, something that transcends both of them and that places them in the path of a single lightning bolt. That's why, even after they break up, lovers go on being captivated by the beauty of their first meeting, because it produced a state of rapture that can never be repeated, and because it's the only pristine reality that survives love's destruction.'

I expected him to describe some rendezvous or tell me a story. Instead, he said, 'All beginnings to love are wonderful. But the most wonderful of them is ours.'

'Really?' I said, feigning surprise.

'Of course,' he replied, 'since it's a miracle that repeats itself every time we see each other.'

And that was all he said. However, his statement led me to the conclusion that we must have met before that film showing. But where, and how? These were questions he didn't seem prepared to answer. He'd entered into a state of silence, placing between us declarations as opaque as a cloud of smoke.

I studied him for a while as he sat there distracted from me by thoughts of us, or of her.

I broke the silence with the first thought that crossed my mind.

I said, 'A man who wears black puts distance between himself and others. So there are questions I don't dare ask you, however simple they might be. You don't seem to like questions.'

'Who said I didn't like questions?' he asked abruptly, seemingly taken aback.

For a minute I thought I'd made a mistake. But then he continued, 'I like big questions, scary questions that don't have any answers. As for nosy, naïve questions, they irritate me, and I think they irritate other people, too.'

'So how do you answer the questions people around you ask?'

He took a deep drag on his cigarette as though he hadn't expected my question. Then, with a touch of derision, he replied,

'People? The only questions they usually ask are stupid ones, and they force you to give them answers as stupid as their questions. They ask you, for example, what work you do, not what you would have liked to be. They ask you what you own, not what you've lost. They ask you about the woman you married, not about the one you love. They ask you what your name is, not whether this name suits you. They ask you how old you are, not how much of your life you've actually lived. They ask you what city you live in, not what city lives in you. They ask you whether you pray, not whether you fear God. That's why I usually respond to questions like these with silence, because when we don't say anything, we force people to correct themselves.'

This man was astounding. His words were as unsettling as his silence, his logic was as complex as it was simple, and his answers were nothing but the outlines to more questions.

And although he left me no room to ask him any 'normal' questions, I discovered that, by the laws of his own logic, I could legitimately corner him and draw him into telling truths that could only be extracted from him in an upside down, backwards sort of way.

So, a bit sarcastically, I said, 'You're a man who tries to get other people to ask questions in reverse. So, would you have the guts to answer my questions?'

'Well,' he replied with a playful defiance, 'that depends on how smart you are!'

So, upping the ante, I asked my first question: 'What name would you have liked to have?'

His reply bowled me over: 'The name you chose for me in your book suits me quite well.' He giggled as he said it.

I couldn't believe my ears. What he'd said meant that he knew who I was. But who was he to be talking to me as though he'd just stepped out of a story I'd written?

'I haven't chosen a name for you yet!' I retorted playfully.

'So be it,' he quipped back. 'It's fine with me to remain nameless!'

'But,' I admitted, 'this bothers me. Can't you take off your cloak of mystery for just a little while?'

'Only love strips us naked, Madame!'

'Am I to understand from this that you aren't in love?'

I could see my question dangling from his silence. So I posed it in a different way: 'Has love ever stripped you naked?'

'It did happen once. After that, I put on my disappointment, and I haven't taken it off since.'

With girlish triumph, I said, 'So, there's no woman in your life?'

'Madame,' he replied, 'how much silence do I need to answer your questions?'

What I was supposed to understand him to mean was, 'Madame, how much patience do I need to put up with your nosiness?' or perhaps, '. . . to answer your stupid questions?'

It wasn't this politely worded insult that drew me up short, but, rather, a certain polite word he'd used.

'Why do you call me "Madame"?' I asked. 'Who told you I was married?'

He smiled and said, 'There are women who were born to be addressed with this title, and to call them anything else would be an insult to their womanhood!'

Before I had a chance to take satisfaction in his reply, he continued, 'Apart from that, your marital status doesn't matter to me any more.'

The way he'd worded his last statement took me by surprise. It seemed to conceal precedents of some sort, or something he wanted to divulge.

'Why do you say "any more"?' I asked.

'Did I really say that?' he replied mischievously, answering my question with a question.

Then he said nothing more.

It was obvious that he knew something about me. The worrying thing was that I still didn't know anything about him. So I decided to carry on with the challenge, adopting his own topsy-turvy method of posing questions.

I said, 'I've never met anybody like you in this city. So I'm curious to know what city lives in you.'

As though he'd divined the aim behind my question, he retorted, 'My answer to a question like that won't do you any good. Like authors who live in one city in order to write about another, I live in one city so that I can love another, and when I leave it, I don't know which of the two cities had been living in me, and which of them I'd been living in. At present, I'm a vacant flat. I left Constantine for love, and she left me out of disappointment!'

'Are you from Constantine? That's strange. I thought you were from somewhere else.'

'Let's say I am.'

'So, what kind of work do you do? I mean, what would you have liked to be?'

Chuckling at the way I'd rephrased the question and the sarcastic tone in which I'd corrected myself, he said, 'Actually, I wanted to be an actor or a novelist so that I could live more than one life. One life isn't enough for me. I belong to a generation that's suffering from an age crisis, one that's spent its life even before it's lived it.'

Then he added, 'In any case, I'm an artist, and quite satisfied with my profession.'

'You're an artist?' I blurted out in amazement.

'What did you expect me to be?'

'I don't know, but . . . '

'But what . . . ?'

'I used to know an artist from Constantine. I just now thought of him. He was so obsessed with the city that all he used to paint was . . . '

'. . . bridges!' he said, finishing my sentence for me.

'Did you know him, too?' I cried.

He smiled and said, 'No, but I'd expect an artist who loves this city to do something silly like that.'

'Why do you call it silly?'

'Let's just say I don't like bridges.'

'Strange. He spent months trying to get me to love them. I thought all artists would like the same landmarks.'

He put out his cigarette as if to avoid an unpleasant subject and said, 'Who knows! He might have changed his mind since then. The only people who never change their minds are dimwits!'

Sensing that it bothered him for me to talk about Constantine, I tried to think of something else I could draw him into a conversation about. Before I'd opened my mouth, he looked at me and said, 'I like you in that dress. Black suits you.'

'Really?'

'Really. But more than that, I like the fact that we both happened to wear the same colour today. I still remember the dress you were wearing the first time I saw you. Like Cinderella's

63

prince, who has nothing but a shoe to guide him to the girl of his dreams, I think that if I'd seen a woman wearing a muslin dress, I would have run after her, sure that she must be you!'

He slowly knocked the ashes off his cigarette and continued, 'What saddened me that day was that I didn't get to exchange a single word with you. All the lights were against us, maybe because we were the best-looking couple at somebody else's wedding. The band had been playing lively music when all of a sudden it stopped and struck up the wedding march in announcement of the bride and groom's arrival. Women lined up on either side, decked out in their finest traditional garb and beating on ben-idirs and tambourines. Just when you and I happened to come in, both of us wearing black, the women starting to ululate. We weren't the bride and groom, of course. We were there at that moment by sheer coincidence, just steps ahead of the bride and groom, but it was the loveliest possible mistake. Next to us, the actual wedding procession looked downright dull! It was as though they'd been escorting you to me in that black dress as my imaginary bride, and the scene stayed with me for years afterwards.'

He puffed on his cigarette. Then he continued, 'I remember how we were so flustered, we split up after that. You struck up a conversation with some other man, and I began talking to another woman, making a point of seeming interested in her. Wanting to avoid more lights and mistakes, each of us found a place in a different group. Even so, we couldn't get past each other. Even while we were deliberately ignoring each other, we were still face to face. I don't think you felt any desire for me at first, and I didn't feel any for you. It was love that desired both of us, dreaming of a pair of characters like us to play these outlandish roles.'

I just sat there listening, not daring to interrupt him with a single word. In silence I found a refuge, a way of creating the impression that I already knew everything he was saying. Besides, silence imbues situations like this with a special sort of beauty.

I felt sure he must be talking about some other woman. I couldn't recall ever having gone to a wedding by myself wearing a dress like the one he'd described. I didn't even have one in my wardrobe. Besides, if I had ever walked into a wedding by accident with a strange man as striking as this one, it wouldn't have slipped my mind. Nor would this scandal-mongering city have given me a chance to forget it!

I was afraid to be honest with him, since it would have destroyed so much of the beautiful illusion each of us harboured about the other. So I kept quiet, enjoying my ambiguous position between two women, one of whom he was pursuing because she was wearing black, and the other of whom was pursuing him because he'd said, 'Not at all'!

Each of us was, to the other, both Cinderella and the prince, and this was the strangest thing about our story!

I had only one comment to make on what he'd said, and it was a statement that I wanted to be subject to multiple interpretations.

I said, 'So we might have all sorts of beginnings for a single story!'

'Yes,' he concurred. 'And that's why I was so sure we'd meet up. In fact, I'd imagined us having a time together just like this one!'

He paused slightly before asking, 'Do you know why I risked ruining our first date by letting the taxi driver decide where to take us?'

Before I had a chance to say, 'Why?' he went on, 'Because in love, more than in anything else, you've got to have a relationship of trust with Fate. You have to turn over the wheel without giving it any particular address or telling it what you think is the shortest way to get where you're going. Otherwise, life will amuse itself by working against you, and either your car will stall on you or you'll get stuck in a traffic jam, and at best, you'll arrive late for your dreams!'

'Something like that takes a lot of patience,' I said, 'and I'm no good at waiting!'

'You've never experienced love, then!' he said.

'Yes, I have!' I objected. 'It's just that my experience of it has only made me more impatient. Maybe that's why I've got it wrong so many times. Love taught me not to believe it, but I believed it anyway. It taught me to recognize it before celebrating it, but I couldn't. So I'm still waiting for love's train. Every time a passenger gets off, I think love has arrived. So I carry his bags for him and ask him how his trip was. I ask him his profession, the names of the cities he passed through and the women who passed through his life. Then, as he talks to me, I discover that he got on the wrong train and ended up in the wrong station. So I head for another passenger and leave the first one sitting on his suitcase!'

He was listening to me with interest, perhaps on account of the possibility that he, too, might be sitting on his suitcase without realizing it. Maybe this is why, as he flicked his ashes into the ashtray with studied leisure, he said, 'I hope you'll leave that station and never go back.'

Some silence passed between us, and I didn't know how to break it with anything but a question which, after what he'd just said, struck me as naïve.

It would have made more sense for me to ask, 'How?' But instead I said, 'Why?'

66

The reply came with an unexpected sternness. 'Because,' he said, 'I'm the last passenger to get off that train. I had to travel a long way to get to you, and now that I'm here, trains have stopped running. So, wait no longer, Madame. I've declared you a closed city!'

How could a woman resist a man so intoxicated with conceit? Is there anything more wonderful than a love that's born out of the fervour of jealousy, out of the conviction that we have a legitimate claim over someone who doesn't belong to us, and whom we're seeing for the very first time?

There was an alluring, unstudied manliness about him as he delivered this first romantic pronouncement. He uttered the words with a composure so disconcerting and so utterly self-assured that it left no room for a logical question such as, 'By what right do you say such a thing?' By virtue of a single sentence I'd fallen under the sway of love in all its insanity, and I began conversing with him outside the bounds of logic.

'But I don't know anything about you,' I said.

'That makes it all the nicer.'

'And all you know about me is whatever illusions you harbour about muslin.'

'It doesn't matter.'

'Do you believe you can keep the trains from whistling inside me?'

'Absolutely.'

'And do you think it will be easy for us to be lovers at a time like this that's so opposed to love?'

'Of course.'

'But we're headed for a romantic involvement . . .'

'Quite necessarily, Madame!'

By the time I'd gathered my astonishment-scattered wits to say something else, he was signalling for the waiter to bring the bill and call us a taxi.

Within minutes we were headed for a farewell when we were still approaching love's door.

Like my voice, his cologne wasn't high-pitched this time.

'When will we see each other?' I asked.

'I'll call you,' he said.

He left me no room for anything but an exclamation mark.

'Call me? How?'

'Don't worry. I know everything.'

'But . . .'

'I know.'

As the taxi descended with us towards Constantine's usual noisy bustle, we, with one bend in the road after another, were climbing love's steep mountain path, whose silence grew ever deeper as we ascended.

Then suddenly, as we were waiting at a traffic light, he asked the driver to let him out. As I looked on in amazement, he handed him a note and told him my exact address, instructing him to deliver me to my doorstep. He leaned towards me as though he were going to plant a kiss on my cheek. Instead, he whispered in my ear, 'It's better for us not to come all the way back together. It's safer for you this way.' As an afterthought, he added, 'I'll miss you.'

Then he got out, leaving me in a state of stunned surprise.

* * *

It was love, then. This was the way it always presented its credentials.

In a state of emotional fluidity, along would come a man against whose directness and unpretentiousness I'd taken no precautions. I'd reassure myself that nothing was in the offing, since he wasn't that handsome or charming. Then, when I was least expecting it, he would say something confusing that no man had ever said before, and suddenly he would become the most important of them all.

It was usually when I was in a state of bewildered amazement over him that catastrophe would strike. After all, love is nothing but being struck by the thunderbolt of surprise!

So here it was again, going away and leaving me hanging on question marks. I found myself in a state I'd never experienced before. As I got out of the car, a mix of peculiar sensations suddenly came over me and I rushed into the house as innocently as a woman who's just come back from a shopping trip or a visit, not from a tryst in an unknown location with a man she doesn't know but who knows her!

I closed the door to my room and hurriedly took off my black dress as though I were trying to cast off an accusation.

I sat down on the edge of my bed: exhausted, scattered, my eyes darting to and fro. I was trying to understand exactly what had happened to me, to recall everything that man had said over the past hour and a half. I wanted to recover all the details of our conversation, in the course of which he hadn't asked me more than one or two questions whereas I had plied him with one question after another. But my interrogation of him had been to no avail, since I'd ended up with even more questions than before, among them: Who could this man be? Where had he got all that information? How did he know my address?

Logically speaking, of course, I should have known a lot more about him than he did about me if he was nothing but a character out of a story I'd written.

However, my creativity had been reduced to nothing but attempts at outsmarting him now that I'd discovered my 'other' story as told by him, such as his description of our first meeting and the black muslin dress I'd been wearing. I might have believed in the possibility of such an encounter if I'd had such a dress in my wardrobe. But I didn't!

I'd purposely not interrupted him or commented on his story. I'd just listened, keeping my amazement to myself while secretly envying the woman who had once released all those wonderful feelings in him.

This pang of envy led me to a surprising discovery: that my story with this person had also been born in a moment of jealousy. He was the man I'd been looking for, the man I could measure myself by. So from the time I met him, I'd felt both envious of him and possessive towards him. I'd also wished I could kill that other woman and take her place without leaving my fingerprints on her neck.

She'd been my sole preoccupation from the start. I'd even asked him twice whether there was a woman in his life. Both times he'd replied in the negative, and this denial of his might have been the nicest thing that came out of his mouth.

There hadn't been any justification for my happiness, of course. When he saw how gleeful I was, he said, 'Don't be too happy now! It's better for you to love a man with a woman in his life than a man with a "cause" in his life. The former, you might succeed in making your own, but the latter will never be yours, since he doesn't even own himself!'

And I never did make him my own. A cause took him away from me for ever. Still, I didn't benefit from the advice he'd given me. In real life, I still fall in love with men who have a cause in their lives, and in novels, I fall in love with characters who have a woman in their lives.

If only I did just the opposite!

At some point it occurred to me that this man might also have some cause in his life. If he did, this would explain his extravagant sorrow, his bouts of silence, and his tendency to evade questions, all of which were traits I'd observed in this type of person.

At the same time, however, I thought it unlikely. Gone were the days of earth-shaking causes, the worthy causes that made an entire generation of men seem more youthful and glamorous than they really were.

In the political marketplaces run by rulers who shrewdly had outbid us with respect to every cause that comes along, they sold us 'the mother of all causes' as well as other, newer ones, packaged according to the dictates of the new world order and ready for local and national consumption. As for us, we took the bait with singular stupidity. Then we died, poisoned by our own illusions, only to discover, after it was too late, that they and their children were still alive, celebrating their birthdays over our dead bodies and making plans to rule us for generations to come.

So, since the days of that cause, dreamers have gone extinct and the knights of romanticism have fallen off their mounts!

Thoughts like these led me to my husband, whom I'd also failed to possess, not because I was sharing him legally with another woman, but because he was possessed by responsibility, and since his only 'cause' was that of remaining in a position of power.

In the end I nearly reached a frightening conclusion: that love is a purely feminine cause which, if it concerns men at all, concerns them to the most limited degrees between two lifetimes or two disappointments, and only when the other, 'major' causes have gone bankrupt.

So was this why women suffered such grief when it came to love?

Suddenly I felt afraid of this story, which was bound to cause me pain. I expected to be swept away by it, no holds barred, and without benefiting from anything I'd learned in life.

In the face of love and death we're all equals. In these confrontations nothing is of any avail to us: neither our culture, nor our experience, nor our intelligence, actual or feigned.

Yet I, who had always confronted love unarmed, expected it to take into consideration my craze for its defeats, and to compensate me for every loss it inflicted with another loss no less lovely.

Consequently, I'd never cared where love's unruly steed was taking me as long I knew I had the freedom to choose one of two fates: death because of it, or death without it!

My real worry was how I was going to go on writing this story of mine with any semblance of fairness or objectivity. How was I to be narrator and novelist in relation to a story that was my own? A narrator, after all, doesn't just narrate. She can't just narrate. She has to fabricate as well. In fact, fabricating is all she really does, clothing the truth in a fitting garb of speech.

This being the case, a novelist resembles her lies the way one resembles one's house. This idea came to me when I was thinking back on something I'd read about Borges. When he was in his fifties he began gradually losing his sight. Whenever he went to an unfamiliar home, he would ask his escort to describe for him the colour of the sofa and the shape of the table, nothing more. As for the rest, it was, as far as he was concerned, 'mere literature'. In other words, it was a place he could furnish in his darkness however he pleased.

When I went more deeply into Borges' logic, I discovered that a novel is nothing but a flat furnished with little lies of décor and deceptive details. The writer's purpose is to conceal the truth, which takes up no more space in a book than a sofa and a table would in a house. Around that sofa and table we furnish an abode of words which, chosen with the intention of misleading, encompass details as small as the colour of a carpet, the designs on a curtain, and the shape of a flower vase.

This is why I've learned to beware of novelists who include too much detail, since they're sure to be hiding something! Similarly, I'm amused at readers who fall so completely for a novel's word tricks that they fail to notice the sofa of truth they've been perched on since the moment they started reading.

For as long as I can remember I've been looking for a reader who will challenge me, one who can tell me where the 'sofa' and the 'table' are in whatever book he reads.

My husband, for example, has never been able to distinguish the 'real furniture' from the 'fake furniture' in anything I've written. At one point he started expressing irritation at my sitting for long hours writing rather than spending my time on some child that never came. He couldn't admit that what irritated him was the writing itself. He was annoyed by this act of confrontation and silent artifice whose credibility he couldn't verify despite his advanced espionage capabilities.

Instead of telling me what he really thought, he began sending me from doctor to doctor and city to city, hoping to turn motherhood into my first concern. I lost count of all the doctors I went to with special recommendations, and all the shrines my mother made me visit for this or that saint's blessing. For two years she and I made the rounds of Algeria's shrines even though I wasn't convinced of the value of what we were doing and didn't even want to be 'cured' of my barrenness.

I confess to having gone with her out of mere curiosity, and maybe as a way of following the path of least resistance. I confess, too, that sometimes I like just to give in. It gives me the chance to reflect on the world calmly and at a distance, as though it were no concern of mine.

When I reflect on the world this way, I start writing without putting anything down on paper. One evening, for example, I decided to indulge in my habit of writing in my head while I watched my husband take off his military uniform and put on my body for a few moments before falling fast asleep.

He'd always been an officer with a predilection for quick victories, even in bed, and I'd always been a woman with a predilection for pleasant defeats and romantic raids that are neither preceded by warning sirens nor followed by ambulances, and that leave the ground littered with lovers' dead bodies.

I have a fascination with random blitzes in which the innocent die of passion, just within desire's reach, and without having time to ask, 'Why?'

I'd always been taken by his power, and sometimes I wished he would make love to me without taking off his uniform, since maybe, with his uniform on, he would make his way into my body by force. But he wasn't about to do it on that night, or on any other, for that matter, probably because he was afraid it would get creased. Or maybe it was just because he was a man with no imagination or, rather, a man who exhausted all his imagination and intelligence somewhere other than in our bed.

After all, men who were made to occupy a seat of power weren't necessarily made to occupy a bed, while the ones who dazzle us with their clothes on don't necessarily dazzle us with them off. The problem is, we don't discover these things until it's too late!

So that night, like other nights, I watched him furtively as he took off his power and put on his nightclothes. As I did so, I thought back on the charming dialogue in Albert Camus's play, *The State of Siege*:

'Take your clothes off! When men of power leave their uniforms, they aren't nice to look at.'

And the reply comes, 'Perhaps. But their power lies in their having invented those uniforms!'

Of course. Clothes are nothing but a statement we want to make to others. Like rumours, they convey the intent to deceive, as when that man with the extravagant sorrow wore a happy colour as a way of concealing his sadness.

The genius of the military lies in their having invented a uniform that intimidates people. Similarly, the cunning of the clergy lies in their invention of pious-looking robes that make them look purer and more godly than everybody else, and the shrewdness of the wealthy in the invention of signatures for big-name designers so that they can wear clothes that place an unmistakable distance between themselves and others.

And this man, why had he chosen to wear black?

Was it to signal unmistakably to me that he was 'him'?

Or was it in order to match a colour I'd been wearing by coincidence when I encountered him, a colour life had chosen for me with the intent to deceive him into believing that I was 'her'?

* * *

Ten days passed in silent anticipation.

I tried to pretend I wasn't waiting for anything, but waiting was all I could do.

For some mysterious reason I was sure he'd contact me, one way or another. But as the days passed, life gave the lie to my intuition.

The only thing he'd said as he bade me farewell was, 'I'll miss you.'

Besides, he was a man who lived outside of time. So how could I have interpreted these words of his as some sort of promise?

Little by little, despair began to seep into me until it had taken over vast regions once filled with expectation. Even so, enough hope remained that I started staying home for fear that his call would come while I was out.

But all the phone brought me was my mother's chatter and her mundane projects.

One day she called to tell me she'd be coming to spend the day with me since my husband was away. The minute I opened the door for her, she began barraging me with questions. Looking at me in horror as usual, she said, 'What's wrong with you, girl? You don't look good!'

'What's wrong with me?' I nearly laughed out loud at the question. Like that man, she should have posed it in the opposite way, since then I could have answered by telling her what *wasn't* wrong with me, which would have been a lot easier than telling her what *was* wrong with me.

I kept quiet, since she wasn't going to understand no matter what I said.

She continued, 'I brought you some basisa that I made for you yesterday. We can get you a bowl of tammina to go with it. The minute you eat it, you'll be strong as a horse!'

Who'd told my mother that I wanted to be as strong as a horse?

I couldn't help but smile when I saw her storm into the kitchen, thinking that my problem could be solved with food and that no one cared enough about me to cook me the things I liked. Since I happened to have liked tammina in the past, my mother was sure to go on chasing me down with it until my dying day, or hers, whichever came first.

Tammina is a dish made from a mixture of honey, clarified butter, and chickpea flour. It's served to women who are post-partum to help them get their strength back after delivery. It's also served to the guests who visit her after the baby is born to congratulate her and make sure she's all right.

I don't know how much tammina I ate with breakfast and afternoon coffee without stopping to wonder, the way I do now, whether my mother was making it just to feed me, or to lure Fate into blessing our household so that she could serve it to guests who had come to check on me and her grandchild!

In any case, there we sat, with our cups of coffee and plates of tammina, checking on each other as though we hadn't been

77

talking on the telephone every day, or as though there were anything in this city worth talking about in the first place.

She asked me about my husband, and I said he was fine. I almost didn't reply, since I remembered how the man in black had told me that he responded with silence to stupid questions, such as when people ask you about your wife and not about the woman you love.

But how was my mother supposed to ask me about a man whose name I didn't even know? And how was she to know that I loved him?

What would she have said if, in a fit of madness, I'd told her I was in love with another man? Had she experienced love herself? Otherwise, how would she understand what it felt like? The fact is, she'd never even known what marriage was – she'd only borne its consequences.

How many times had she made love in her lifetime? During their five years of marriage, my mother had lived in one country and my father in another. He would only come back from the front to Tunisia once every few months to spend a few days with her. Then he would head back to the freedom fighters' bases, where he was responsible for directing operations in Eastern Algeria.

Then one day he went to Algeria and didn't come back. At last he'd had the honour of suffering martyrdom, and she suffered the fate of being widowed at an age when other women were just getting married.

When she was twenty-three years old, my mother shed her dreams. She shed her youth and her aspirations and put on the clothes of mourning, thenceforth to carry a name that was beyond her years and beyond her size. She'd fallen into the trap of big names, having fallen before that into the trap of arranged marriage. This time also, no one consulted her. No one asked her whether this big name was worth the black dress she would be consigned to wear for the rest of her life. No one asked whether she might have preferred to be the wife of an ordinary man rather than the widow of a national symbol. Instead, she found herself confronted with a fait accompli, which included two young children and a big name.

So she'd carried on: with a body that didn't belong to her and a fate that satisfied the pride of the homeland – the homeland that possessed the exclusive right, whenever it pleased, to strip you of everything, including your dreams. It had stripped my mother of her womanhood, and me of my childhood. Then it had walked away.

And here it was, still walking: trampling on my body and hers, on my dreams and hers, the only difference being that in my case, it wore army boots, and in her case, the stilettos of history.

I sat pondering her, with her damaged womanhood, her placid beauty, her down-to-earth gaiety mingled with sorrow. She was mysterious and calm like the Mona Lisa. But I don't like the Mona Lisa! I don't like calm features, placid femininity and frigid bodies. Where had my mother got all her frost? From her capitulation to Fate, or from her ignorance?

And where had I got all my fire? From my rebellion against everything? From the verbal volcanoes that were continually erupting inside me?

How could the ashes seated across from me in a black shawl have given birth to all the flames that burned inside me?

There's a saying that goes, 'Fire gives birth to ashes.' Well, sayings get it wrong a lot of the time! Here was a pile of ashes that had given birth to red-hot embers, to torrents of molten lava that had incinerated everything inside me: all the ready-made convictions, all the lies that women had inherited.

These thoughts led me back again to that man, and I thought of an idea that I'd been resisting for the past ten days. Taking advantage of my mother's visit, I suggested that I ride back home with her, after which I could ask our driver to take me on a tour of the city.

I knew that my chances of coming across that man in a city the size of Constantine were slim at best. But why not give it a try? I had nothing to lose but some time, the one thing I had too much of.

So I quickly put on a pretty dress and spruced myself up in anticipation of a possible encounter.

Not long thereafter I found myself in a government car, seated next to a driver to whom I'd turned over the wheel of Fate. I felt at ease, since I'd made no effort to determine where this rendezvous would take place. As long as the little details were Fate's responsibility, I'd let it dispose of my affairs however it pleased. I was determined not to intervene in deciding which direction the driver would go, and I wouldn't suggest any particular way for him to get me to my destiny.

The car sped along towards the unknown. The driver, who was well acquainted with both me and the city and whom I affectionately called Uncle Ahmad, had been baffled when I said, 'Take me wherever you like. I want to see the city.'

He was a retired soldier who was used to taking orders and carrying them out. As such, he wasn't really qualified to play the role of Fate, and he wouldn't understand why I might want to imitate some man who had asked a strange taxi driver to take us wherever he wanted and give Fate a chance to drive the car for us.

After taking me down half the streets in the city thinking that I'd wanted to look at the shopfronts, he asked suddenly, 'Where shall we go now?'

Hoping to get him to choose a place, I said, 'I don't know, Uncle Ahmad. I'm a little nervous. So if there's somewhere you like yourself, maybe you could take me there.'

Surprised by my request, he replied, 'I love everything in Constantine. It's my home town.'

Determined to corner him one way or another, I said, 'What's your favourite place in Constantine?'

After a brief silence, he replied, 'I love its bridges. No place has bridges like Constantine's.'

His answer came as something of a disappointment. But, determined to play by the rules of the game, I said, 'Well, then, take me to whichever bridge you like the most.'

The car took off again, speeding along from one bridge of illusion to another, suspended between the sky and the valleys into whose depths my slim hope of finding that man had plunged.

He'd said he didn't like bridges. Or maybe he'd said he didn't like them any more. So why had I come looking for him on a bridge, of all places? Was it an exaggerated attempt on my part to be fair to Fate so that I could prove to it that my intentions were honourable and that I trusted it completely?

Or was it because I believed that in spite of his dislike for bridges – or even because of it – I might actually find him there, since we sometimes frequent places we don't like any more simply to justify our dislike for them? If so, this kind of behaviour would suit him to a tee!

Actually, I didn't believe he really disliked bridges. In spite of what he'd said, I felt he was just like that artist I'd once known, who'd been madly obsessed with them.

He'd loved me as much as he'd loved bridges, and whenever he did a painting of one, he would insist that I was just like it.

The fact is, I didn't love them, nor was I like them. Rather, I loved him, and I was like his poet friend. That was all. On second thoughts, maybe it was the other way around. Maybe I was like that artist and loved his friend or, maybe I was like myself, and loved them both!

Be that as it may, we parted. There was an excess of love in our story. There was also a kind of counter-fate at work. The poet died a Constantinian death, and the girl married in traditional Constantinian fashion.

As for the artist, he disappeared. It was as though he'd decided to die in absentia. He could have come back on any pretext he chose, since he was a man in whose face no door ever closed. But he stayed away.

He left the way he'd come, without a fuss, and left me a painting that hung on the reception-room wall. It depicted a hanging bridge – hanging, like our story – suspended from steel ropes.

Before seeing that painting I hadn't liked iron bridges, the towering types that are like questions that dangle out of answers' reach. Now, too, when I was faced with this real bridge quite unlike the oil colours I'd grown accustomed to, I was gripped by a vague, inexplicable aversion to it.

I asked the driver to stop, hoping to find some explanation for this feeling. It also occurred to me that I might just find that man among the scores of people going back and forth across the bridge. Sometimes it happens that life gives you the thing you most love in the very place you most hate. In fact, life has often amazed me with its unexpected logic.

I got out of the car and went over to the bridge's iron railing. Never before had I got such a breathtaking view of Constantine from the top of a bridge. It was a chasm filled with frightening rocky valleys, deep as deep could be, and with the approach of sunset, it looked all the eerier and more desolate.

As people around me scurried in all directions as though they were afraid of bridges, or as though they were afraid of Constantine at night, I thought of some lines from Walt Whitman's poem, 'Crossing Brooklyn Ferry':

> Flood-tide below me! I see you face to face!
> Clouds of the west – sun there half an hour high – I
> see you also face to face.
> Crowds of men and women attired in the usual
> costumes, how curious you are to me!

Suddenly I felt dizzy the way I always do when I'm on a bridge. My legs could hardly hold me up as I stood there, terrified, at a height of seven hundred metres trying to reclaim a man who had left, and waiting for a man who would never come.

I was happy to see the driver get out of the car and come and stand beside me. This way I wasn't as likely to arouse the curiosity of passersby, who would find it strange to see a government car parked along a roadside and an eccentric woman getting out to look at a bridge!

I felt the urge to strike up a conversation with the driver, who lit a cigarette and stood looking at the bridge as though he, too, were discovering it for the first time.

As if to justify this madness of mine, I started to chatter. I said, 'You know, Uncle Ahmad, this is the first time we've ever come here. Whenever I stand on a bridge, I get dizzy. Bridges scare me.'

In fatherly fashion he replied, 'Don't be afraid, child. Believers aren't afraid of anything but God.'

As if to reproach him for having chosen such a place, I went on, 'I can't imagine why you like bridges. To tell you the truth, I hate them!'

With the logic of the simple-minded, he replied, 'Nobody would ever hate his home town. And what would Constantine be without its bridges? Just imagine if this bridge could speak!'

He fell silent, and I left him to his thoughts.

I decided not to argue with him. The logic of the elderly and simple-minded has a way of robbing you of your own, so it's better not to quarrel with them over convictions they've held all their lives. After all, no matter what you say, they're too old to change their minds!

As though he'd noticed something, he said unexpectedly, 'Come on, let's go.'

Seeing how late it had got, I said, 'That's right. It's nearly nightfall!'

As he went ahead of me to the car, I cast a parting glance at the barren valleys. I'd concluded now for sure that I really did hate this bridge and that whatever curiosity I'd had about it was dead and gone, just like my hope of meeting up with this man that I'd spent over two hours searching for in vain.

My sadness was made all the more acute by an overpowering sense of disappointment, since I'd lost the crazy bet I'd made with Fate.

Had I arrived too early for love, or too late? Or, rather than my having been too early or too late, had Fate's timing been right on the mark, the way Death's is?

I was suddenly wrenched out of my reverie by the sound of gun shots. The report shook me with such force, it was as though the bullets had gone right through me.

I jumped. Terrified, I looked behind me. All I saw was a young man, now a few metres away from me, shooting like an arrow through the crowd and disappearing down a side street.

I looked for Uncle Ahmad, but I didn't see him in the car or anywhere else. I took a few steps in the other direction, and what should I find but his body sprawled on the ground, with blood oozing out of his head and his chest.

I felt as though I was about to faint. At least, I wished I could faint so that I wouldn't have to see anything that was happening around me.

I saw the pool of blood spreading, and felt my voice escaping from me.

Passersby began gathering around, and someone asked me what had happened. Others had no need to ask, since they'd either witnessed it or figured it out for themselves.

I heard some of them uttering prayers for God's forgiveness as they shook their heads in disapproval, cursing a government that would let armed men roam so freely, while others stood looking on in silence. As for me, I was dumbstruck. A police car finally drove up and two officers got out and made their way through the crowd, their siren still screaming.

All I could think of to say when they asked me what had happened was, 'Take him to the hospital. Please!'

Seeing that he had a bullet in his head and another in his chest, they called an ambulance even though, as one of them put it, 'He won't make it.'

The officers were visibly tense. Both of them were young and clutched their pistols nervously. It was as though, now that they knew there was no hope of saving this man's life, their sole concern was to escape from the circle of human beings gathered around them, in the midst of whom might lurk another murderer only too happy to bag a policeman.

One of them began examining the car, and took a close look at its number plate. From this he easily concluded what rank and position its owner had occupied. He then went over to the body lying on the ground and extricated the keys from its closed fist. It was as though Uncle Ahmad had been in a hurry to open the car and whisk me away from the danger he had percieved with his military sixth sense, or as though, like a good soldier, he'd wanted to die in the line of duty, weapon in hand.

All of a sudden this government car had become more important than the person who'd driven it for years, and making away with it more important than saving the life of a man who lay dying in a pool of blood.

I don't know how long it took the ambulance to get there, but as far as I could tell, it was taking its sweet time. As we waited, one of the two policemen stood near the wounded man brandishing his pistol and ordering the crowd to scatter, while the other inspected the car and its contents. When at last a military vehicle arrived, the matter was settled. I watched them hurriedly move Uncle Ahmad to a stretcher and place him in the ambulance. Meanwhile, a soldier got in the car and drove it back to the house – without me.

Someone asked me to accompany him to the police station to make a detailed statement about the incident. I tried in vain to convince them to let me go with Uncle Ahmad in the ambulance, but they refused, saying that my presence wouldn't be needed.

'Where are you taking him?' I asked.

'To the military hospital,' someone replied impatiently, from which I understood that the matter wasn't open to discussion.

As they were about to shut the ambulance door and be on their way, I had a feeling I might never see him again. I ran over to the ambulance, took his hand and started kissing it. I buried my tear-stained face in his hand as though, since I hadn't shared in his death, I wanted to transfuse him with life. After all, I was the one who'd brought him to this place.

At the same time, I felt as though I were kissing the hand of death, the death that was about to take him, and that was waiting out of mere politeness for me to remove my lips so that it could snatch him away.

I heard him mumble something, though I couldn't make out the words. I think he said something like, 'It's all right, child' or maybe, 'Don't cry!' But I was crying anyway, since no one could see me in that car-turned-hearse.

A soldier was waiting impatiently for me to get out so that he could close the door. So, followed by Uncle Ahmad's vacant stares, I had no choice but to leave. After I let go of his hand, it dangled off the edge of the stretcher, his forefinger pointing forward as though he were uttering the testimony of faith during a ritual prayer.

As the car ejected me at the entrance to the police station, I entered a state I'd never experienced before. It was a blend of sadness, stupefaction, dread and nausea. I found myself together with a motley crowd the likes of which I'd never encountered in all my life. They were scary-looking, their faces expressionless with the exception of their intimidating gazes. Some of them were wearing ordinary clothes, while a number of bearded men clad in what appeared to be Afghani attire were wearing their beliefs on their sleeves. A man in a track suit with a shaved head had his hands bound with iron chains behind his back while another, seated, had been beaten so badly that his features were barely recognizable.

Masked military personnel milled about the place. Resembling woollen stockings, the black masks pulled over their heads concealed everything but their eyes and their mouths, which appeared through three openings that allowed them to speak and see out without being recognized.

What kind of a nightmare was this?

I concluded that this miserable-looking room with its bare walls and its filthy tile floor was an indiscriminate gathering place for a criminal, a suspicious-looking student, a citizen that had shown up for who knows what reason, a newly arrested thief, and me!

I'd ended up there because I was in love with a fictitious man, because I hated iron bridges, and because I'd wanted to make sure that I hated them as much as I thought I did. By some strange coincidence, the room was furnished entirely in iron chairs, the men sitting behind its desks were made of iron, and they were interrogating other men bound with iron chains.

So this was the Iron Age, then, a fact I could only have discovered by putting down my notebook.

After I'd been standing there for a few moments, a policeman noticed my anomalous presence and escorted me to a small side office where I was to wait. I was happy to have some time to myself, and to get away from those men's curious, unfriendly stares. They betrayed a hostility I could see no justification for apart from my being a woman, and my differentness.

Constantine is a city that watches your every move. It lies in wait for your every moment of happiness, interprets your every moment of sadness, and calls you to account for being different. So in order to survive, you have to rethink your wardrobe, your hairdo and your vocabulary and try to look as ordinary and miserable as possible, since the one thing the state will never forgive you for is being different.

What is freedom, in the end, but your right to be different?

Another thing I couldn't see any justification for was the fact that I had to wait so long in that little office. It was as though I was of no concern to anyone, or as though everyone was too busy with more important matters to concern themselves with my case.

From time to time I'd hear a young man screaming. I concluded that they must be interrogating him in their own way, which made me feel all the more pained and helpless.

For a moment it occurred to me that they might have caught the murderer, although I didn't think it likely, since they'd never caught a murderer that fast before.

Suddenly a policeman came in and asked me to follow him.

This time I was ushered into an office whose furnishings were nicer, in keeping with the rank of the officer who occupied it. Above his desk hung a picture of President Chadli Bendjedid. When I came in, the officer stood up to shake my hand and invited me to sit down.

'Have you found the murderer?' I asked him.

'No,' he replied as he arranged some of his papers. 'We're counting on your testimony to help us do that.'

I gulped.

'All the details are important to us,' he went on, 'so try to remember everything you can.'

'I'll try,' I said.

He took out a piece of paper in preparation to write down my answers.

'First,' he said, 'did you see the murderer?'

'I was looking towards the bridge when I heard gun shots. When I turned around, I saw a young man running and disappearing down a side street.'

'Do you think he was alone, or that someone was with him?'

I answered, 'I only saw one man running. I don't know whether there were others with him, or waiting for him somewhere.'

'Approximately how old would you say he was?'

'Somewhere between twenty and twenty-five, maybe.'

'Could you describe him for me?'

'I don't know how to describe him, actually. I only glimpsed him from the back.'

'While you and the driver were on your way to the bridge, did you notice a motorcycle or car following you?'

'I don't know. I was looking ahead. All I know is that while we were standing on the bridge, there was heavy traffic. There were a lot of people around us and, as you might expect in that sort of situation, some of them turned and stared at us out of curiosity.'

'Did you stand there for very long?'

'I don't think so. Not more than around ten minutes. I remember the driver saying all of a sudden, "Come on, let's go," as if he'd noticed something. Then he headed for the car. I'd just started towards the car after him when he was shot.'

'Do you go there regularly?'

'No, not at all.'

'Did you inform anyone in advance that you would be going there?'

'No.'

'The maid, for example. Didn't you tell her where you were going?'

'No. As I always do, I told her I was going out, and that's all.'

He paused briefly, fiddling with a small piece of paper in front of him. Then he asked me, 'And your brother? Is he aware of your comings and goings?'

'My brother?' I asked, surprised. 'He doesn't live with me.'

'I know,' he said.

Then he continued, 'Had you noticed any change in the driver's behaviour of late? Any visible nervousness or anxiety?'

'No. He was a calm, peaceable sort of person, and during that last outing of ours, he was his usual talkative, jovial self.'

After jotting down some comments, he got up, shook my hand again, and said, 'We may be in touch with you again if we need to investigate any of these details further.'

Then he added, 'I've learned that your husband is on a mission in the capital at the moment. I'll send him word of the incident through the Ministry. Then I'll give him a report.'

He walked with me to the door, asking a soldier to escort me home, and we shook hands again. In a voice that wasn't mine any more, I said, 'Thank you.' Then I left the world of iron for the world of bewilderment and grief.

* * *

Writing is always scary, because it makes an appointment for us with all the things we're afraid to face or understand too deeply.

The day I began writing in that notebook, I hadn't intended to invest things around me with some profound philosophical significance. Yet now I'd discovered that this man's death was bigger than me. It transcended the limits of my understanding. It transcended my logic, because it had happened outside of my notebook. Or, rather, it had happened on the margin of the page, along that fine red line that separates life from words.

The freakish, painful thing about his death was that he'd died because of a fictitious character, a creature of ink. Never before had death been this accessible to either words or imagination!

This man who hated bridges, who hated questions, it was his love that had brought me up against questions that had no answers.

And Uncle Ahmad, why had he died? Why today? Why now? Why in that particular place? Why him, and not somebody else?

I'd worked to get him to choose an address for my fate, and he'd chosen one for his own.

I'd told him to take me to the place he loved most in this city, but death had abducted my question and escorted it to its final answer.

Which of us was the prime suspect in a crime like this? Was it Fate, to which I'd turned over the wheel and with which I'd concluded a pact of trust, only to have it betray me? Was it I, who'd gone running after a fictitious man beyond paper's borders only to find that I'd turned the game of writing into a game of death? Or was it that fictitious man, who'd persuaded me to put my trust in Fate, then abandoned me so as to teach me a lesson in story writing?

It all boiled down now to two questions: Had this man's death been a crime of Fate, or of literature? And to what extent had I been responsible for it?

For my husband, who rushed back the following morning, things couldn't possibly be viewed from such a simplistic perspective, not only because he wasn't aware of the story I'd been writing and living and that had caused me to end up on that bridge but, in addition, because he was, first and foremost, a military man for whom what mattered were purely factual questions that left no room for Fate or literary creations. And this was the type of question that, like the ones I'd answered the day before, would rain down on me again, only this time in an irritable tone and with certain additions.

'Why did you go there? Have you lost your mind? Why on earth would you have a government car pull up along the side of the road, get out to look at a bridge and then, as if that weren't enough, carry on a conversation with the driver where everyone could see you?'

93

'I just wanted to see the bridge up close, that's all. I always see it in the painting in the reception room, the one Khaled Ben Toubal gave us on our wedding day. We happened to be passing that way, and since we were taking a tour and had the time, I thought: Why not get out and look at the bridge?'

'Taking a tour, you say? Is this a tourist city? And is this a time for sightseeing? This entire country is in a state of open siege, and you're out taking a tour? Don't you read the newspapers? Don't you talk to people? Every day they lead policemen away, slaughter them like sheep, and throw their bodies off bridges!'

'But I don't understand what Uncle Ahmad had to do with any of that. What had he done to deserve such a fate?'

'He was driving a military vehicle, which made him a military official!'

'But he wasn't in uniform.'

'That makes no difference. He was in the service of the state, and that was enough to make him suspect in some people's eyes. Unless, of course, they thought he was me, in which case they would have had more than one reason to kill him.'

He fell silent for a while. Then he asked the most important question of all: 'Where were you sitting?'

'In the front seat,' I mumbled, 'the way I sometimes do.' (The fact is, I *always* sat in the front seat.)

We sank together into an awkward silence as his thoughts and mine went to the same place. In the beginning my husband had objected to my sitting next to the driver. But with Uncle Ahmad in particular, I couldn't bring myself to sit in the back seat. He'd been like a member of the family. Besides, there was something so loyal and kind-hearted about him that, especially given the fact that he had once served in

94

the military, I would have been ashamed to demote him to the status of a mere chauffeur or porter when we were away from home.

I respected the patriotic service he'd performed in years past. I respected his seasoned hands. I respected his hoary head. It didn't matter to me that his towering height made him look younger than he was or the fact that sometimes he even looked as though he might be my husband. Nor did I care about the looks of shocked amazement that I got from other officers' wives when they happened to see me sitting next to him.

In fact, my quarrel with my husband might be summed up in this one issue. His ambition was to sit behind a chauffeur in a government car, whereas mine was simply to sit next to a man in a car, any car.

His dreams and mine had been separated by nothing but the distance between one car seat and another. Even so, it was a distance that turned out to be greater than I'd thought. I'd never realized that our decision to sit in one seat rather than another could expose something as deep as our convictions and aspirations in life. Nor had I realized that such a decision might cause the death of an innocent man because, without changing his place, it had changed the way he was perceived.

So here I was, confronted with another possible explanation for Uncle Ahmad's death, and it didn't relieve me of responsibility any more than the other one had. By sitting beside him I'd transformed him in others' eyes from a mere driver into a military officer and, as such, into an ideal target for their bullets.

How amazing, I thought suddenly, that Fate had done such a superb job of writing an end to this man's life. After living his

95

life as a simple soldier, he'd died at the age of fifty under the guise of a high-ranking officer.

He'd died under suspicion of being what he'd always dreamed of being, and he may well have been pleased by such a suspicion because, if only at the last moment of his life, his dreams were realized. Hadn't he died as a high-ranking officer on one of the bridges of Constantine that he'd loved so much?

The bridge on which he died was the very place where, in all likelihood, he'd fought and risked his life repeatedly thirty years earlier. However, death hadn't taken him then. It hadn't wanted him as a soldier disguised in the hooded cloak of a freedom fighter, nor as a martyr in a commando operation. That would have been too ordinary.

Rather, death chose to take him thirty years later: a soldier sitting in the seat of an Algerian officer who would die by Algerian bullets.

Only a death like this would be truly extraordinary!

My thoughts carried me far away, somewhere between irony and pain, as I travelled from one way station of regret to another.

I'd killed this man, not only with my insanity, but with my kind-heartedness, with an overdone humility that had prompted me to sit next to him in order to give him an illusory sense of being my equal.

Actually, the word 'humble' doesn't quite fit me. As I understand it, 'humility' means believing you're important for some reason, then relinquishing your status and making yourself other people's equal for a period of time, yet without entirely forgetting that you're more important than they are.

I've never felt more important than anybody else. I've always been so unpretentious that all the simple folks and nobodies around me thought I was one of them. And there's no hope of my changing – I've looked at things this way for as long as I can remember. I love these people. I learn more from them than I do from anyone else, and I'm more comfortable with them than I am with anybody else. Relationships with folks like these are easy and straightforward. In fact, they're downright wonderful, whereas relationships with important people – or people who appear to be important, at least – are tedious and complicated. In other words, they're pointless!

So, I'd had a relationship with this man, and only after he was gone did I see how beautiful it had been in its spontaneity.

* * *

Uncle Ahmad's death turned our lives upside down.

Given his certainty that he'd been the assassin's intended target, my husband took new security measures. The first of these was to give up his government vehicle and begin using an ordinary car, which he replaced from time to time. The second was to hire a new driver who would accompany me only when necessary, and to insist that I sit in the back seat and not engage him in any conversation.

My comings and goings were to be restricted that week to a visit to Uncle Ahmad's house to offer condolences to his family. My husband sent them a sheep and, I believe, also went to visit them one morning.

My only other outing of the week would be to visit my mother to see her off on the pilgrimage to Mecca. It was her third pilgrimage, or maybe her fourth. I don't remember exactly. Nobody around here knows any more how many times anybody else has gone on the pilgrimage, since it's become the fashion to try to outbid others when it comes to pious appearances.

I was so stressed that week, I nearly had a nervous breakdown. I made my way from a dismal household which, after losing the sole provider for a family of seven, was filled with the sound of the chanting of the Qur'an and the wailing of women clad in black, to a house where I found my mother flitting about in a white robe and white shawl and surrounded by women of all ages. After putting on all the jewellery and fashionwear they could find in their wardrobes, the women had come to see her off for the umpteenth time or, rather, to convince her for the umpteenth time that they were no less well-off than she was and that, like her, they had the wherewithal to go on the pilgrimage as many times as they wanted to.

Some of them, of course, were officers' wives who'd come out of consideration for me and who were sure to ply me with questions about the incident for fear that some similar 'surprise' might await their husbands.

However, I hadn't felt like talking for days, and their plush presence only exacerbated my grief.

They were women of ennui with houses so neat they looked as though nobody lived in them, who cooked only the most complicated dishes, whose words were as insincere as they were polite, whose bedrooms were as frigid as they were luxurious, and whose exorbitant wardrobes concealed bodies that no man had ever set on fire.

As for me, I was the woman of worry, the woman of blank pages, unmade beds, dreams that simmer over a low flame, and the chaos that engulfs the senses at the moment of creation. I

98

was a woman whose clothes consisted of tight-fitting words and statements barely long enough to cover questions' knees.

I'd been a skinny little girl with big questions surrounded by women full of loose answers.

They were still hens that turned in early, clucked a lot, and fed off men's crumbs, pecking at the remains of the love meals they were served when they happened to be available, whereas I was still a woman of silence, a woman of sleeplessness.

So where would I find the words I needed to speak to them of my sorrow?

Fortunately, I was saved by Nasser's arrival. Using him as an excuse, I left the women's gathering and went to sit with him.

So here he was again, at last.

During my five years of marriage he hadn't visited me more than once a year. Our other encounters had taken place either at our house on holidays, at family gatherings, or by mere happenstance (as on this occasion), as though we didn't live in the same city. The last time I had seen him was on the previous Eid al-Fitr. He would usually kiss me warmly when we saw each other. We'd exchange our latest news, and sometimes we would laugh and reminisce together. But that day he'd seemed withdrawn and anxious. Seeing that he didn't seem to want to talk, I'd respected his mood and left.

Nasser was three years my junior, but he'd always been my soulmate. He'd always shared in my joys and sorrows, and in my rebellions, too.

Then suddenly, when I got married, something was broken between us. What we'd had before was replaced by a kind of unspoken reproach on his part. At first I interpreted it as jealousy, since Nasser had been attached to me: I was his whole family, all his convictions, everything he had to be proud of. He hadn't excelled in school, and when his peers were still pursuing their educations, he was becoming a businessman. He'd rejected the idea that some strange man could come along and rob him of the one thing he'd had to himself. In fact, he rarely uttered my husband's name, as though he didn't want to acknowledge his existence.

I remember bringing it up with him a couple of years ago. I said, 'I've been married for three years now, and it's time you accepted it. It had to happen.'

His response took me by surprise. 'It had to happen?' he said ruefully. 'For them to plunder the country, empty out our bank accounts, commandeer our dreams, then show off their wealth when they can see how miserable we are, maybe that had to happen. But for the bastards to marry our women and trample our martyrs' names in the dust, that didn't have to happen. You made that happen yourself!'

Nasser is twenty-seven years old. He's three years younger than I am, and a cause older.

He came into the world bearing a cause the way we bear names that we didn't choose but that we live up to in the end. During Algeria's war of liberation, my father had developed a fascination for the figure of Abdel Nasser, and he'd wanted to give his son a name that reflected his pan-Arab aspirations. So, without realizing it, he gave him two names of renown: his own name, as that of one of Algeria's most celebrated martyrs, and that of pan-Arabism's greatest leader.

Nasser had shared with the homeland both its orphanhood and a name that was no longer his. Nasser Abd al-Mawla had been the national memory's pampered child. However, he hadn't necessarily been the child of a pampered nation. He'd been born with a name which, bigger than he was, had draped a cloak of distinction over his shoulders.

And herein lay his tragedy.

It's no easy thing to be the son of a national symbol, and you're bound to feel a chill inside the thick, luxurious coat of fame. What might he have worn under that coat to keep warm in times of disappointment?

What might he have been hiding beneath the burnoose of silence?

I kissed him fervently, speaking to him, as usual, in a Constantinian dialect infused with the vocabulary of motherhood. 'How are you, little mama?' I gushed. 'I've missed you so much!'

'I'm fine, may God give you life,' he replied.

He sat down across from me in his white jubba. I presumed that he'd just come from the mosque or was about to go there, since whenever I saw him he was either between one prayer and another, or between one cause and another.

Wanting to make conversation, I said, 'I came to say goodbye to Ma. It looks like she'll never get tired of making the pilgrimage!'

'I told her she'd get a greater reward for donating the money she would have spent on her pilgrimage to the poor in Iraq, but she didn't believe me.'

I didn't say anything more, not knowing how to continue the conversation with him.

Nasser still hadn't recovered from the Gulf War. When Iraq first invaded Kuwait, he'd been divided and unsettled. He'd go to sleep supporting Saddam Hussein, and wake up defending the Kuwaitis.

When worse came to worst and things moved in the direction of a military confrontation with the international alliance against Iraq, he sided once and for all with Saddam, captivated by the notion of 'the mother of all battles'. Like so many others, he was betting on the impossible, and dreamed of some huge battle in which we'd liberate Palestine!

But after the first missiles Iraq dropped on Israel fell in the middle of the desert, he called me one night and said, 'So is this the Scud missile Saddam's been threatening the world with? It's nothing but a suppository that Israel's stuck in its rear end!'

I laughed. I hadn't expected the war to have such an impact on him.

Those days were the only period in which Nasser came to see me regularly, maybe just because he needed somebody to vent to. After all, he knew it would be easy enough to infect me with his gloom.

One day, for example, he dropped in and was surprised to find me sitting at my desk writing. We were in the throes of the Gulf War and the insults that came with it, and he started raking me over the coals as though I were committing some sort of crime.

He said, 'I don't understand how you can go on writing as though none of this were happening! The earth is shaking under your feet and destruction awaits an entire people, and you sit here at your desk. Stop and look at the mess around you. Can't you see there's no point in what you're doing?'

'But this is what I do,' I said apologetically. 'I'm a writer!'

'And because you're a writer you should shut the hell up or go commit suicide!' he sputtered. 'Within the space of a few weeks we've gone from being a people that had a nuclear arsenal to one that's been stripped of everything but a few knives. And you sit here writing! We've gone from being a people that had the largest financial reserve in the world to being pathetic tribes that go begging for crumbs in international forums. And you sit here writing! The people you're writing for – do you think they can spare the price of a book? They're waiting for somebody to come give them medicine and a few loaves of bread. As for the rest of them, they're dead. Even the ones who are still alive are dead. So you should mourn them by declaring silence!'

Little did Nasser know that, by saying these things that he may well have changed his mind about since, he would change the course of my writing and force me to keep silence for two whole years.

During those two years I came to despise all those writers who, blithely publishing piece after piece in newspapers and magazines, shamelessly carried on with business as usual as Arabdom lay dead at their feet.

I would turn on US television stations to find 'live' coverage of Arab soldiers trudging through desert sands on the verge of starvation, falling like flies in trenches of degradation and being sprayed with the shells of meaningless death without knowing why these things were happening to them.

I'd see caravans of refugees fleeing in trucks from one Arab country to another, leaving everything behind after a life of misery and without understanding why.

I'd see Kuwaitis dancing in the streets, waving US flags, kissing pictures of Bush and offering General Schwarzkopf a handful of Kuwaiti soil, and wonder how we'd come to this.

A man who couldn't have cared less about us, who'd never lost a loved one in any of the wars he'd improvised or lost an ounce of his weight during any of the world's famines, would appear on our television screens in swimming trunks and casually promise us more victories.

During that entire time I couldn't stop thinking about committing suicide, and the only thing that kept me from it was the grief I knew it would cause my mother.

As a matter of fact, I'd dreamed of some sort of big, showy death. I didn't want to die like Khalil Hawi, who'd shot himself in the forehead with a nondescript hunting rifle. As his brothers and neighbours looked on, he'd killed himself on 7 June 1982 in protest against Israel's invasion of Lebanon. Before pulling the trigger he'd said, 'What's become of this nation of ours? After this pitiful show of weakness, I'm ashamed to call myself an Arab.'

If I had killed myself, I would have wanted to do it in a way that did justice to the grief I felt. I would have wanted my death to be something in the order of the suicide carried out by Japanese writer Yukio Mishima who, shortly after delivering to his publishers the fourth and final book of his *Sea of Fertility* tetralogy, headed out one Sunday morning to complete the final chapter of his life according to a carefully thought-out plan. He'd decided to commit ritual suicide in protest against Japan's humiliating defeat by the United States in World War II and the loss of its national identity in the face of Western supremacy.

Mishima had prepared for his death ahead of time. He'd taken private lessons in wrestling, equestrianism and body-building, which helped to prepare him for a coup attempt in the course of which he went to the Tokyo command of Japan's Ground Self-defence Forces and, together with four of his followers, took its commandant captive. He then delivered a heartfelt speech to more than a thousand Japanese soldiers gathered there, urging them to reject the post-World War II constitution that prohibits war and forbids Japan to form an army.

When his words failed to meet with the hoped-for response, Mishima went back to the room where he and his four followers had barricaded themselves. He donned a traditional Japanese garment, tying its sashes and securing its buttons with perfect self-composure. He then invited photographers to take pictures of him together with the four chosen members of the small, one-hundred-man militia he'd trained to defend the greatness of Japan. With the photographers still looking on, he stood grasping his banned samurai sword in preparation to commit hara-kiri before kneeling to commit the gruesome deed. He was then decapitated by one of his followers.

I tip my hat to you, Mishima!

Wherever you are, friend, I kiss the brow of your severed head, cast at the feet of your homeland in November 1970 in undying rejection of the ignominy of bowing before America's might.

And I still wonder: Were we being optimistic, or just plain naïve, to ally ourselves with a people so stubbornly determined to go on being defeated that they would achieve one stunning failure after another?

During those days I needed to see Nasser every day if I was to maintain my commitment to Arabdom. He would challenge everything I said, and he refused to let me badmouth any particular Arab regime. His rule was: Either you badmouth all of them, one after another (for reasons he was quite willing to recite to me in great detail, at great length, and ever so persuasively), or you keep your mouth shut! As far as he was concerned, lambasting one of them and not another was a worse offence than not saying anything at all.

Sometimes he would pass by and spend time with me. Then he would take off, saying, 'God help this people. Half its leaders are collaborators, and the other half are crazy.' Then, as an afterthought, he'd add, 'Of course, it would be even worse if they were collaborators, and crazy, too!'

Then suddenly Nasser changed.

He stopped talking to me about the 26 billion dinars that had disappeared from the Algerian state treasury. He stopped talking to me about his friends who, like thousands of students and other young people of Constantine, were prepared to suffer martyrdom in defence of the Iraqi flag. (After the Gulf War began, the phrase *Allahu akbar*, 'God is greater', had been added to Iraq's flag. This had prompted certain sceptics to suggest that we add the phrase *Allahu ghalib*, 'God is victor', to the Algerian flag, meaning, in effect, 'We can't do a thing for you'!) Nor did he talk to me any more about rumours to the effect that Israel had obtained a missile that could reach Algeria, and that it was getting ready to attack Constantine.

The rumour had gained such credence, in fact, that for nearly a month people were poised for war as though they actually hoped it would happen, whether for the satisfaction of fighting for a just cause, or out of a passion for martyrdom.

I don't know whether he'd lost his appetite for conversation, or whether I'd lost my enthusiasm for causes in general, having got to the point where I didn't know what to do with myself.

Given his disappointments on the national level and his disillusionment with pan-Arabism, Nasser had washed his hands of

Arabdom, or rather, he'd found his new cause in Islamic funda-
mentalism, which meant washing his hands five times a day as
part of ritual ablutions.

I, who'd always been one cause behind him, couldn't figure
out what was happening to him. But every time we saw each
other he seemed more distant than the time before, to the point
where he seemed like a complete stranger.

I didn't dare laugh or joke with him the way I'd done before.
I didn't even dare disagree with him for fear that he'd start
debating with me based on a logic I didn't know how to
respond to.

Hoping to draw him into a conversation, I said, 'You saved
the day by coming by just now. I can't stand women like this!'

'Well,' he said, 'it was your choice to join this club, so you
might as well get used to it.'

I nearly exploded in his face. But instead I said pitifully,
'Nasser, you know very well that this atmosphere doesn't suit
me, and I don't want to go into this again. I'm worn out. Uncle
Ahmad died before my very eyes just a few days ago. What
happened to him was horrible, beyond belief.'

I expected him to say something comforting, or to call down
God's mercy on Uncle Ahmad's soul. But he didn't say anything
at all. Was it because he was so overcome with emotion? Because
he didn't care? I had no idea.

My thoughts wandered away with me, and for a moment I
started imagining the craziest scenarios. I had a sudden flash-
back of my exchange with the police officer who'd questioned
me after Uncle Ahmad's murder: *'And your brother? Is he aware of
your comings and goings?' 'My brother?' I said. 'He doesn't live with me.'
'I know.'*

After a long silence, Nasser's voice broke in, saving me from a near heart attack: 'May he rest in peace. He was a nice man.'

I was so relieved I nearly thanked him for what he'd said, and before I knew it I'd flung myself at him, sobbing, and begun showering him with kisses. As for him, all he could do was take me in his arms.

Wet with my tears, his beard clung to my cheek. It felt strange, as though he were my father rather than the son he'd always been to me.

Still holding me, he asked, 'What's wrong, Hayat?'

I didn't answer. I was enjoying his embrace, his unanticipated affection. Suddenly I realized how much I'd needed affection without knowing it, and that it had been years since anyone had held me with tenderness – just plain tenderness, untainted by lust or desire.

'Nasser,' I said to him through my tears, 'treat me with affection. Does your religious law allow that? You're all I have in this world. Don't be on my side if you don't want to. But don't be against me. It's too painful. You're always letting Baba's death come between us, and you try to outdo everybody else in glorifying our martyrs. But Baba would never have wanted things to be this way. I don't want the day to come when we're enemies just because we don't think the same way.'

Which of us was crying at that moment? I don't know.

All I know is that I could hear laughter coming from the other room where the other women chattered happily away, awaited outside by a driver who hadn't died yet, and that I'd decided to leave without telling them goodbye.

I don't remember any more exactly which event it was that caused me to collapse and robbed me of my appetite for life.

Nothing held any attraction for me, nor did my life matter to anybody.

My mother was too preoccupied with her pilgrimage to be thinking about me, my husband was distracted by his responsibilities, my brother was busy with his cause, and the country was absorbed in its confrontations. And when I'd tried to find an illusory man for myself, somebody had come along and shot my illusions to death.

This city isn't content to kill you day after day. It also kills your dreams, sending you off to a police station to give your testimony about a crime in which you've been implicated by the act of writing.

My husband, who didn't have time to try to understand me and who didn't know what to do with me when he saw me closing up like an oyster, decided to send me to the capital to rest for a while near the sea until the storm had blown over.

It was the nicest idea he'd had for a long time, and an unexpected gift from Fate.

Chapter Three
Of course

THE JOYS WE WAIT for rarely arrive, and rarely would it happen that, when we have an appointment with someone, Fate would cause either him or us to miss it.

Consequently, I started living without an engagement diary, hoping in this way to save myself a lot of pointless waiting.

But after I decided that no lover was worth waiting for, love stationed itself at my door. In fact, love itself became a door that opened automatically the moment I approached it, and over time I've learned to be amused at love's droll counter-logic!

I'd come to the capital without plans and with hardly any luggage. I'd packed my suitcase with a few clothes that I'd chosen more or less at random as a way of convincing myself that nothing but the sea awaited me. The sea had an indisputable right to see me scantily clad. Consequently, I'd brought the scantiest items I owned and, I admit, a bit of unspoken collusion, since I didn't know whether I'd really come for the sea's sake.

When we take a trip, we're always running away from something we know. However, we don't necessarily know what we've come looking for.

I flung my suitcase on to an enormous bed that no one but I would be occupying and went to explore the house where I'd be spending the next week or two. Actually, I wanted to gauge the place's mood, its vibrations.

I loved the house. I loved its architectural design and the garden at the back. The garden was dotted with orange and lemon trees that beckoned me to sit on a stone bench shaded by a blossom-laden jasmine vine. So I took a seat and gave myself over to daydreams.

Like people, there are houses that you love at first sight, and others that you'll never love even if you live with them for years on end. There are houses that open their hearts to you the minute you walk in the door, and others that are darkened, closed in on their secrets. They're abodes to which you'll remain a stranger even if they belong to you.

This particular house was a lot like me. Its windows didn't open out on to any neighbours' yards, its furniture hadn't been chosen with the intention of dazzling anyone, and it had no secrets to hide. Everywhere I turned, it was light and spacious, bounded by nothing but the greenness of the trees and the blueness of the sea and the sky.

It was a house that invited you to do nothing but love, lounge and, just possibly, write.

As I sat there pondering the house, I wondered who had furnished it and taken such good care of its grounds over the last quarter of a century or more. It was easy to see that it dated back to the days of the French occupation, when powerful French feudalists had built opulent summer residences along Algeria's coastline not far from the plains and agricultural lands they owned.

After independence the Algerian government took over the vacant properties French builders had abandoned and made them into summer headquarters for its senior officers and officials, who now had a legitimate and permanent presence on the shores of Moretti, Sidi Fredj and Club des Pins. This villa, I surmised, was among the properties that Algerian officers had taken turns occupying each summer until someone had come along and reserved it for himself based on either his military rank or his political influence. And, thanks to a certain new law, this person would have been able to buy the house for nothing – amazingly – but a token dinar.

When had my husband acquired this villa? And how? They were questions I didn't care about the answers to. However, they brought my husband to mind, and suddenly I remembered that I hadn't called him to let him know we'd arrived safely as he'd asked me to do as soon as we got there.

It would actually have been more comfortable and convenient for Farida and me to have travelled by air. However, my husband had insisted that the chauffeur drive us up so that he could be at our service and guard the large house, where it would have been unthinkable for us to stay alone while we waited for other family members to join us.

I had a few days ahead of me before other people arrived, and I didn't know how to spend them. In any case, I decided to start by taking a warm bath and going to bed in celebration of my freedom.

*

I was in a hurry to fall asleep, but without falling into the trap of dreams. There are rooms that are so beautiful they seem to border on melancholy, and whose beds punish you by making you dream!

Even so, by the following morning I still hadn't escaped from my body. When I woke, desire woke with me. Enveloped by the scent of my craving, I stayed for a while, scattered, under the sheet, not wanting my lazy woman's slumber to come to an end.

An unexpected, pleasant sensation tempted me to stay where I was. I hadn't sought it out. Rather, the sea had brought it to me serendipitously as I lay in bed.

I'd wakened unusually early that morning, as though I wanted to make the most of every drop of this freedom that might suddenly be taken from me.

Then all of a sudden I was smitten by an irresistible morning hunger. My appetite for life seemed to have grown exponentially in this new venue. So I sent the driver out to get what we needed for breakfast while I stayed to look at the sea. After a whole night of ebbing and flowing, its salty fragrance crept towards me like a wild animal stalking its prey, inflaming my senses with a subtle craving for love.

I ignored its scandalous confession to having spent a night of love right next to me, busily taming its waves while I was busily taming my senses and running away from the worries that had been trailing me in my slumber.

Nevertheless, I'd slept more soundly that night than I had in days. I'd experienced such complete tranquillity, it was as though I'd left everything behind and flung myself on to a vast bed that had no memory. And now the only thing I wanted to do was to have breakfast and go on a walk with Farida to explore the neighbourhood.

*

Even before Sidi Fredj's marina drew me in with its tourist attractions and yachts, I was astounded by the way I always seemed to end up coincidentally in places so steeped in history, the types of places that brandish their memories in your face at every turn.

After all, Sidi Fredj isn't just the name of a saint whose tomb people visit to this day in search of his blessing but, in addition, the name of the port at which France first entered Algeria. It was here that France's warships set down anchor on 5 July 1830 after crushing all the humble defences that had been set up in the Sidi Fredj mosque and turning the mosque into a command centre for its military personnel.

By the will of Fate – or, rather, of the Algerian negotiators – France left Algeria on this very day a hundred and thirty years later, and 5 July also became its independence day.

Indeed, there was a time when Algerians insisted on writing history with their egos! The legendary incident in which Hussein Dey, Ottoman ruler of Algiers, slapped the French consul with his fan – and which France used as a pretext for going into Algeria to restore the French honour after being so rudely insulted – bears eloquent testimony to our pride and our fanatic zeal for our dignity, not to mention our innate insanity.

Possibly as a way of thumbing their noses at history, the Algerians displayed consummate artistry in designing the Sidi Fredj port following independence. To wit, they constructed it in the form of a modern-day fortress, with a tower and lighthouse so high, one suspects there were still people who thought an enemy would approach from the sea. Since that time, however, no enemy has approached from the sea, nor even necessarily from outside the country!

*

One day I went on a morning outing that did my spirits good. I took off walking without any particular destination in mind, starry-eyed as though I were discovering the world for the first time. Then Farida and I came back to the house with the things we'd bought, each of us cherishing her own dreams.

I felt as though I'd made a little dream of my own come true. It was a dream that, simple as it was, hadn't seemed within my grasp before, and which consisted of nothing more than walking down a street with peace of mind.

Farida and I began settling into a rhythm suited to life in a summer getaway, and the days we spent in the villa were more peaceful than any I'd ever known before.

Despite our previous disagreements and the difference in our ages, cultures and tastes, we were happy to be together. We'd become co-conspirators in the enjoyment of the momentary freedom that had descended upon us even though, under the circumstances in which we found ourselves, it meant different things to each of us.

For Farida, who'd spent a lifetime trapped in a marriage that had ended with her return to her brother's household as a divorced woman, freedom meant nothing more than being able to look out over a seaside balcony and experience the vicarious pleasure of watching others swim, roast in the sun and just live their lives. In short, freedom consisted of nothing more than her right to dream.

As for my freedom, it was opposed to the very logic of hers. I'd become a free woman precisely because I'd decided to stop dreaming!

I discovered this when I opened my black notebook one day, after having neglected it somewhat since our arrival, to jot down an idea I'd arrived at. The idea was: 'Freedom is to expect nothing.' I could have worded the same thought in a different way. I could have said, for example, 'Expectation is a state of enslavement.' In fact, I'd arrived at the first idea by means of the second.

But no sooner had I been liberated from my enslavement to expectation than I fell slave to writing. When Farida saw me staying in the house and scribbling away all day long, she got worried.

She felt responsible for me in two respects: as my elder, and as someone who had been assigned by her brother to watch out for my well-being. Consequently, she began encouraging me to watch television and to get out of the house.

One afternoon I decided to go out in an attempt to escape from both sleep and writing, which generally took turns trapping me at that particular time of day. I'd found that in this new location, a state of physical restlessness would come over me in the late afternoons, when most people were taking a nap. No matter what the weather was like, the feeling would dog me until sunset. And every day it would inspire the same questions: What do people do with themselves at this time of day? What do they do with their bodies? How do they spend these hours? Why is it that, in the late afternoon in particular, the rooms where women lounge around, bored, in house dresses are charged with such powerful vibrations of lust?

It wasn't the right time for me to find answers to all these questions. So I just put on the first dress I saw in the wardrobe and left the house, fleeing from my body!

I walked lazily down our street looking at the white houses with blue and green window frames, houses whose nap-time was tranquil in a way I'd never experienced myself.

Nothing about this place bore any resemblance to Constantine with its traffic jams, crowded pavements and noisy bustle. Everything here was nice, neat and tastefully engineered as though it belonged to another world, or as though it had ended up where it was by accident. If it hadn't been for the presence of a few cars parked along the sides of the street or the occasional sight of someone coming back from a bakery or a tennis court, a passerby would have thought nobody lived here.

It was a street that spent its every waking moment in a state of urbane serenity that placed it at the farthest possible remove from the shouting of hawkers, the squealing of young children and the call of the minarets with which the streets of Constantine began their day.

As I passed a bakery I was accosted by the aroma of freshly baked bread. I went in, surrendering to a sudden bout of hunger, and picked out an assortment of pastries and two loaves of bread. Then, remembering that I still had somewhere else to go, I asked the bakery attendant to keep them for me. I continued on my way in search of a newsstand. Once there, I began leafing through the newspapers with the curiosity of someone who hadn't read the news in a week. Suddenly everything I saw made me feel like reading, as though I'd woken up that morning to discover the world.

I chose a women's magazine and a political magazine, as well as a few newspapers in Arabic and some others in French. I didn't ask myself whether I was actually going to read them. After all those years of having newspapers come to me already paid for and chosen in keeping with my husband's tastes and interests, I took satisfaction in the mere act of acquiring them!

As I stood looking at one of them, I heard a voice behind me say, 'Never mind getting any newspapers. There's nothing worth reading these days!'

I started. Then I turned around, and who should I see but 'him'.

Frozen in place, I stood there in a state of sweet speechlessness, staring at him in disbelief. For a few moments we just looked at each other, bowled over by the coincidence.

I have a feeling my cheeks were red by this time even though I'd forgotten to put on any blusher, and I spontaneously reached up to put some locks of hair back in place. As if he wanted to unnerve me even more, he didn't take off his shades, and as he had the first time we'd seen each other, he gazed at me from behind his dark lenses.

Suddenly he said, 'I have to admit, I didn't expect to find you here.'

As if to apologize for my appearance, I said, 'Neither did I!'

'Didn't I tell you to learn to trust Fate?' he said with a grin.

'I remember that. But let's just say I've been having a crisis of confidence.'

Given the fact that we were his only two customers, the newsstand owner seemed to be taking a special interest in our conversation. Wanting to avoid any further eavesdropping, I asked my interlocutor to buy his newspaper so that we could leave.

Instead, he smiled and said, 'I didn't come to buy a newspaper.'

'What did you come to do, then?' I asked as we walked out.

'Now, I *could* say that I'd come to see you. The fact is, though, I only came to buy cigarettes.'

Then he added as he opened the pack, 'I don't trust anything any more, either.'

He lit his first cigarette, and we took a few steps together without any particular destination in mind, thereby exposing our madness to public view. Then we stopped in our tracks, weighed down by a load of unasked questions.

As we stood there he grabbed my arm unexpectedly as though he wanted to jolt me awake, the way you might do with someone who's been sleepwalking.

'I want to see you,' he said.

My body was electrified by his touch.

'But . . .'

'That word has no place between us. It's enough that it surrounds us on all sides.'

'I don't know how that could happen,' I said.

He took a newspaper I was holding. Then he took a pencil out of his breast pocket and scribbled a telephone number on one edge of the paper, saying, 'Call me at this number, and we'll agree on the details.'

I took the newspaper from him, not believing what was happening to me. With feigned spontaneity I asked, 'This number . . . what is it? Is it an office number, or a home number?'

'It's my number,' he replied.

Trying to get him to reveal more, I said, 'If somebody else happened to answer, who would I ask to speak to?'

Ignoring the meaning behind my question, he said, 'Nobody but me would answer the phone.'

In a single statement he'd closed off the path to any further questions, including the most important one of all. So I wasn't going to find out his name this time, either.

As we parted, I was just as flustered as ever, and he was just as self-assured as ever. He didn't press me to contact him as soon as possible. Rather, he seemed to know it was going to happen, and that was that. He didn't ask me what had brought me to this city or how long I'd be staying. Such details were apparently of no concern to him. Then again, maybe he already knew my schedule from A to Z!

All he said was, 'You look ravishing today.'

Then, as his gaze rolled down my black dress, the same one I'd been wearing the first time we met, he added, 'I love you in that dress.'

After a brief silence he continued, 'And I envy it!'

We parted without saying goodbye just as we'd met without saying hello. This was the way things always happened with him.

Neither of us tried to get the other to stay with either a word or a look. We had a mutual feeling that we were headed for an even lovelier encounter.

I have to admit, I would have liked him to stay longer, to say more than he did. However, I accepted the encounter the way it had come: amazing, surprising, fleeting. It had been an encounter with the lifespan of a cigarette. He'd lit it as we met, and as he put it out with his foot he'd said, 'And I envy it!' and was on his way.

This man, who was envious of my simplest dress and who'd said things to me that I would never have expected – did he mean what he'd said? Or did the fact that I'd happened to wear this same dress again arouse him because he thought I'd worn it deliberately, as a way of luring Fate in a certain direction? I hadn't done any such thing, of course. If I had, I would have prepared for our meeting a lot better than I did.

Love is astounding. It always comes out of the blue, in the place and at the moment we least expect it to, which is why we so rarely give it a fitting reception.

I know now what fashion designer Coco Chanel meant when she advised women always to look their best whenever they leave the house. Each of us should go out looking as chic as she'd hope to look if she bumped into the man who was destined to change her life. Otherwise, it's bound to happen on the day when she's neglected her appearance!

So, was this love? A mere word from him, and I'd become another woman. The woman who'd left the house in an ordinary dress, her nails unpolished and her features worn and haggard, had come back more beautiful than ever. Life, too, seemed beautiful and ravishing.

Even more beautiful was the fact that life is always so full of surprises. At any turn in the road your life could change. You might have an accident. You might also encounter a man who causes a marvellous earthquake in your being!

When I got back to the house I found Farida sitting in front of the television (as if she hadn't spent her entire life there), watching the same silly soap operas she always watched (as though they wouldn't be waiting for her when she got back to Constantine).

I felt sorry for her for being so stupid. How was I supposed to explain to her that we have to live life to its fullest, that we have to fill our lungs to capacity, taking in all the things we come across with our senses and our emotions fully engaged, since they may never come our way again? How could I persuade her to love the things that she would only see once in a lifetime, not the things she saw every day on a television screen?

I wanted to infect her with my happiness, with my appetite for life. However, she was an unimaginative woman of limited intelligence. I could also see that her naiveté was a blessing of sorts, since it would keep her from noticing what was going on with me.

She looked up from the television and asked me if I'd brought the bread. With a gasp I said, 'I forgot it at the bakery!'

As I headed to my room to change my clothes, I thought about how I'd now officially entered the phase of sweet follies and that if I'd forgotten some pastries I'd spent half an hour deciding to buy, then from now on I was likely to forget other things as well, and to take up residence on some other planet that had nothing to do with the details of my earthly world.

As soon as I'd changed, I picked up my newspapers and headed out to the garden, not to read the newspapers but so that I could be alone and leaf through the pages of my story with this man whom I'd chased down the streets of Constantine and who, after I'd despaired of finding him and come to another city, had found me here.

Life seems to operate by a strange sort of counter-logic. You go running after things, and they run away from you. Then the minute you sit down and convince yourself they aren't worth the trouble, they come running after you, and you don't know whether to give them the cold shoulder or welcome them with open arms as a gift straight from Heaven. After all, they might be your bliss, or they might be your ruin.

In situations like this it's hard not to think of Oscar Wilde's quip that, 'There are only two tragedies in life: one is getting what one wants, and the other is not getting it'! I wondered to myself which of the two types of tragedy this man would be. Or what if he started out being the first type, and ended up being the second?

I inspected the newspaper he'd written his telephone number on, trying to decipher what Fate held for me with him through those six digits. It had a lot of zeros in it, which scared me. But the rest of the digits, all of them odd, made me feel better. I like odd numbers. They're a lot like me.

At the same time, I couldn't help but wonder why he'd written it in pencil. Was it because artists usually write with pencils? Or was it because things with him were liable to be erased at any moment? Then again, maybe it was just because this was the Age of Lead, which writes some stories and erases others!

Evidence in favour of the last possibility lay in the fact that his telephone number was written in a narrow white margin of the front page of a newspaper that was filled with news of national and pan-Arab tragedies.

Why did his love have to run parallel to the tragedies of the homeland, as though there were nowhere left for it on the pages of our lives but a tiny, nearly invisible space? Wasn't there any place left in this country for a normal, happy love?

As I sat there bursting with joy, the newspapers of sorrow lay in wait for me on the garden table. Even before reading them, I regretted having bought them. I remembered somebody once saying, 'Every time I buy an Arabic newspaper, I end up regretting it!'

I turned the pages hurriedly, afraid that their contents would ruin my mood. But some of the headlines arrested me and drew me into reading entire articles in a kind of masochistic orgy.

If you'd bought an Arabic newspaper in June 1991 as a way of reading the Arab world's future, you would have risked giving yourself a heart attack. If, on the other hand, you'd bought an Algerian newspaper on the very same day, your worst national and pan-Arab nightmares splayed across its front page, you would have risked losing your mind.

Before you'd even opened the newspaper, the homeland would have assaulted you with its headlines: 'Military Authorities Suspend Curfew Until After Eid al-Adha'; '469 Arrests Over the Past Three Days'; 'Salvation Front Declares Civil Disobedience'; 'Strike and Open Vigil Begin'; 'Heavy Military Presence Around Government Buildings and Mosques'; 'Municipal Transport Buses Seized in Preparation for Large March on the Capital'.

If you'd fled to the bottom of the page, you would have been met by other homelands that you'd thought were your own. At least, that's what you'd been told when you were little by a certain naïve poet who died singing, 'All the Arabs' lands are my lands!' But by 15 February, 1991, he wasn't around any more to read the headlines, which ran: 'Palestinian Miya Miya and `Ayn al-Hilweh Camps Still Surrounded by Lebanese Army'; 'Iraq Arrests and Tortures Scores of Egyptians'; 'Executions of Arab Citizens in Kuwait Ongoing'; 'US Firms Monopolize Kuwaiti Reconstruction' and 'Egypt's Debts Forgiven'.

The good news in all of this wasn't the last headline. Rather, it appeared on an inside page, written large: 'On the occasion of Eid al-Adha, Algeria's National Livestock Office has imported 220,000 sheep from Australia, most of which have arrived safely.' The word 'safely', of course, meant nothing more than that they were still alive despite having spent a month in transit, packed like sardines into the hull of a ship, and even though most of them had nothing to look forward to but the mercy of being slaughtered on the morning of Eid al-Adha. In this respect they differed little from the hundreds of Algerians who'd been jostling and shoving each other for months in front of the Australian Embassy, waiting for the mercy of obtaining an escape visa to a country that was falsely rumoured to be needing workers!

Upon the arrival of the ship laden with its blessed cargo, the newspaper had devoted an entire page to a discussion of how to resolve the juristic question raised by the fact that, unlike the sheep Algerians were accustomed to with their long, fat tails, the Australian sheep had had their tails docked. The question was whether it was permissible to slaughter such sheep as sacrifices for Eid al-Adha. The upshot of the debate was a legal ruling that said, 'If, whether as a result of a birth defect or human intervention, a sheep has no more than one-third of a tail of normal length, it is to be considered blemished and unacceptable for slaughter as a religious sacrifice.' The question then became, 'What shall we do with the sheep, then, and what are we going to slaughter on Eid al-Adha?'

However, the real difficulty lay not in what to do with some Australian sheep whose tails had preoccupied Algeria's jurists and laymen alike for days on end, but rather in what to do with the human sheep piled in front of the Australian Embassy, and in how to answer the worrying question: How could a country that once exported revolution and lofty dreams have come to the point where it exports human beings and imports sheep?

* * *

Of course . . .

It wasn't a time for love. But doesn't love's greatness lie in its ability to survive even in the times most opposed to it? And

126

wasn't this evident in the fact that nothing I'd read and nothing that had happened to me because of this man had made me give up on loving him?

Then one evening, something started urging me in his direction. It picked me up, ran with me, and plopped me down in front of the telephone.

I sat down on the edge of the bed, barely touching it, as though I were sitting on the edge of my fate. Some other woman then dialled up a man that might be 'him', a man whose name was 'him', and who would at last put on his own words rather than hers. He would become a voice over the telephone line. He might say, 'Hello.' He might say, 'Yes?' He might say, 'Who is it?'

A woman in a hurry dialled his six-digit number, then waited for him to speak. Remembering that I didn't know exactly who I was calling, I'd made up my mind not to say anything when he picked up the receiver.

Then suddenly his voice penetrated my silence. He didn't say, 'Hello.' He didn't say, 'Yes?' He didn't say, 'Who is it?'

He said, 'How are you?'

To my amazement, he added, 'I've been waiting for your call,' and, after inserting a bit of silence between one statement and the next, 'It's nice that your call came at night.'

I hadn't said anything yet, and he was talking to me as though he could see me through a kind of sensory overlap. His voice collapsed the distance between one sense and another, repunctuating sentences, repunctuating dreams.

I recognized him from the ellipses in his speech. I recognized him and loved him with his sultry new telephone voice.

Then I said the first thing that came to my mind: 'I love your voice.'

'And I love your silence,' he replied.

'Should I take that to mean that you don't like me to talk?'

'Rather, it means that I like to hear whatever I want to hear from you, not what you're saying.'

'But I haven't said anything yet.'

'So much the better. Did you know that the reason animals don't lie is that they can't talk? Human beings are the only species with the capacity for hypocrisy, since they're the only species that can speak. In other words, humans are actors by nature.'

'How can you say a thing like that?'

'I can say it because I know what life is like, and because I know what you're like.'

'And what do you know about me?'

'I know enough to beware of you, and enough to be in love with you.'

'Should I beware of you, too?'

'Rather, you should beware of love, and you should love me.'

'I do love you.'

'Really?'

'. . .'

'Notice that you've started to withdraw into silence. Nice words spoil fast. That's why they can't be said any old which way!'

I didn't know how to go on talking to him, since everything I said was bound to collide with that sharp wit of his, and with his one-of-a-kind way of looking at things.

But I did say, 'I want to learn your philosophy of life.'

'Me, teach you my philosophy of life?' He chuckled. 'You're asking the impossible! All I can give you is the broad outlines. We can't learn life from others. We have to learn it through our

128

bruises and scratches, and from all the parts of us that stay on the ground after we've fallen and got back up again.'

'Is that what always happens?'

'Of course. You're going to learn how to let go of a part of yourself with every new trial. With everything you go through, you have to leave somebody or something behind. We come into life like people who are moving house. We're loaded down with furniture and stuff – our ideals and big dreams – and we're surrounded by family and friends. But as time goes on, we lose things and we leave people behind until all we have left in the end are the things we consider most important for the simple reason that we've lost the things that were more important than they were!'

The things he was saying gave me an idea of how I might get him to talk about himself.

'So what have you left behind?' I asked.

When he didn't say anything for a long time, I remembered that this was how he responded to questions that weren't worth answering, so I corrected myself.

'I mean, what's most important to you now?'

'You,' he replied in an absent sort of voice.

His reply took me by surprise.

I expected him to add, 'And what's most important to you?' But instead he went on, 'I'm waiting for the illusions around you to die. Maybe then I'll become the most important thing to you, if not by merit, then by coincidence!'

'I don't need any more disappointments in order to love you,' I interrupted. 'You're all I've got.'

'That's not true. You've got your writing; that is, the illusion of superiority. So we'll never be equals until our story is written not by you, but by life!'

'Have you come back to poke fun at me, then?'

'No, I've come back to love you. I've missed you like mad all this time, and I don't understand why our story has to be so complicated. You know? If we were illiterate, we'd be happy with our love. The illiterate man knows what he wants from a woman, and the illiterate woman knows what she expects from a man. As for us, we've been lured into the game of words, so we're hard on love in honour of literature. Imagine: If we were a couple of illiterate folks, I would have told you right up front, "I want you," and that would have been that. But instead, here we are talking on the telephone past midnight, not to love each other, but to make sense of our love.'

'Let's be a couple of illiterate folks, then!'

'We couldn't do it. Ignorance is a luxury we can't afford any more.'

'What do we do, then?'

'Let's just be a man and a woman, plain and simple. Let's be together by the logic of love, not by the logic of literature. It wouldn't do for us to come out of the darkness of ink just to end up in the darkness of the night. I want our love to see the light of day. I want to see you, touch you, tell you things that don't require either of us to say a word.'

'But I don't know where we could meet.'

'There are lots of nice cafés and restaurants in your area. We could meet there.'

'But all my neighbours are officers, and they know my husband. I wouldn't dare risk meeting you around here.'

After a pause, he said, 'If you'd like, we could meet at my house. But I live an hour's drive from you. Would that suit you?'

'Give me a day or so to think. I'll manage it.'

Then, as if I'd just remembered something, I added, 'But before that, I want to know who you are.'

As if the matter were of no importance, he said, 'Love me without questions. After all, love doesn't have any logical answers.'

'How do you expect me to visit a man whose name I don't even know?'

'You'll know everything when the time is right.'

'I'm no good at waiting.'

'That's a shame, since things acquire their value from our having to wait for them.

'And by this criterion,' he went on, 'you're the most desirable woman of all, since you're the one I've waited for the longest. I've waited a lifetime for you. So you could manage to wait for a few days or weeks. Let the illusion last a little longer.'

I don't remember what he said after that. We suddenly found ourselves in a word-induced state of passion which he prolonged to the maximum by the mere force of his desire to be nothing but an illiterate man who wants a woman!

I woke up the next morning in a state of sweet infatuation; that is, until the news broadcast ruined my mood, at which point I decided to call my husband to find out what was happening in Constantine. I picked up the receiver only to discover that the phone was dead, which worried me even more. So I headed over to the house next door to see if I could use the neighbours' phone.

I got a cool reception from the lady who came to the door, and the disdainful way she looked me over totally unnerved me. At first I interpreted her look as due to the fact that I'd come in house clothes rather than being dressed properly for a visit.

Still standing outside, since she hadn't invited me in, I began explaining that I lived in the villa next door to hers and that my telephone was out of order. Before I could finish, she interrupted me cattily, 'So, you're the new neighbour. Well, every day's a party around here!'

Thinking that she might have mistaken me for somebody else, I said, 'I live in villa No. 68 to your right. I've only been here a week.'

'Most women around here only stay for a night or two!' she retorted sarcastically.

I froze, as though her words had slapped me across the face. I mustered the courage to say, 'I'm the general's wife. I only came to ask you why the phone wasn't working, since I haven't been able to contact my husband in Constantine. I have no idea what was going on in this house before I got here.'

Visibly flustered, the woman suddenly opened the door and apologetically invited me in. My unkempt appearance must have led her to believe that I was one of the various fleeting visitors to the house, and she obviously regretted the things she'd said. Fumbling for words, she tried to convince me that she'd thought I was staying in some other villa. She also explained that since most of the villas in the neighbourhood stood empty for most of the year, some people had taken to bringing their lovers and girlfriends to their summer houses, which irritated her because she lived there all year round.

I assured her that I understood completely. Then, apologizing for the disturbance, I said a polite goodbye. However, she kept insisting that I call my husband from her house, saying there was no need to trouble him over the matter of the telephone since her husband could contact the relevant authorities and get it fixed right away.

When I got back to the house I didn't tell Farida what the neighbour had said. I kept the insult to myself. Besides, what would she have said if I'd told her? She was sure to believe deep down that her brother was entitled to behave however he liked, not just because he was a man, but because he was a man of state.

Oddly, I didn't feel jealous. What I felt was more like nausea than anything else. I didn't want to think about the women who'd taken turns occupying the bed I'd been sleeping in, and I didn't bother to put features to their faces.

What they looked like didn't matter to me, though I imagined them to be the floozy, naughty-looking sort. They might have been plastic blondes. That was the type my husband usually went for. Maybe all men did, for that matter, which I could understand.

What I couldn't understand was why my husband had married a dark-skinned woman if fair-skinned women were his preference. And why had he taken a second wife if the only thing that satisfied him was the snacks he picked up while he was out?

I thought of a friend of mine whose husband was enamoured of blondes. It got on her nerves to hear people whispering things like, 'We saw your husband with a blonde the other day!' So the poor thing went and bleached her hair, not in hopes of seducing him or getting him back, but just so that it would seem to people from a distance that he was with her – as though the only thing that mattered was keeping up appearances!

In any case, the worst punishment I suffered that day wasn't what I heard the neighbour lady say, but, rather, not being able to hear that man's voice.

The next morning I was wakened by the voice of my husband, who'd called to tell me that the phone lines were working again.

His voice jolted me out of the previous night's nightmares, but without putting any sweet dreams in their place.

Dreams had another voice. I'd called that voice a nameless 'him', who was nothing but the four letters that make up the word 'love' with a question mark at the end. He was nothing but four letters and six digits. However, they weren't the six digits that made up his telephone number. Rather, they were the six digits on the lottery ticket I was using to gamble on my fate.

'I've missed hearing from you. Why didn't you call yesterday?'

'The phone was out of order.'

'Have you figured out where you want us to meet?'

'Yes. If it's all right with you, I'll visit you at home this afternoon.'

'You're the only thing on my schedule,' he said after a slight pause. 'You can come whenever you like. But . . .'

'But what?'

'The situation doesn't look safe today.'

I reassured him, saying, 'It couldn't be any worse than it's been in Constantine.'

'I don't think you know how bad it really is, then.'

'What's going on?' I asked, my curiosity piqued.

'Last night the capital's squares turned into huge bedrooms. The Islamists spread out everywhere, and didn't get up till this morning to shout slogans and threats and recite loud prayers.'

'When did this all start?'

'Yesterday. Busloads of them, both men and women, rolled in.'

'Women, too?' I asked, incredulous.

'They came in minibuses with the curtains drawn. All you could see was copies of the Qur'an being raised outside the windows.'

My enthusiasm waning a bit, I asked, 'Are these things happening near you?'

'Of course,' he said. 'I live on Larbi Ben M'hidi Street. It branches off Emir Abdelkader Square, which is where they're holding the vigil.'

'I know that street!' I interrupted.

For a moment I was about to give up on my crazy adventure. But I was so frustrated that as far as I was concerned, not being able to see him was the worst thing that could possibly happen to me.

I thought he'd be surprised when I said to him, 'I'll come by way of the Central Post Office. Just give me the address.'

But, with an excitement that made me happy, he said, 'That's what I expected you to decide. It's just like you!'

Then he added, 'Do you understand now why I love you?'

'No,' I said jokingly. 'You'll have to explain it to me when I get there!'

* * *

At long, long last three o'clock rolled around.

You took so long to get here, love, why are you rushing me now?

At breakneck speed, the driver took me halfway to my heart's desire. I would then have to go the rest of the way alone, frightened and on foot. As I made my way down the pavement, I dodged the glances of drivers who made it their profession to spy on others, and of passersby who had nothing better to do than mind other people's business. On the other hand, who would be

135

perceptive enough to recognize the footsteps of a woman on her way to or from a rendezvous with love?

Unlike those who have time to squander, love is an impatient teacher that brooks no nonsense. It teaches you everything at once. Whatever it shows you, it shows you its opposite through the same experience. And by instructing you in how to be yourself and somebody else simultaneously, it makes you into a first-rate actor.

I crossed Emir Abdelkader Square with a steady gait, walking along in my cloak and long headscarf as though I'd been wearing them all my life.

I felt safe in the midst of the crowds of men that surrounded me with their bizarre get-ups and hostile faces. Shouting and chanting religious and political slogans, they were too preoccupied with their otherworldly concerns to pay any attention to my worldly ones.

I would have liked to avoid the square, but I had no choice but to pass through it, since all the streets that led to my destination were so busy that if I'd come by way of any of them, I would have been at least an hour late for my appointment.

I couldn't remember ever having passed through this square without being taken aback at the minuscule dimensions of Emir Abdelkader's statue. The sight of it had always given me a bad case of nerves. This time, too, hurried as I was, I couldn't help but notice it as it stood there engulfed by a sea of people, above which it rose by a mere metre or two. The statue was so short that some people had climbed on top of it without difficulty and draped it with green and black flags.

It kills me to see the gargantuan statues that adorn Arab capitals in honour of rulers who've given their peoples nothing but blood and destruction, while this man – who gave us a reason to be proud of our history by founding an Algerian state that dazzled France itself, and who wouldn't have demanded that we bring his remains back from Syria or that we erect a statue of him in a square that, large as it is, will always be dwarfed by his greatness – has nothing but a puny little statue to his name.

(It's a strange time indeed, when values are turned on their heads and people make statues for their leaders in celebration of their crimes rather than their greatness!) No wonder, then, that for twenty-five years Emir Abdelkader had been registering his displeasure at being among us by standing with his back turned to the Liberation Front Party headquarters and his face to the sea, a fact that had become the stuff of many a political joke among residents of the capital.

There was a time when we Algerians had been masters of irony. So how had we lost our sense of humour? Where had we got these expressionless faces, these hostile temperaments and these strange fashions that had never suited us?

How had we become strangers to ourselves and each other? We were alienated to the point of being afraid of each other, taking precautions lest others look at us askance, and terrified every time we heard footsteps behind us.

As I walked through the square, hidden safely inside clothes that I'd borrowed from Farida and that weren't the least bit like me, fear prompted me alternately to speed up and slow down. I found myself living back and forth between two people, one of whom was practised in seduction, the other in piety. One time I went to meet this man wearing a skin-tight black dress, and the next, a loose cloak and a headscarf that left nothing but my face showing. In short, I was being occupied in turns by two different women, both of whom were me.

Because we tend to think and act in keeping with what we put on and take off, I passed through the crowd in a kind of vague collusion. In fact, I might have joined in their excited shouting if I hadn't been so engrossed in looking for the building where that man was waiting for me. Meanwhile, I kept wondering: Why is he always alongside of politics? Why does he come back according to history's timing? And why is it that, when I relate to him, my joy is constantly on guard against sorrow?

As I walked warily past the Milk Bar Café, I suddenly remembered Djamila Bouhired. It's said that one day during the revolution, she came to this café dressed in European clothing and ordered something. Before leaving, she put her bag under the table. It turned out that the bag was filled with explosives, and when they went off, the resulting blast rocked all of France, which, after having demanded that Algerian women remove their hijabs, discovered that European dress might be used to conceal a freedom-fighter!

And here I was, forty years later, Djamila Bouhired's legitimate heir, passing the same café disguised in the garb of piety, since women had discovered that this very garb might conceal a lover whose body is set to explode with passion.

I walked past the café with the same fear, the same defiance, and the same determination, knowing that love had become the biggest freedom-fighting operation any Algerian woman could carry out.

*

138

I've always told myself, 'Don't jump life's red lights, and learn to stop at destiny's checkpoints. There's no point in rigging traffic signals, since destiny can't be taken by force.'

I used to tell my heart, 'Try not to be like me. Don't be in a hurry. Look right and left before you cross life's streets, and don't try to jump on to this runaway train when it's moving. Dreamers travel standing still, since they know they always arrive one disappointment later than everybody else!'

And my heart would reply, 'Everybody you've ever known has seen his dreams crushed under the homeland's wheels, and all the people you've ever loved have been scattered all over destiny's train. So cross wherever you like, since either way you're bound to die in some accident of love!'

At last the building appeared.

When I stepped inside, I felt myself leaving one world and entering another.

I wasn't bothered by its filthy staircase, I wasn't put off by its broken-down lift, and the four flights I had to climb only added to my excitement.

Love's sweetest moments are when you're going up the stairs!

Outside a door behind which the unknown awaited, I caught my breath and tried to make sure I looked all right. But before I knocked, I saw it opening before me, and a familiar figure withdrawing slightly behind it as though it were gesturing for me to enter.

So enter I did, and the door closed behind me.

Having experienced the whole spectrum of love, I of all people know that it doesn't stay in five-star hotels or in houses that are fancy but frigid, so it pleased me to find that this house was as unadorned and cosy as a nest.

Without bothering to ask permission, I headed, exhausted, for the nearest room. I flung my bag on to the sofa and was about to fling myself down beside it. Instead, though, I stayed where I was for a moment, contemplating him, as though I were searching him for something that would justify all this madness.

He came up to me and removed the headscarf that I'd forgotten to take off. He smiled. Then, after some hesitation, he confessed wistfully, 'How I've missed you!'

'I've missed you, too,' I replied. 'What else would have brought me all this way? If only you knew what a time I had getting here!'

He sat down on the sofa across from me, fiddling quietly with the headscarf. He pondered this apparel that bore no resemblance to me, as though he were trying to decide who I was, while I in turn pondered the room where we were sitting. Its simple furniture, chosen with bachelor-ish taste, consisted of nothing but a large velvet sofa, a table, and a bookcase that extended the length of the opposite wall. The books arranged neatly on its shelves left room for nothing but a television and a tape player from which emanated the soft strains of a Richard Clayderman piano piece.

I loved the way our tastes seemed to match. More than that, I loved our shared propensity for acting contrary to logic, such as listening to a piece of music like the one that was playing on a day marked by such outright lunacy. The only thing that surprised me was the absence of any pictures in the house, which deprived me of an important avenue for getting to know him better.

'What do you consume besides cigarettes?' I asked him.

'Patience . . . and silence,' he replied with a chuckle.

'And how can you draw with such icy sensations?'

'And who told you I drew? To draw is to remember, and I'm a man who tries to forget.'

'I'd like to see some of your paintings,' I said. 'Would that be possible?'

'No, actually,' he said. 'I don't have any of them here.'

'What did you do with them?'

'I left them in another city.'

Suddenly I felt suspicious of what he was saying. I sensed that he was hiding something, or lying, and that he'd never been a painter.

'Where did you learn to draw?' I asked.

'Oh,' he said dismissively, 'the worst thing that can happen to an artist is to go to art school!'

I wanted to argue this point with him, maybe just to get him to talk more about himself. But he fell silent, and didn't say a word for some time. When he did open his mouth again, it was to talk to me about the political situation and to ask me whether I'd had trouble finding his house.

As he spoke I was distracted from his words by listening to his hands, since they were the only thing that told me very much about him.

First of all, they told me he was lazy, since he only used one of them: the right one.

I took a long look at his fingers, which seemed to have a lot to say about who he was as a man. He had a way of trimming his fingernails to a studied roundness as though he didn't want to cause anyone pain, even in romance. This was reassuring to me. It also whetted my appetite for intimate touches, though it didn't help me in the least to figure out what his actual profession was.

This man was no artist. His hands were too calm and collected for someone who lives with the nervous rush of creation.

We recognize a pianist by his lithe, agile fingers. We may recognize the hands of a carpenter, who more often than not will have lost a finger or two. Similarly, we might be able to identify a house painter or a butcher by certain features of their hands. We recognize a teacher by the chalk dust clinging to his palms, the farmer from the dirt trapped under his finger-nails, and a printer from the tell-tale signs of ink in his fingerprints.

What a remarkable world, the world of hands. It's remarkable in its scandalous nakedness, a nakedness that reveals who we are. No wonder, then, that artists and sculptors spend so much of their time studying people's hands, since it's through these that they enter into their paintings and sculptures. Renowned French sculptor Auguste Rodin, who himself devoted no little attention to hands, once summed up his obsession with them in the words, 'There are hands that bless and hands that curse, hands that exude a sweet perfume and hands that quench a burning thirst. And there are hands made for love.' How, then, could he sculpt one type and neglect another?

Hands have a lot to say about our intimate secrets. They hold our memories, the names of those who've embraced us, the people whose bodies we've passed over with tender touches, or on which we've left a scratch.

Our hands reveal the age of our bliss, and of our misery. They expose the true age of our bodies. They make known all the professions we've practised and all the love we've made, and not made.

Consequently, there are hands that, like their owners, aren't worthy of life because they've done nothing with their lives.

As I looked at him, I knew I was seeing hands that had experienced life, hands that had woven life and kneaded it to the point of impassioned identification. It was clear from their calculated indolence that they'd given pleasure to many a woman, and that life had given them many a disappointment.

Here were hands that had dallied, fondled, discovered, hands that had set fire to untold numbers of women, and which were setting fire to me now from behind the smoke wafting off his cigarette as he sat there in silence.

They were also setting fire to my questions, stoking the flames of my jealousy. These hands to which nothing had clung, had they ever clung to anyone? What was the name of the last woman they'd loved? The last women they'd undressed? How old was their bliss?

I could tell he was a man of many lifetimes. Consequently, I might have asked him, 'How old are your eyes?', 'How old are your lips?' or, 'How old is your silence?'

But instead I asked him, 'How old are your hands?'

I thought he'd like my new way of condensing questions and turning them upside down the way he always did.

However, seemingly unimpressed by my query, he replied, 'They're as old as my disappointment.'

'But I still love them,' I said.

Getting up suddenly to turn the tape over as though it were a way of changing the subject, he replied, 'You've always loved my neuroses!'

I didn't understand what he meant, and I didn't try to. I just got up and headed over to the bookcase, which I'd been wanting to take a closer look at. It was to my advantage that he didn't seem to have heard of Roland Barthes' apt observation that 'one should hide from others both one's medicine cabinet and one's library!'

I glanced at their titles, exultant that now at last I could acquaint myself with this man, who, seeing me distracted by his library, withdrew, saying, 'I don't suppose you'd miss me too much if I went to make you some coffee!'

'Of course not!' I said, laughing. 'Books can only bring us closer!'

From the very first glance, I was bowled over by the breadth of the subjects covered by his book collection, which bespoke a highly cultured individual conversant in two languages, with diverse political and historical interests that I hadn't expected this man to have.

At the same time, I was amazed not to have seen a single book on the fine arts or drawing in the house of a painter whose library reflected such wide-ranging interests. There were books on the lives of historical figures, the Arab-Israeli conflict, and even the global hegemony of multinational corporations. However, there seemed to be no room for creativity in the entire collection with the exception of a lower shelf filled with small, pocket-sized volumes of a contemporary French poetry series. I found Baudelaire's *The Flowers of Evil*, Rimbaud's *The Drunken Boat*, something by Jean Cocteau, and books by other poets.

As I stood leafing curiously through some of the books, I happened upon one by Henri Michaux entitled *Corner Columns*. It was a book I'd never read or even heard of before even though there'd been a time when I loved this poet.

I don't know what led me to this book in particular. However, of all the books I'd looked at, it was the only one this man had written in, adding occasional comments in the margins and highlighting specific passages.

As I leafed through it, I suspected that I'd found the key that would unlock his secret.

I was sure that Roland Barthes had been right in what he said. After all, just as our medicine cabinets will tell others what sorts of illnesses we've suffered from, our bookshelves might tell them more about us than we'd like them to know, especially if they come across a book that we've shared in writing by scribbling in the margins.

I was still looking through it when he came back with the coffee.

'Would it be all right if I borrowed this book?' I asked.

'Of course,' he said, without bothering to ask me its title.

As he set the coffee on the table, he continued, 'Your requests are very modest. I'd been hoping you'd ask for something nicer!'

As I returned the other books to the shelf, I replied, 'I'm fine with the modest requests. The nicest things can't be asked for.'

As if in correction, he said, 'The nicest things always come last, Madame!'

His voice was so close, it seemed to be stroking my ears. No sooner had I turned to look behind me than I found myself up next to him. He was just breaths and a kiss away. However, he didn't kiss me. With his right hand he reached out and caressed my hair. After gliding slowly down my neck with a maddening flirtatiousness, his hand slid towards my ear and removed one earring, then the other.

In what appeared to be a kind of romantic ritual, he placed the earrings on one of the bookshelves with the unthinking spontaneity of someone who was accustomed to removing small items from women's bodies. Then his lips began where his hand had left off.

They passed over me with deliberate slowness and at a studied distance in order to produce the maximum arousal. They grazed my mouth without quite kissing it, slid down towards my neck without actually touching it, then ascended again with the same deliberate slowness as though he were kissing me with nothing but his breath.

He was a man who knew how to touch a woman, and words, with the same hidden blaze. With a kind of studied lethargy, he embraced me from behind the way he might embrace a fleeing sentence. I stood in surrender against the wall, numbed by a storm of pleasure. I didn't ask myself: What is he doing to me? Is he drawing my body with his lips? Is he plotting my destiny? Is he dictating to me the next thing I'll write? Or is he cancelling out my language?

How was I to resist a man who, with a single kiss, or without kissing me at all, could write me and erase me? How was I to resist him as he traversed desire's hidden passages with his lips, then assaulted me with sudden ferocity, devouring my lips and swallowing everything I'd been about to say to him?

I discovered that only now was he starting to kiss me. As he grasped me by my hair and mingled his saliva with mine, I broke out in a sweat so profuse that my body odour drowned out the fragrance of his cologne. Meanwhile, our mouths were locked so tightly that I felt as though I were breathing through him and with him.

I wished he would draw me closer so as to keep me from falling. But he seemed to derive such enjoyment from overpowering me with his manliness that he preferred to hold me with only one arm.

146

Then, in what might best be described as an erotic cluster-bomb attack, he began blanketing my neck with staccato kisses that descended in rapid succession as though he were placing ellipses at the end of a text he might return to later. Then he withdrew.

As I caught my breath, I noticed that the cloak I was wearing was drenched with perspiration. Meanwhile, I saw him take off his jacket, light a cigarette, and sit down on the sofa to drink his coffee.

My questions came back to me as I looked at him.

Like a gypsy woman reading someone's palm, I stood there reading his features with nothing but my intuition and my senses. At that moment I cared less about discovering his past than about discerning my own destiny as it related to him. Like a forty-year-old man, it was a destiny with tired lips, tousled hair, lazy words, confusing touches, unexpected kisses and conflicting desires.

'What are you thinking about?' he asked.

'I'm thinking about how I love forty-year-old men.'

He smiled and said, 'But I'm not the man you think I am!'

Flicking his ashes into the ashtray, he held out his hand to me and said, 'Come over and sit next to me.'

I hesitated a bit. Then I confessed, 'I'm all sweaty. I've had this cloak on for hours.'

I expected him to say, 'Take it off,' or some such thing. Instead, he drew me towards him, saying, 'I like the way you smell. I've always liked the way your body expresses itself!'

Then, as if to reassure me, he added, 'An odourless body can't talk!'

Sitting down beside him, I said, 'I'm afraid the day might come when my body is more eloquent than I am!'

'Whatever happens,' he said, 'your body is more truthful than you are. It's only our senses that don't lie.

'The strange thing,' he went on, 'is that I keep feeling as though I've met you before in some other house, that I've kissed you at some earlier time, that I recognize this odour of yours from some other embrace, and that I've tasted your lips in some other kiss. How do you explain the fact that we can forget a body we've possessed, but not one that we've only desired?'

Of course I had no answers to questions like these, especially since I didn't share his feeling that these things had happened before.

All I said was, 'It's lovely to feel so much desire. There's a kind of heroism in the ability to remain faithful to . . . an illusion!'

He put his feet up on the table in front of him and, puffing his cigarette smoke in my direction, said a bit sarcastically, 'What heroism? You're still approaching life as though it were literature. People like stories with sad endings where the hero sticks to his principles till the very last page, since they don't how to stick to their own principles in real life.'

Then he added, 'Gone are the days of great causes. Heroism in real life has let us down. So let's go for a better type of heroism in novels. All the heroism of virtue and all the victories of wisdom are nothing compared to the greatness of surrendering to the one we love in a moment of weakness. Falling in love is our most enduring victory!'

He took my hand as though he wanted to keep me from going anywhere and said, 'This time I want us to settle for a heroism that's sweet and simple, one that's within everyone's reach, like, for example, trying for the longest kiss in the history of Algerian literature!'

Then he asked, 'Do you know what I was thinking about when I kissed you a little while ago?'

'What?'

'I was thinking about how our life together began with our imitating literature, as though love had motioned to us to carry on, in real life, with a kiss we'd begun in a book. Just like in that novel, we're having the same first date and kissing in front of the same bookshelf after you look at the books and ask if you can borrow one of them.'

He went on, saying, 'I love the fortuitousness of kisses that travel from one story to another. Imagine how wonderful it is for there to be a kiss that's begun by a fictitious man in a book, and that's continued in real life by another man who's so much like the first that he even knows what the woman's lips will taste like. In the age of superhuman feats, intercontinental ballistic missiles and interplanetary satellites, the achievement that one can take the most pride in is a kiss that can travel from one time to another, from one novel to another.'

'That's all well and good,' I said. 'But I don't understand why you're so bent on breaking this record in particular. Men usually pride themselves on breaking other types of records!'

He chuckled, seemingly surprised by my question. After a pause, he said, 'The reason is that kissing is the only romantic act in which all the senses take part. Unlike having sex, kissing someone requires all five senses. A kiss exposes us, because it reflects a state of sheer romantic transport that has nothing to do with the sexual urges that we have in common with all other animals.

'That's why we can have sex with someone that we have no desire to kiss, whereas we might be content with nothing but a kiss from a woman whose lips alone give us a fever that couldn't be generated by the bodies of all other women put together!'

I could feel myself blushing. His words had set me all aflutter, and my body was electrified. But I didn't say anything. It was as if I'd become another woman all of a sudden.

He pushed back a lock of my hair that had fallen out of place, saying, 'I've had a lot of sex, but I just now realized that I haven't kissed a woman for a long time, and that the last time I was in bliss was when my lips were pressed against yours on page 172.'

I nearly asked him what book he was talking about, and how he could remember the exact page where the kiss he remembered had taken place. But I couldn't think of anything to add to what he'd said. So I stood up, as if I were in search of an answer that I thought I might find more easily on my feet.

Apparently having misunderstood the reason for my getting up, he looked at his watch and asked me, 'When's the driver coming for you?'

'He'll be waiting for me on the back street at five o'clock.'

'You've got fifteen minutes. So you'd better be going.'

I didn't argue with him. I was used to his ending our time together at its sweetest moment, the way the electricity goes off in the middle of a celebration.

Then, as if he'd recalled matters that love had pushed temporarily out of his consciousness, he added, 'The situation's bad, and in the next few hours there might be confrontations between the protestors and the army.'

As if I were looking for an excuse to stay, I asked him, 'Why today? Why now?'

'Because the leader of the Islamic Salvation Front made a speech today in which he described Chadli as a nail in Algeria's heel that had to be removed. An Islamist march is heading towards the presidential palace demanding that the presidential elections be moved forward.'

Seeing my astonishment at the news he'd just announced, he said, 'Don't you listen to the radio?'

'There's no radio where I'm staying,' I said apologetically. 'And since you advised me not to read the newspapers, I've been isolated from the world over the past couple of weeks in that summer house.'

As he looked on, I spruced myself up in front of a mirror and put the scarf back on my head.

Then I headed for the door, about to leave behind the simple surroundings for which I so envied him.

He stopped me, handing me the book I'd asked to borrow, and said with a wry wink, 'It seems that here, too, I'm like Khaled in that novel of yours. But there's no danger in my lending you this book as long as it isn't one of Ziyad's poetry collections!'

I was amazed that he would remember so much from one of my novels.

I reassured him, saying, 'Henri Michaux died several years ago, so he poses no threat to you!'

'I don't know,' he quipped back. 'I've learned not to be complacent when it comes to the things you read!'

I giggled.

I remembered how Khaled lends the novel's heroine a poetry collection written by a Palestinian friend of his named Ziyad. Khaled has been gushing to her constantly about Ziyad and his poetry, confident that nothing could happen between the two of them since Ziyad is away on the war front. Then Ziyad happens to come to Paris for a few days on a visit from Lebanon, and the heroine ends up falling in love with the poet and ditching the artist, who loses her from the minute she begins reading that collection.

At the door that was still closed on our secret, he embraced me without a word. It was as though the scarf that now covered my head had relegated us once more to the realm of strangers.

We parted without a kiss, without a word of farewell.

All he said as I left the house was, 'I'll be waiting for your call. Ring me as soon as you get back so I'll know you arrived safely.'

'I will,' I replied absently.

Once outside, I paused to look back at the door as it closed behind me on a moment stolen from destiny. Then I walked down the stairs like a thief who's certain that everyone he sees is eyeing him with suspicion, and who himself has begun to be suspicious of his own happiness. He suspects a pleasure which, now past, no longer seems to merit all the risk he took on its account, and the long-awaited moment of passion which, within the space of the instant it takes for a door to close, has suddenly become a thing of the past.

If the truth be told, there's no one more miserable than a lover going back down the stairs!

I went home by the way I'd come, but with more fear and less enthusiasm. There was a blurred space in me for joy, and another for regret.

Suppose you have a couple of hours to yourself in a car being driven by a military chauffeur who, bringing you back from a romantic tryst, takes you down the streets of wrath and the alley-ways of death. Those two hours will set the stage for a heartbreaking plunge back into reality, and give you plenty of time to regret what you've done.

The process is catalysed by the garb of piety you're wearing for the occasion and which, before you know it, has started wearing you, with the result that your own thoughts turn on you!

The minute I got back I hurriedly took off the cloak and returned it to its owner in the hopes of being reconciled with my body.

A hundred years ago, in order to be able to write, French novelist Amandine-Lucile-Aurore Dupin took the pen name George Sand. She even adopted men's attire inside of which she lived as a woman. Since that isn't an option for me, I've always had to borrow some other woman's clothes so that I can go on writing inside of them.

Literature teaches us to borrow other people's lives, convictions and outward appearances. But the hardest part isn't to break into other people's private spaces. The hardest part comes when we close our notebooks, take off what doesn't belong to us, and go back to living inside of bodies that don't recognize us any more because of all the times we've dressed them up in someone else's clothes!

I put on a summer house dress and sat down to think about what had happened to me.

Like pain, pleasure forces you to re-examine your life and your convictions. In fact, it might make you go so far as to ask the crazy question: 'What use is my life now?'

There are kisses which, if you don't die during them, you don't deserve to survive. But either way, you make an astounding discovery: namely, that up until that existence-defining pleasure or pain, you hadn't yet lived.

It reminds me of a man who used to defy death and who, when I worried about him, would make light of my fear, saying, 'I need to die sometimes in order to realize that I'm still alive.'

Now that life had brought me this much enjoyment, I was afraid of the realization that before it, I'd been among the living dead.

A single kiss, and I found myself discovering life all at once. I also discovered the enormity of what I'd been missing.

I wished I could fill that whole black notebook of mine with nothing but a description of that defining moment, the moment that had marked the end of one lifetime and the beginning of another. I wished I could freeze it, or embalm it inside of time.

I wished I had the hands and the talent of Auguste Rodin so that I could immortalize two lovers for whom time had come to an eternal standstill in a moment of passion that took them up into another world, fused in a kiss of stone. If only, like Proust in his masterpiece, *In Search of Lost Time*, I could spend twenty pages doing nothing but describing a single kiss!

Was it because Proust's kiss hadn't really happened and had ended, after his lengthy narrative, on the beloved's cheek, that he was able to describe it in such detail?

And was it because Rodin wasn't entirely devoted to Camille Claudel, the sculptress whose stormy affair with him may have contributed to her ending up in the mental institution where she died, that he wanted to compensate for her absence by creating a statue which, in its unsettling nakedness, immortalized a kiss they would never again share?

Is an early experience of betrayal a condition for creativity? Is coming back empty-handed the only thing that can fill a book?

It didn't matter to me to answer such questions. Besides, I couldn't have answered them even if I'd tried.

The desire that had now taken me over was preventing me from thinking. It was setting me on fire, singeing my fingers, making it impossible to write. Of course, it might actually have forced me to write if it hadn't been for the telephone that sat nearby and which, by means of a magical six-digit number, could provide me with an instant dose of love and affection that would make it pointless to conjure my beloved by sitting in front of a piece of paper!

So I went over to the telephone to call him. As I did so, I thought about what a loss to literature had been caused by this modern gadget. How many an exquisite text and how many a love letter will never be written because of that deadly word, 'Hello'!

Before I'd lifted the receiver, the phone rang. I jumped. It was my husband on the line. So the word 'Hello' can put illusions to death, too!

It was a hurried exchange, as though we were continents apart, or as though his telephone bill weren't paid by the government.

So be it, then! I thought. He was always in a hurry. Maybe it was events around him that were in a hurry, since he was telling me to come back to Constantine in two days' time. He told me that given the deteriorating security situation in the capital, I'd be flying back rather than returning in the car.

When I asked him what to do about the driver, he said, 'He'll bring the car back after taking you and Farida to the airport. I've reserved seats for the two of you on the 9:30 a.m. flight.'

He hung up, and I sat there, frozen.

I'd been expecting to return to Constantine, of course, with Eid al-Adha just three days away. However, I'd expected some miracle or emergency that would make my husband ask me to stay until my mother got back from the pilgrimage, which would have given me a chance to see that man again, if even just once.

With time close on my heels, I was all the more anxious to call him.

Six digits later, the telephone began to ring. And only two rings after that, as though it had been waiting for me, a voice came over the line, saying, 'Did you get home safely?'

'Yes. How about you?'

'I haven't left the house. I decided it would be better to soak up certain places' memory of you. This house is still haunted by your scent. It must be your polite way of punishing me!'

'I didn't punish you on purpose.'

'Well, you might have, if you'd read about what Josephine did to Napoleon when he forced her out of the palace.'

'What did she do?'

'She sprayed her perfume all over his room to make sure he'd be surrounded by her for a full fifteen days even though he was with another woman. And before that, Cleopatra used to spray the sails of her ship with her perfume as a way of leaving a trail of fragrance behind her wherever she went.'

'All right, then,' I said, laughing. 'I'll keep that in mind for the next time!'

After a pause, he replied, 'There won't be a next time.'

'Why?' I asked, distressed.

His voice even despite my agitation, he said, 'Because I'm leaving tomorrow.'

'Are you going to Constantine?'

'No, to France.'

'To France!' I cried, incredulous. 'What are you going to do there?'

'What everybody else does when they go there,' he said with a laugh.

'But you . . . .'

'But I'm not like them,' he said, finishing my sentence for me. 'Isn't that what you were going to say? I'm a creature of ink that travels between your notebooks and in your company alone. I might go back and forth between Constantine and the capital, but I wouldn't go anywhere else. And I have no right to buy a ticket for myself and go somewhere without you.'

After a pause, he continued, 'But I'm not the hero you think I am. Your heroes and heroines don't get sick or grow old. As for me, Madame, I'm sick and tired.'

Suddenly alarmed, I said, 'What's wrong?'

He replied with a kind of sorrowful derision, 'I'm tired of standing up. I've spent my whole life standing up, since I'm no good at sitting on principles.'

I didn't try to understand what he was saying. The only question that mattered to me was, 'When are you coming back?'

'I don't know. I'm a man who's always in transit.'

'But I care about your life.'

'Which life do you mean?' he shot back sarcastically.

I didn't say anything. I didn't understand what he meant.

'I haven't been successful in life,' he went on, 'so my hope now is that I might be successful in death. Could you give me a sweet death if life lets me down in the last scene?'

'What are you saying?' I shouted. 'Just a few hours ago we were happy, talking about love. So where did all this pessimism come from?'

'Since you care about love, you must care about death, too. Love and death are the two greatest puzzles in the world. They're alike in their inscrutability, their fierceness, their unexpectedness, their meaninglessness, and the questions they raise. We come and we go without knowing why we loved one person and not another, why we die on one day and not another, or why we die here, now. We also don't know why we're the ones who die, and not others. This is why love and death alone fuel all the literature in the world, since apart from these two themes, there's nothing worth writing about.'

What he'd said got me to thinking, and I sank into a silence that was interrupted by his voice:

'Do you know what I thought about as I was kissing you today?'

'What?'

'I thought about how, if kisses die the way we do, then the best time to die would be during a kiss.'

'Amazing. Would you believe that when I got back to the house I got out my notebook and wrote, "There are kisses which, if you don't die during them, you don't deserve to survive"?'

He registered a moment of silence, as though he were savouring the idea, delving deep into it.

Then he said, 'You've realized on your own that unless we come straight up against death, we'll never experience a love sublime enough to be called true passion.'

I sat there without saying anything, like a student who's trying to memorize a lesson being taught by a professor whose entire curriculum consists of his shifting moods, and who, in the space of a single day, has to master one lesson on desire, a second on death, a third on love, and a fourth on how someone can kiss a woman with perfect passion, then abandon her with perfect indifference!

This is all I can recall of that conversation.

I don't remember him saying anything romantic after that or leaving me a new telephone number or address.

All he said was that the fragrance of that stolen time still hung about him. Then he drew the conversation to a close by saying apologetically that he needed to get some sleep before his trip.

I understood from what he'd said that I'd be able to call him the next day so that we could talk one last time.

At seven o'clock the next morning, still half-asleep after a troubled night, I dialled his number. The ring of the telephone sounded like someone crying, with no one on the other side of memory to silence it. It was the tragicomedy of love, repeating itself without end.

Only now would silence be able to weep.

Chapter Four

Inevitably

WE ALWAYS ARRIVE AT love just a bit late.

Then we knock cautiously on somebody's heart, apologizing before the fact for a sentiment that we know will vanish the minute it appears.

Love repeats itself in various forms, with beginnings that give birth to lofty dreams, and with precipitous, excruciating endings. So we learn to expect love's drunken driver to deliver us to disappointment's door.

The dream matures by necessity, but before the time is ripe. So what use is it for the heart to grow up so fast?

When Eid al-Adha arrived, Constantine was awaited by another sort of occasion.

I returned to the city, my heart suffering from multiple fractures. As I struggled out from under the wreckage of a dream, gasping for breath beneath a massive heap of illusions, Constantine presented me with a face I didn't recognize. Its streets were piled high with refuse, since the Islamists had commandeered the rubbish collectors' dustcarts to force them to join the open strike, leaving the city's stray cats to celebrate the holiday alone.

I was in a hurry to get back to my house, where all I could hear was the city's loud bustle as it prepared for its holiday, and the bleating of the sheep awaiting slaughter the next morning.

I'd always hated holidays, and this one promised to be the saddest of them all. It was a holiday of absence. The feeling of absence came over me as I woke up on the morning of Eid, since there was nobody in the house, other than the maid, to wish a happy holiday. There wasn't anybody to call, either, except for Uncle Ahmad's wife, whose voice over the phone made me feel all the sadder since it revived my feeling of guilt towards her.

My husband had left the house early in anticipation of possible demonstrations or unrest after the end of the holiday prayer. Farida had gone as usual to spend the day with her family. My mother wasn't back from the pilgrimage yet, and Nasser wasn't at home to answer the telephone when I called. Even the sheep, which had been outside in the yard, weren't there any more. Or, rather, all that was left of them were blood stains on the ground and carcasses hung up on hooks and being skinned by a butcher.

What do people do on the morning of the holiday but attack sheep's carcasses: skinning them, cutting them to pieces, dividing them up? No one here, no matter how limited his means or humble his abode, could conceive of Eid al-Adha without slaughtering a sheep. So I was used to seeing people scurrying around on the morning of Eid al-Adha, the men to the open areas set up specially for the ritual slaughter, and the women to their kitchens, where they would divide up the animals, keep the parts they needed, and distribute the rest as alms.

That particular year I expected the need for alms distribution to be greater than ever. The price of a single sheep came to over 10,000 dinars, which meant that an animal purchased as a sacrifice for the holiday was now worth more than a human being, who could be slaughtered for the price of a bullet.

I called my husband to wish him a happy holiday. I sensed that he was surprised by my call, and maybe even pleased. When I asked him if he'd sent anything to Uncle Ahmad's house, he said he'd been so busy he'd forgotten, so I told him I'd take care of it. Before I could say anything else, another telephone rang in his office and our conversation was cut short.

I asked the driver to take half a sheep's carcass to the poor man's house. Then, when he was about to leave, I ran after him and asked him to take me to the cemetery first.

Only rarely have I visited my father's grave on the morning of Eid al-Adha. I've always preferred to go there alone, the way one goes to a love tryst.

I don't like to visit him on social occasions, maybe because of all the times I've had to share him with others. Often, when I've crossed a street or passed a school named after him, I've been stricken with a sense of orphanhood so overwhelming that it's nearly drowned out the pride I feel in bearing his name.

Between me and the man resting beneath that marble headstone there'd been a kind of tacit understanding. After he died, I'd built a little shrine to him inside of me that had nothing to do with the prestige attached to the standing he'd enjoyed in our society. It was a shrine that grew in size with every passing year with the result that, in his absence, he became larger than life, and larger by far than the living who surrounded me.

Every now and then I would sit at that shrine the way some women sit at the shrine of a saint, telling him their woes and asking for his blessing and for strength to cope with life's tribulations.

Sometimes I'd close the door to my room and, opening my memory chest, tell him about all the things that grieved me and the mistakes I had made. I'd invite him to sit on the edge of my bed and tell him things that had happened to me. I'd ask for his advice, expecting him to answer me, and when his picture didn't say anything in reply I'd burst into tears.

I'd be afraid that I'd told him too much about myself. I'd be afraid I'd lost his approval. After all, there's nothing more difficult than to remain in the good graces of the dead.

Now, too, like all the times when destiny had caused me anguish and life had let me down, my steps led me to that same patch of ground, where I went digging for answers to my endless questions.

But this time I found no answers. All I found was Nasser, who was about to leave the cemetery. What made it even more surprising to see him there was that it had never been his custom to visit our father's grave on holidays. In fact, my mother had once told me that he'd given her a legal ruling according to which visiting graves and shrines was objectionable.

As usual, I didn't argue with him about his beliefs or ask him why he'd come. Instead I simply expressed my surprise at finding him there, and told him how happy I was to see him. However, as I kissed him, I couldn't help but comment on the fact that he looked different somehow, although I couldn't put my finger on what it was that had changed.

With a touch of sarcasm he replied, 'I've lost a lot of weight lately.'

Then he added, '. . . so that I wouldn't lose my beliefs!'

Not understanding what he meant, I said brightly, 'Well, that's better. You look younger this way.'

In the same sarcastic tone he said, 'And what's so great about looking younger?'

So here he was again, drawing me into a conversation about something that wasn't going to be easy to talk about. It reminded me of the time, a few years earlier, when I'd asked him to take the wall clock to get it fixed because it was losing a few minutes every week or so.

In a mocking sort of tone, he'd said to me, 'Come on, you! We're a whole century behind the rest of the world, and you're sitting in front of a clock counting minutes? If we took it to the repairman, he'd die laughing. After all, people in this country only bring him clocks when they're about to go to jail!'

I wanted to avoid getting into an argument I knew he was sure to win. He responded to my way of thinking about life with his way of coexisting with it, so he always had right on his side.

'I've been on a trip,' I said apologetically. 'I just got back a couple of days ago. I called you this morning to wish you a happy holiday, but you weren't home.'

'I'm not staying in the house,' he replied. 'As you can see, we're all on a trip. The dead are the only ones with permanent addresses now!'

Then, after a slight pause, he went on, 'That's because they don't have anything to worry about any more, and nothing to be afraid of.'

'So what are you afraid of?' I asked.

'Of God! And God alone!' he shot back confidently, as if I'd been accusing him.

'We're all afraid of God,' I said.

'How can somebody who obeys his enemies claim to fear God?'

I kept my mouth shut, not because I didn't have a reply to what he'd said, but because as far as I was concerned, arguing at a graveside on a religious holiday was nothing short of madness. After all, we hadn't come here to fight. We'd come to recite the Fatihah over our deceased father's grave. But politics seemed to haunt us wherever we went: in our beds, in our notebooks, even in cemeteries.

Finally I said, 'Nasser, dear brother, people come together today to wish each other a happy holiday, to make up, to forgive each other. But I've barely said hello to you before you blow up in my face. Can't you please just be my brother, if only on this holiday?'

'What holiday?' he said, Scrooge-like. 'Look around you at these graves. They're all new, fresh. Every day this cemetery receives a new batch of innocents.'

'And what fault is that of mine?'

'Your fault is that you share a bed and a house with the Devil!'

I said, 'I don't know whether this man is an angel or a devil. As far as I can see, the only difference between him and others is that he's a high-ranking officer who's responsible for defending the homeland, and I believe in the homeland more than I believe in either angels or devils.'

'Doesn't it bother you to be held by somebody with blood on his hands? On his orders innocent people are thrown in prison and these graves are filled to overflowing. What's the use of all you've learned about people's freedom to choose their destiny?'

166

'What I've learned hasn't done me any good. I don't know how to choose my own destiny, much less anybody else's. There are more than sixty officially recognized parties whose job it is to represent the people and defend their choices. But I don't have a party to defend me. Even you, you've never asked me my opinion on anything. So why are you so surprised that I don't have an opinion now?'

He kept quiet at first, as though he didn't know what to say, or didn't see any use in talking.

Then, his voice tender as though he were whispering a farewell, he said, 'I'm afraid for you, Hayat.'

'Afraid of what?' I murmured.

'Of everything.'

With the same tenderness I replied, 'You've always worried about me.'

'But this time,' he said, 'I know what I'm talking about. Leave that man. Since you don't have any children by him, ask for a divorce.'

I smiled. Then I laughed out loud at what he'd said.

'What's so funny?' he demanded.

'Well,' I said, 'I was just thinking about Ma. If she heard you say what you just said, she'd blow her top. My being married to this man is the biggest feather in her cap!'

'Don't worry about our mother. Her whole life revolves around one thing: what other people think. But the wall she's leaning on for support is just one big illusion. Lean on God in all your decisions, and He won't let you down.'

'I've always leaned on Him,' I said, 'and on the person lying in this grave. And this is what's led me to where I am. I would have liked you to be my support, too. You're all I've got in this world. But here we are, bumping into each other in a cemetery by coincidence like strangers. You don't call and you don't come to see me. And when I come to see you, you're not around.'

'One of these days,' he interrupted me ruefully, 'you won't have any trouble finding me. I'll have a permanent address right here.'

'What are you talking about?' I cried. 'Are you out of your mind?'

'Death is closer than you think,' he broke in. 'Would you like to see the grave of a friend of mine who was murdered a few days ago for no reason? He was near a policeman, and they got suspicious of him because he put his hand in his pocket and looked as though he was about to take something out of it. So they shot him. Then they discovered that he hadn't had anything in his pocket. Imagine: You could die not because of some crime you committed, but because, if you happen to look a certain way when you're in a certain place at a certain time, you're assumed to be a criminal. In other words, we're all potential suspects. All it takes for them to convict us is for time, place and appearance to work against us!'

I said, 'I don't think people want to hurt each other or commit murders just for the fun of it. But everybody thinks it's either kill or be killed. We don't trust each other any more. We're living in a time when evil's pull is stronger than ever, and we've got to resist being swept along with the tide. Life is good, Nasser. Believe me. We've just got to put a little love into it.'

Nasser was quiet for a while. Then he put his arms around me and said, 'Sometimes I wish I were like you.'

'I always wish I were like you. Life has pulled us apart sometimes, but nothing will ever separate us. Isn't that right?'

'Right. We'll never let that happen.'

He started to walk away. Then he came back as though he'd remembered something, or as though he'd decided to tell me something he'd been hesitating to mention. He whispered, 'Try to come to the house in the next couple of days. Ma's due back from the pilgrimage the day after tomorrow. Once she's back, I'll be leaving, and I want to say goodbye to you.'

'You're leaving?' I asked, astonished. 'Where are you going?'

'I'll tell you later. Don't say anything about this to anybody.'

As soon as he'd disappeared, I collapsed at the foot of the grave, and before I knew it, I was in tears.

What kind of a time was this, when a brother and sister would meet up by chance in a cemetery on Eid al-Adha morning, fight and make up within ear's range of the dead, then part, not knowing when they'd be seeing each other again, or in which world?

* * *

I, who had gone that day looking for answers, came back with more questions than ever. I'd spent half my day consoling Uncle Ahmad's family, and the other half consoling myself over men who came just to leave again, who greeted me just to say goodbye, and who couldn't seem to talk to me without introducing death as a third party to our conversations.

I couldn't help but wonder whether there was some contagion going around among the men of the country that made them all say the same thing, and dream of nothing but leaving!

That evening I sat down to supper with my husband out of politeness. Actually, I'd already decided not to eat the meat of those poor sheep, whose heads had been bobbing for several days from the seasickness that had stricken them during the month and a half they'd spent crammed into a ship's hull.

My husband for his part was so exhausted that he didn't notice my lack of appetite. We exchanged ordinary chit-chat about nothing in particular, and the minute he finished eating, I saw him head for the bedroom and take off his clothes as though he were casting off a burden he'd been carrying around all day long. Then he flung himself on the bed.

As I hung his clothes up for him, I said, 'I'd been hoping you'd spend the day with me. I don't understand why it is that you have to spend every day in your office, even holidays.'

He replied, 'If I spent the holiday with you, who would guarantee security in a city whose smallest university has a student population of over 23,000? And then there are the mosques. God knows many there are in the city, and new ones are springing up every day.'

'What I meant was that we don't see each other at all any more. Even your days off, we spend apart.'

Our conversation reminded me of Nasser, and I thought back on my conversation with him. I kept his travel plans to myself. However, without thinking I found myself telling my husband about seeing him that morning at the cemetery. In general my husband avoided talking about Nasser, as though reciprocated my brother's dislike for him.

But to my surprise, he said approvingly, 'It's nice that you saw him.'

Then he added, 'How did he seem to you?'

A bit startled by his question, I said, 'He was his usual self. He might have lost a little weight, but he was in good health.'

'Didn't he tell you anything?' my husband asked.

His question flustered me, and my mind started going in a million directions.

Did he know about Nasser's travel plans? Had somebody been eavesdropping on us at the cemetery? I hadn't seen anyone. And what if he was trying to find out things he didn't know?

Finally I said, 'No, he didn't tell me anything except for the fact that my mother will be back from the pilgrimage the day after tomorrow.'

Shifting on the bed, he asked, 'Didn't he tell you he'd been arrested?'

'Arrested!' I cried. 'Why? When did this happen?'

'I didn't tell you about it when you were away so as not to worry you.'

In a daze, I wondered: Is he involved in some dangerous organization? Did they find documents or arms in his possession? Whatever the case, they must not have found enough evidence to condemn him. Otherwise they wouldn't have released him.

'What did he do?' I wanted to know.

'A good deal of suspicion hovers around him because of his ties to fundamentalist groups.'

'But,' I said testily, 'just because he sympathizes with them doesn't mean he's a terrorist! Nasser would never take up arms to kill anybody. I know my brother.'

His voice stern, my husband interrupted, 'Your brother talks too much. If it weren't for his big mouth, he would have saved both me and himself a lot of trouble. He thinks his family name gives him some sort of immunity, and that it entitles him to badmouth the authorities and incite others to do the same. I intervened this time to get him released. But I can't do that all the time. We've got a tense security situation on our hands, and

171

exceptions shouldn't be made even for the people closest to us. You'd better explain this to him!'

I hadn't expected the news of Nasser's detention to put me in such a muddle, and I had no idea what I was supposed to explain to him.

In any case, I said nothing as my husband flexed his muscles in front of me, metaphorically speaking, and reminded me how much I owed him. I had no desire to get into any arguments. Nor was I prepared to end the holiday by squabbling with my husband after having started it off with a spat with my brother.

Suddenly I saw him fall fast asleep. All I could do at that point was to slip into bed beside him, feeling helpless and confused, and try to get some sleep myself.

I don't know how my rage died, but only then did I realize that it *had* died, and that I'd lost that marvellous spark that had so often set my pen ablaze and set me ablaze in confrontation with others.

When you've lost the ability, and even the desire, to get angry, it means either that you've got old, or that those inward conflagrations have burned out, one disappointment after another, to the point where you don't have the passion to argue about anything any more, not even about issues that once seemed so earthshaking, and ideals that you held so dear that you would have been willing to die for them!

All that mattered to me now was my mother's homecoming. I didn't know exactly what had made me so anxious to see her: the fact that I'd missed her, my need for her, or my desire to see Nasser and find out what surprises he had for me.

Since I was used to my mother going on pilgrimage and coming back again, it didn't surprise me to see her sitting in the living room in her white pilgrim's garb and her white head covering. What surprised me was to find her, for once, without the usual entourage of women who came either to see her off or welcome her home.

I was happy for the chance to be alone with her and get up close to her. I guess I wanted to soak up some of her spiritual blessings before she went back to being an ordinary woman again.

The minute she saw me she said, 'You don't look good. Is something wrong?'

'No,' I said.

'Your trip to the capital didn't do you a bit of good. You're paler than ever! Maybe the sea doesn't agree with you.'

'It agrees with me just fine,' I said. 'It's this city that tires me out.'

Once she'd reassured herself that there hadn't been any problems while she was gone, she went on to talk about her trip. She talked about the unbearable heat in Mecca, the pilgrims who'd been trampled to death, the collapse of the Algerian dinar, and the rise in gold prices.

'Ma,' I said after a while, 'did you pray for me when you were there?'

'Of course, sweetheart,' she replied, taken aback. 'I always do!'

I felt an overwhelming urge to cry, as if I'd just been waiting for her to come back so that I could break down. But I fought it off and went on listening to her talk while I cried on the inside.

Meantime, a neighbour lady arrived, followed by a number of other women, so I withdrew and went to be with Nasser the way I usually did on such occasions.

I loved Nasser's taciturnity, and the manly features and tower-ing height he'd inherited from our father. Today in particular he seemed beyond his years.

I felt him to be a man above complexes, above suspicion. He had nothing in common with people for whom fundamen-talism was nothing but a handy solution to all their male hang-ups or earthly problems and who used their extremism as a way of compensating for some emotional deficit, exacting revenge for social injustices, or venting their patriotic frustrations.

He'd chosen this path and left everything else behind, while others had followed him simply because they had nothing to lose. He could have had any girl he wanted, any job he wanted, any fortune he sought. But he'd turned up his nose at them all. I wondered what kind of inward wealth he drew on, what cause he'd married in secret, what country he emigrated to every day as he sat sipping his coffee in silent discontentment. My mother was always trying to get him to find a job and take advantage of the opportunities at his disposal. She'd needle him by comparing him to people who, although they'd started out in circumstances less fortunate than his, had succeeded in life.

But had they succeeded? Hardly. The people my mother had in mind had succeeded in sparing themselves life's hardships by plundering the country wherever they went and shamelessly flaunting their spoils. Within the space of a few years, they'd erected huge mansions with fancy cars parked outside, and their wives had made it their pastime to travel to Europe whenever they wanted to buy themselves new wardrobes.

What my mother didn't realize was that she was only deepen-ing his sense of failure, and encouraging him to defy her even more.

174

As the days went by I saw him lose his ability to respond to her. He was also losing his elegance. It was as if he'd gone on strike against both life and elegance, since the homeland wasn't as elegant as his dreams!

Had he decided to join the Silence Party and give up his voice, the way others suddenly give up their slogans and shave off their convictions for fear of prisons that lie in wait for men with beards?

The time had come for razorblades – which, with a sudden decline in values and in the value of human beings – were finally available on the market. So, was this the time for the homeland to renounce its claim to be of some value?

As values went downhill, slogans came down off the walls, marking the beginning of a time of tribulation as prisons filled up with bearded men and with those who'd been arrested by accident, caught in the crossfire the way people so often are in times of war.

In a low voice I asked him, 'Do you really have to leave, Nasser? Have you thought about what will happen to Ma if you're not around?'

'I'm only leaving to come back,' he said. 'But if I stayed, you might lose me for good. I can tell you this, of course, but not Ma. I'll keep her in the dark about it and go meet my fate on some nice-sounding pretext. She'll tolerate my not being around better than she'd tolerate finding out that I'd been arrested or murdered.'

'Are your options really that limited?' I asked.

'Of course. Gone are the days of fleeting disappointments. Now's the time for prisons, sudden death, and fabricated assassinations.'

'My husband tells me you were arrested while I was away.'

'And did he also tell you he'd intervened to get me released?' he interjected.

'Is that not true?'

'It's true, all right. It's just that it was a political ploy with multiple aims. First, it puts me in his debt. Second, it calls my integrity into question, since it causes my friends to doubt my opposition to the state. After all, I was only in jail for a couple of days, whereas they might be there for months or even years. Not to mention the fact that if they release you, it means your problems have just begun. They've started releasing the ones that irritate them the most so that they can kill them on the outside and claim that it was some random crime. So what choice do I have but to leave?'

I listened to him incredulously. It was as though somebody had lifted the lid of a chest in which I'd deposited my dreams, thinking they were in a safe place – a place I'd called my 'homeland' – only to find that they'd turned into a stinking mess!

All I wanted to do now was run away with him to some other country, any other country, or some other continent or planet until this crazy train had passed.

Although I wasn't convinced of the logic of a man who had gone off and left me, I *was* convinced of the logic behind this man's wanting to leave home, and I soon found myself helping him invent lies and excuses to persuade my mother of the same.

I went home that day laden with kisses and instructions from Nasser and with presents from my mother, foremost among them some water from the Well of Zamzam, which she brought me every time she came back from the pilgrimage in anticipation of the day when I got pregnant and used it during childbirth.

Meanwhile, I was pregnant with that man. He was the only thing that kept growing inside me. As the days passed, his presence overshadowed even Nasser's departure and life's other disappointments. At the same time, I couldn't understand how, in spite of all the tragedies happening around me, he managed to go on living in me and keeping me from concentrating on anything but him.

More than his words, what clung to me was his scent. It was mingled with a kind of perfume, with the smell of a certain tobacco, and with the odour of a certain perspiration which, taken all together, made up a presence that awakened my senses. It was a presence that had no name. Or maybe its name was simply 'him'.

I remembered how Diderot had proposed a hierarchy of the senses, describing sight as the most superficial, hearing as the most conceited, taste as the most pessimistic, and touch as the most profound. As for smell, he described it as the sense of desire; that is, a sense that can't be classified because it's governed not by logic, but by the subconscious.

The frightening thing about this man was that he'd led me to discover my senses, or, more precisely, my womanly fear of them. In fact, he'd cast me into a chaos of the senses so extreme that I feared the day when I wouldn't be able to describe him or even recognize him, my knowledge of him having passed out of the realm of logic.

So one day I decided to devote my time to reading the book I'd brought back with me by Henri Michaux, the one he'd marked with notes and comments of his own. Since I'd failed to unlock this man's secrets through real-life observations, I wanted to see if I could unlock them outside the realm of his concrete presence, with the calmness of someone getting to know a character in a book.

Being swept off your feet by someone whose inscrutability makes him not only alluring, but even obnoxious at times, may be your chance to write a great novel – that is, if you're a novelist. If, on the other hand, you're a lover, the beloved's inscrutability will be your torment and your curse, since love will turn you into a part-time detective.

Like everyone in love, you want to know everything about your beloved. You want to know his past, his present, the names of the people he's loved and who have loved him, where he's lived, the cities he's visited, the professions he's practised, the places he frequents.

You ply him with questions about his sign of the zodiac, his hobbies, his associations. You might even bring a book home from his library just for the pleasure of finding out what sorts of things he reads!

Love will turn you into a sneak, a spy, a snoop. However, questions will only draw you more deeply into your romantic morass, and herein lies lovers' tragedy!

My first question was: What had drawn this man to Henri Michaux? And why had he chosen this particular book to record his own thoughts on? The only answer I could come up with was that, like him, Henri Michaux had been an artist.

At that point the question became: How can I understand a man through a poet who was himself a mystery? He was, in fact, a poet whose questions only led to more questions. His life was founded upon never-ending attempts to penetrate life's outer façade. He steadfastly rejected literary prizes, he refused to have his picture taken, and he refused to allow his books to be published in large quantities. Instead, he wanted no more than five copies of any given book of his to be printed. He was haunted his entire life by a sense of meaninglessness, a sense that makes itself felt from the first idea he records in this book. He writes, 'In your belief that you place others in your service, it's more likely that you yourself turn gradually into a servant. But the servant of whom? The servant of what? Search, search.'

In the margin someone had written, 'Don't search. You only place your intelligence in the service of insanity.'

This was followed by another thought: 'In the absence of the sun, learn to grow ripe in the cold.'

Below it he had added in blue ink, '. . . or in a newspaper!'

The next comment was: 'If you're embarking on failure, then don't fail any old which way.' The pen went on to say, 'If, on the other hand, you're embarking on death, don't worry!'

Reading a book in which somebody has recorded some of his own opinions and ideas or highlighted certain sentences is like getting to know him by looking into his briefcase or spying on him unawares.

Intimate realities are more easily written about than spoken of, since writing is a kind of silent confession. So I felt a bit embarrassed in the presence of a book that wasn't meant for my eyes. In fact, I didn't understand how he could have lent me this book with no hesitation whatsoever. In any case, I found myself reading it from two different angles at the same time.

I love texts that have been written by two pens. They're similar in their effect to a piano duet. In a solo played to the rhythm of Henri Michaux, the first player seems to say, 'Rest assured: some purity still remains in you.' Then the second player comes in on an unexpected note, as if to say, 'Is that so?'

In the violent passion of his earthshaking La Symphonie Fantastique, Berlioz says in effect, 'What have you left once you've destroyed the impregnable wall of your own knowledge?'

In reply, confident fingers come in once more in blue ink: 'Rather, it's a wall called fear.'

Then the piano falls silent, and the blue pen continues apace, underlining verses and ideas that have arrested its attention.

'Don't despise your mistakes, and don't be in a hurry to correct them. After all, what will you put in their place?'

Or . . .

'It wasn't long before I noticed that I wasn't just the ant, but the ant's path as well.'

Or . . .

'Sleep in the end is your most enduring disappointment.'

Next to this a question had been penned in a tone of even greater disappointment. Like the opening bar of Beethoven's Fifth Symphony, it seemed to say, 'And what about love?'

Then the blue pen fell silent.

I spent days rereading Michaux's little book, at first merely out of curiosity. As I read it I was taken by how similar these two men were in numerous areas, including their love for drawing, and their fondness for the colour black, in which and against which Michaux did most of his paintings. Add to this their mutual dislike of big names and being in the spotlight, and their obsession with death.

My other discovery was that this man worked for a newspaper, that there had been a major emotional disappointment in his life, and that he had a rather sardonic style which served to conceal a profound bitterness and an acute intelligence. In short, he was just the kind of man I tended to fall in love with.

Perhaps because I was possessed by thoughts of Nasser, I found myself reading it again and again with alternating ideas in my mind.

There are books that enable you to make the most amazing discoveries. In them you discover yourself, and regions within your being that you'd known nothing about.

In other books you discover someone else you hadn't expected to find. In fact, they might lead you from one person to another. Thus it was that I found myself thinking of Nasser. It even seemed that some of the thoughts I was reading were things he had said. Take this verse, for example: 'I have no name. Rather, my name is a squandering of names.'

After all, wasn't Nasser Abd al-Mawla just a squandering of two dreams and two names: Gamal Abdel Nasser, and al-Tahir Abd al-Mawla?

How could my brother have been born during both the Algerian War of Independence and the Nasserite era without coming to feel that a series of historical coincidences were bound to change the history of his own life?

Before he had ever heard any political discourse, Nasser developed an awareness of his name, half of which had been dedicated to pan-Arabism, and half of which was a repository for the patriotic memory.

Before he was old enough to follow the news or read a newspaper, he had opened his eyes to the absence of his father and to the constant presence of Abdel Nasser, smiling and saluting in that famous picture of his, not only because we didn't have a television in our house in those days, but because, when we were living away from our own country, it was the only picture that graced the wall of our humble sitting room.

I remember how that picture came to us in our place of exile in Tunisia through a friend of my father's known as Si Abd al-Hamid. This man used to come to visit us while my father was on the front. He would come laden with gifts and a sum of money, which may have been from him, or which he may have given us on instructions from the front – I don't know which.

One day as he was playing with Nasser, the man asked him, 'What would you like me to bring you?' Nasser, who was only four years old at the time, cried, 'Bring me Abdel Nasser!' as though he were asking for a toy. My mother has told me how Si Abd al-Hamid was left speechless at first by the little boy's question and how, with the logic of a child, he finally replied, 'I'll bring him to you next time I come.'

This man, who used to go to Cairo frequently to conduct political consultations and was responsible for monitoring Algerian students' affairs there, once brought us a large picture of Abdel Nasser with a number of souvenirs. During some of our evenings in Tunisia, we would listen to *The Voice of the Arabs* from Cairo, which broadcast Abdel Nasser's speeches and rousing pan-Arab anthems. Some of them I still know by heart, since we would memorize them the way little children in those days would memorize songs in kindergarten and never forget them. Then we would go to sleep happy without any need for television.

We used to watch the world on a screen that consisted of a wall on which Abdel Nasser's picture hung. This picture was later joined by a smaller one of my father from a front-page newspaper article from the summer of 1960 announcing the death of one of Algeria's revolutionary leaders at the hands of French paratroopers after a fierce battle in the city of Batna.

I remember keeping that newspaper for days. I would open it up to the front page and sit staring at my father's features, contemplating the way he had looked when time stood still for him for ever. Then one day I surprised myself by cutting the picture out and asking my mother to frame it, whereupon it became the second picture to hang in our home.

Perhaps it was then that I first developed a secret habit which, some twenty years later during the Palestinian intifada, took a new and painful form. I began spending long hours poring over the pictures of martyrs-to-be, who would have their pictures taken individually and in groups as a keepsake before a suicide operation. Newspapers would then publish the photos the day after the operation to announce their martyrdom. I would always keep this page of the newspaper, one operation after another. I finally accumulated such a huge pile of them that I decided to gather them into a bag and put it somewhere far away, out of reach and out of sight, so that I could find some relief.

I had forgotten all about those two pictures which, after our move from Tunisia back to Algeria, had ceased to be part of the decor in our new sitting room, which was too elegant to be decorated by a couple of pictures on that order of simplicity. Then, about a year ago, I came across them entirely by coincidence in a small attic room where my mother hides things she likes to hold on to. She keeps them organized, neatly arranged, and 'buried' in metal lockers of the sort that went out of style when people began to travel by air, and which my mother probably used to move her things from Tunisia to Algeria in 1962 after Algeria's independence.

I remember how delighted I was to stumble across those two pictures. They awakened within me a time that was now so far removed that it seemed never to have been. They were the types of things that my mother used to keep hidden away, because they were too important to throw out but not important enough to take up space in our house. I considered leaving them to gather the dust of oblivion. I also considered taking one of them and leaving the other. However, together they embodied the memory of a single era. They were so fused in my mind, in fact, that my visual memory couldn't distinguish one from the other. So I decided to take both of them back to my house, where, to my mother's dismay and my husband's amazement, they came to occupy a permanent place on my desk.

I didn't feel like explaining myself to anybody. This memory concerned me alone, and possibly Nasser as well. However, Nasser surprised me in the way he related to those two pictures. He met them with silence, as though they were no concern of his.

I didn't want to draw him into childhood confessions that the logic of manhood had rendered invalid. I just pondered his silence, and concluded that he had forgotten his passion for the one, and the other's fatherly passion for him, and had decided to let them be my concern alone.

Even so, Nasser remained my main preoccupation. He had been gone for more than a month, and my mother badgered me with questions about him to which I had no answers. 'Why did he go to Germany?' she wanted to know. 'People usually go to France. I've never heard of anybody going to Germany.'

I didn't know what to say to her. I myself hadn't known where he was going until just a week earlier. I'd been at my mother's house when he called. I asked him if everything was the way he had hoped it would be. 'It's all right,' he said. I asked him if he had an address or telephone number where we could reach him.

He replied that he would call us whenever he got the chance, from which I understood that he didn't want to tell me anything over the phone. When he asked me whether our mother had come to live with me since he left, I told him she'd insisted on staying in her own house.

'Don't leave her alone very much then,' he urged me. 'Please,' he added by way of emphasis.

From the beginning my mother had rejected the idea of coming to live with me while we waited for Nasser to come back. She considered it humiliating to have to live with her son-in-law, especially in view of the fact that she owned a lovely apartment of her own, and that she was quite attached to all of her little trinkets.

But from that time onward she became more and more attached to me. She was constantly visiting me or calling on the phone, she consulted me about everything, and she liked to go everywhere with me. Things got to the point where I felt as though I was *her* mother.

I understood her constant need for my love and affection. She'd been widowed at the age of twenty-three and orphaned as a child. She didn't understand why life had to make trouble for her and even for her children, or why she'd been destined to have a barren daughter and an absent son. So I listened patiently to her grumbling and complaining and to her motherly chatter, and had no choice but to surrender to all her whims.

I even agreed to accompany her that afternoon to the Turkish bath, though I'd never shared in her enthusiasm for the weekly rituals of hygiene that took place there. As a matter of fact, I could understand her logic. The bath was the place where she could meet all the women in the city. Like them, she could gossip freely, talk about whatever was new in her life, and show off her new purchases, her jewellery, and the clothes that no man had ever seen.

It reminded me of the way, in the old days, she'd liked to show off her fancy bathroom set, which included a silver wash basin, a fine-toothed comb made of ivory and silver, plush embroidered towels, imported scented soap, colognes, preparations for removing or dyeing hair, and all sorts of women's accessories that she kept in a fancy pail of engraved silver in the corner of the bathroom cabinet, ready for her weekly show-and-tell session.

Twenty years later not much had changed. The pail had been emptied of its contents and had been moved from my mother's bathroom cabinet into the parlour, where it had been transformed into a fancy pot that held a decorative plant. However, my mother's mind hadn't been emptied of its contents, at least not completely. Nor was it devoid of its original mentality. It had simply adjusted itself to the requirements of the age. There was no longer any need for her handbag with the sky-blue satin lining, which had had the pleasure of rubbing against my mother's lingerie more often than any man had.

As a child I would often sneak a look inside that bag as though it were a chest full of wonders. I would sit on the edge of the bed, dreaming of a women's world that as of yet I knew nothing about. I would look at my mother's things and dream of having a body just like hers on which to sport all that lovely lingerie.

I would dream and dream, close my mother's body up again in the bag, stash it in the wardrobe, and rush out of the room before being taken by surprise by my other mother, the one that had no body.

I found myself now with my mother the 'Hajja', whose body had changed since the days of my childhood. As she had when I was a little girl, she led the way, and I followed her unquestioningly from one room to another through the vast Turkish bath. The rooms of the bath were of different temperatures, growing hotter the farther in one went. My mother insisted on staying in the third, and hottest, of the rooms. I made no objection despite the fact that this was the room I hated the most.

I walked after her gingerly over a wet tile floor that seemed all too ready for someone to slip and fall on it, then shatter into a million pieces. I remembered once seeing a woman fall right in front of me. She'd been holding an infant who fell out of her arms and died within hours at the hospital.

As I entered the room, steam rose from pools situated along its walls. A child's cry could be heard here, women's laughter there.

Without question, I sat down in front of the first pool I came to. Or rather, I did have one question: Why was it that, ever since I'd been a young girl, I hated to sit in rooms that were devoid of anything but steam and water, and whose only furnishings consisted of women's naked bodies? Was it out of respect for femininity, which I had always expected to be more beautiful than bodies that had lost their natural contours? Or was it because from the very beginning I'd been destined to be a creature of paper and ink whose existence was imperilled by these prodigious amounts of water and steam?

My mother sat down beside me and placed her things on the tile floor. As for me, the only things I had were some clothes that I'd left outside, and which I had brought in her honour in case we ran into someone who knew me. Disturbed by the thought of

187

such an eventuality, I wrapped my towel around my body again and secured it mechanically around my bosom.

Suddenly I heard my mother's voice repeating words that I knew all too well from having heard them so many times in this very place. From the time she was a teenager, she'd been ashamed of her femininity and had hidden inside of towels with the insistence of someone denying an accusation.

This is a place where you learn from the glances of others how to deny your body, persecute your desires and wash your hands of your femininity. People here teach you that not only is sex shameful, but so too femininity, along with everything that bespeaks it.

As usual my mother yelled at me, 'Take that towel off!' Her words led me to new questions.

Since she had given birth to me, did she think of my body as a personal possession that she was entitled to flaunt before others as one of her accomplishments, finding in it some solace or compensation for what her own body had become?

Suddenly I became aware of one of the reasons behind my complex, distant relationship to this place. In this city, where there was nowhere that one could describe as intimate or private, the Turkish bath was the place where the sanctity and modesty of people's bodies were routinely violated. They were placed under bright lights and subjected to women's curious stares, while hands passed over them in succession, rubbing, massaging, rinsing and dowsing them with huge quantities of water as though they wanted to purge them of their woman-hood.

So was womanhood a kind of ritual impurity? Or did these women, most of whom went through their entire lives without ever denuding themselves in front of a man, have some sort of libidinous relationship with these huge quantities of water, which they poured over their bodies pail after pail for hours on end with a mysterious sort of enjoyment, and an utter preoccupation with the womanly aspects of their physical selves? It was as though they had come here for a rendezvous with their own bodies, and for no other reason. Or are all women, regardless of their nationality or their age, the granddaughters of Cleopatra, who ruled Egypt during its glory days without ever entirely leaving her bathroom?

Whether collectly or mistakenly, these women were of the belief that after every bath they would go back home to take up their seats on the 'throne' of the marriage bed, whose crown they would wear for a few brief moments – in the dark – before resuming their routine lives again.

The dark! As I sat gazing at these bodies whose femininity had been so disfigured, with their flabby bellies and drooping breasts, I suddenly saw one of the blessings of the dark, and I understood why God in his infinite wisdom had created darkness as a way of making it possible for his creatures to make love when their physical appearance had ceased to be conducive to sexual attraction. Otherwise, what man or woman, however wild their desires and however drunk they happened to be, would feel like making love with the lights on?

I kept these comments to myself. I also kept my towel wrapped around me in protest against being associated with this category of women. Each of them sat beside a small pool surrounded by streams that were either red or black depending on the colour of the henna that she used on her hair, which as she washed it, turned the Turkish bath's tile floor into a multi-coloured Danube.

Suddenly there entered three middle-aged women of mediocre beauty who nevertheless possessed a peculiar allure. They had walked in stark naked, flaunting their feminine charms in everyone's faces, whereas the custom was for women to come in wrapped in a towel, and only to take it off after they were seated.

For a moment they were the centre of attention, and they were pursued mercilessly by curious, disapproving glances from every direction. I gathered from my mother's insulting remarks about them that they were prostitutes. Prostitutes? Did such a profession still exist in this city? Other than on the pavements of rundown neighbourhoods where certain down-and-out women might work the streets, I didn't think it did.

Before I knew it the room had divided itself into two camps, one of them occupied by the 'honourable women', and the other occupied by the 'women of ill-repute'. The former proceeded to make comments about the latter, targeting them with gibes and derisive glances inspired by a sudden exaggerated sense of their own virtue and superiority. The targets of these taunts were unfazed, and the three newcomers acted as though they had the place to themselves, laughing loudly, washing and flirting with each other as if to get a rise out of their critics.

I took pleasure in my anomalous presence between the two sides, since I considered neither of them morally superior to the other. Surrounded by steam, water, unspoken desire and women's hypocrisy, I may have been secretly amusing myself by recording wry comments in my mind. After all, a writer, like any other ordinary human being, stands halfway between purity and sinfulness.

Every virtuous human being has just enough filth inside him that at any given moment it might surface and drown out his virtues, and that deep inside every bad person there is a spark of goodness that's bound to shine out one day at the very moment when he least expects it. Similarly, every woman has the capacity to be either a saint or a whore, since she was created with both potentialities. But the more she leans towards one of the two, the more likely she is to shun and deride the other.

Her patience at an end, my mother began vigorously massaging my arms, refusing to turn me over to a masseuse. Then she went on badmouthing the 'harlots', saying that large families had a custom of reserving the Turkish bath once a week and inviting relatives and friends to come at their expense. They did this in order to ensure that they didn't have to mix with strangers, including the seedy types that had infiltrated Constantine, violated its sanctity and insulted its population.

I was only pretending to listen to her, and made no reply. I was busy thinking about something that Sasha Guitry once said: 'There aren't honourable women and dishonourable women. There are only dishonourable women, and ugly women.'

As I left the Turkish bath that day, Sasha Guitry was still on my mind, and when I went home that afternoon in the rain, I recalled a certain sarcastic comment of his: 'Don't make love on Saturday nights. What will you do then if it rains on Sunday morning?' He was poking fun at husbands and wives who make love out of boredom on Saturday nights, then don't know what to do with themselves if they have to stay home the next day.

Even though it was a rainy Saturday, I decided that evening to go against Sasha Guitry's advice, since in our country Saturday isn't the last day of the week, but the first, which meant that my husband wouldn't be around the next day to share my boredom. Add to this the fact that I was coming back from a

Turkish bath that had set my desires aflame, and I was dying to give my womanhood to a man.

I didn't know, of course, that the mere fact of my intending to fall in love would be enough to turn the country upside down. Nor did I know that history was planning to give Algeria one of its greatest surprises on that day. President Chadli Bendjedid had chosen this particular Saturday, 11 January, 1992, to announce his resignation and the dissolution of Parliament during the eight o'clock news broadcast, a development which would usher the country into a constitutional labyrinth. I didn't blame Bendjedid for dumping cold water on my desires at night. After all, he'd been dumping cold water on the desires of an entire nation for years on end.

Chapter Five
Definitely

TIME ALONE WILL MAKE you sane when everyone else has gone mad. As for history, don't expect it to be in a hurry to say what it has to say in such cases. It's waiting for the right moment.

After a wait of twenty-eight years, an aeroplane landed on the tarmac. A man more than seventy-eight years old disembarked and walked across a red carpet with a bewildered look on his face.

Was it only a one-hour trip between his place of exile and his homeland? Then why had it taken him twenty-eight years to cover the distance?

A thin man with an upright posture, and tall as the truth is lofty, he was slightly stooped over, his hands were dry and rough, and the bones in his face and hands were prominent.

Not long before history began, his name had been Mohamed Boudiaf. He lived in a small city in Morocco where, with his rough and calloused hands, he had run a small brick factory. Since igniting the spark of Algeria's War of Independence in

November 1954, he had lived far removed from all political activity other than the memories of a revolution that had spurned him, and news that drifted in from a country whose rulers had deleted his name even from their history textbooks.

Hence, he no longer had a name, from the time he set foot on the homeland's soil, his name became 'history'. (But isn't history what prevents the future from coming to be?)

He had been ageless before, but now he was as old as his dreams, which had arrived on the scene two or more generations late.

Now at last he was learning to tread over the soil of the homeland in which he had never before walked with freedom or safety. France, which had pursued him doggedly, found that the only way it could detain him and his comrades was to hijack their aeroplane in 1956 as it crossed the Mediterranean Sea from Morocco to Tunisia. It diverted the plane to France, taking Boudiaf and his four companions – Ahmed Ben Bella, Aït Ahmed, Mohamed Khider and Rabah Bitat – with their hands bound towards their various places of detention. It did so to the astonishment of the entire world, which had yet to hear of the innovative practice of hijacking. It was met with outraged demonstrations on the part of the Arab masses, which during that same year had been filled with pan-Arab fervour and zeal by Abdel Nasser's rousing rhetoric.

It was only days before *The Voice of the Arabs* began broadcasting lively tunes demanding the five men's release. These anthems were soon taken up by young and old alike accompanied by women's ululations. One of them ran, 'In the name of the heroes five, O France, we will have our revenge!' And we cried.

*

History, on the other hand, was laughing, since it alone knew what no one else could ever have anticipated. In June 1963, not long after Algeria won its independence and the five revolutionary leaders found themselves free men, the then-new president Ben Bella, who had once been Boudiaf's comrade in arms, had Boudiaf arrested as he left his home. Boudiaf was led from one place to another until he ended up in a prison somewhere in a trackless wasteland. Thus it happened that the Algerian revolution's leading man suffered the disgrace of discovering that he had a homeland more savage than his enemies.

Ben Bella himself made the same discovery two years later when, in June 1965, Boumédienne removed him from power and threw him in prison, from which he emerged fifteen years later a wizened old man. As for Boudiaf, who had never demanded power for himself, but had refused to fight to free a nation from imperialism just to surrender it to the tyranny of a one-party system, he saw no difference between the two rulers who had come to power since the revolution.

On the day he disappeared, none of his comrades asked where he'd been taken. They were too busy dividing up the spoils!

But despite his long absence, Boudiaf re-entered the scene with a powerful presence.

Just like that, after twenty-eight years, his enemies had remembered him again. Sated and bloated, they had filled their pockets at the expense of the Algerian people. Then they had withdrawn, leaving a country that had been mortgaged to the World Bank – though with high hopes – for several generations to come. Boudiaf was the only one with any degree of integrity or self-restraint, and who had never once sat at the table around which dubious power deals had been struck.

Consequently, he was the only one whose name could restore confidence to a people who had lost all confidence in everything and everyone after seeing Ali Baba and the forty thieves lead one corrupt government after another.

They told him, 'Algeria needs you. You're the only one who can save her!' – words to which his ageing frame could only respond with a loving 'Yes!'

The old man rose, washed the clay off his hands, and purged his memory of hatred and bitterness, since he had always been of the belief that you can't build something with hatred. A man with an extraordinary ability to forgive, he embraced those who had exiled him and came home. Never once had Algeria called upon him but that he had answered her call.

Behold the man . . .

He was wearing a suit that he had never expected to wear for an occasion such as this.

He was learning to walk before us, to smile at us. He raised his right hand in a bashful salute, like someone apologizing for a hand that had never held anything but a weapon or fired bricks, and which saw itself as unprepared for such a role.

Behold the man, Boudiaf . . .

He had come to us on foot, treading on dreams. He was received with national flags by a generation that until that day had never heard his name, but which saw in his stature the history of Algeria in its legendary greatness.

Behold the man . . .

It wasn't his feet that kissed the soil of the homeland at every step. Rather, it was the soil of Algeria herself that celebrated his every step and kissed the soles of his shoes. Meanwhile, people's hearts cried, 'Stop, history! One of your men has come to us!'

January 14, 1992 was exceptional even in its weather. The rain that had been falling in torrents for days suddenly stopped, and out came the sun. It was as though Nature was herself in harmony with what Algerians were feeling, or as though she wanted to conspire with history to give Boudiaf the best day of his life.

All afternoon Algerians' eyes were glued to their television screens. They wanted to see and hear this man who had entered the Silence Party thirty years before. What would he say?

Everyone wanted, if only with their eyes, to kiss this man whose comrades affectionately dubbed him 'Mr Kindness and Patriotism' and whom all of us revered in our hearts as a father. Since Boumédienne's death, we had been orphans, suffering an emotional bankruptcy that surpassed the bankruptcy of our economy, and a national deficit of love even greater than the deficit in our budget.

We were looking for a man with the stature of Abdel Nasser, the eloquence of Boumédienne, and the integrity of Boudiaf. We were looking for a man who was as simple as we were, who would run his hand over our heads, pat us on the shoulder, tell us simple things we could believe, and promise us dreams that we knew he could make come true. We were looking for a man who would cry with us for everyone who had died without scrutinizing their political or religious affiliations, a man who would apologize to the living for those who had died, and to the dead for the assassination of their dreams.

We were looking for a man who, from the moment he stepped off the plane, would declare war on those who had assaulted our future and achieved glory for themselves by humiliating an entire nation. We were looking for a man who would say, 'Algeria first!' and awaken our pride, and whose simple words would become a motto to live by.

We, of course, had been waiting for Boudiaf for as long as we could remember, yet without knowing it. But he, what had he been waiting for? One day he had said to his wife, 'Even all this fanfare can't keep them from assassinating me. I don't trust them.' When she asked him if he had come with the intention of committing suicide, he replied – like someone who knows his fate is inescapable, 'It's my duty. My only hope is that they'll give me some time.'

* * *

The next day the city woke up in the mood for a good debate, and I woke up in the mood to write. I couldn't see any better way to celebrate Boudiaf's return than to go back to that notebook of mine.

I opened it at the place where, during a kiss four months earlier, both love and ink had run out on me.

My intention had been to write something about the present, to describe my wonder at the sight of Boudiaf. But my emotions turned my pen back to the past, awakening within me another man, a man who was bound to appear whenever I opened this notebook. It was a man who had once said to me, 'I thought about how, if kisses die the way we do, the best time to die would be during a kiss.' Then he had left.

Ever since that day I had been nurturing memory with his feverish words lest the fires of love be extinguished while I waited for him.

Was it desire? The need to write? Or a kind of fate that makes every individual story parallel to some communal story, though we never know which of them is writing the other?

Otherwise, how is one to explain the surprise that was waiting for me three weeks after Boudiaf's return? Never once had I stopped feeling that I was going to meet him in some public place or other. Instead, however, I stumbled across him where I had least expected him to be: in my own home, on the pages of a newspaper lying neglected on the floor next to my husband's desk!

I love those presents that life gives you without any particular occasion, the kind that turn your life upside down with a simple coincidence. There are some that it flings on the ground in front of you so that when you bend down gratefully to pick them up, you realize you've stumbled serendipitously upon love!

And what if you've stumbled upon something else? After all, I don't think love has ever been in such close proximity to politics!

* * *

In a photo of Boudiaf with members of the National Assembly, I saw him, and could hardly believe my eyes. I fixed my gaze on his face in particular. I knew those features perfectly. That absent look was the same one that had given me pause on the day when he took off his shades to kiss me. The hair, the mouth, everything, I recognized it all. It was him!

I quickly reread the article under the photograph. Then I read it again slowly in hopes of finding some explanation for this man's presence in the picture.

I understood from the article that Boudiaf had decided to form the National Consultative Council, a body that would include numerous politicians who, known for their integrity and patriotism, hadn't been associated with any previous regime, to help him bring Algeria out of its political and legislative quagmire. I continued reading the article on the third page, which included a number of photographs with captions identifying some of the council members. I was impressed by the number of writers and thinkers who had been appointed to the Council, noting that one of the individuals who had headed the Council on a periodic basis was none other than the renowned Abdelhamid Ben Hadouga, and that its membership included numerous women intellectuals, university professors and journalists in a country in which neither intellectuals nor women had ever been asked their opinion.

I looked over all the names and professions, and found not a single artist among them. I almost began to think I was deluded and that I was hallucinating his picture wherever I went, especially since I knew he was in Paris at the time. This being the case, it was highly unlikely that he would be taking part in a gathering of this nature unless he had returned from his trip.

Suddenly I thought of a way to put my doubts to rest. I headed for the telephone and dialled the number that my hand still knew by heart (or that my heart still knew by hand).

It was nine o'clock in the morning. I didn't stop to wonder whether it was an appropriate time to call, or if he would be the person to answer the phone. I didn't even stop to think about whether the number I was dialling with a trembling hand and a racing heart was right or not.

I wanted to hear him. At the very least, I wanted to hear the telephone ringing in the house where I had experienced love. I wanted it to wake up its furniture and bring its memory to life. On the second ring someone picked up the receiver, and my heart nearly pounded out of my chest.

I almost said something, but decided to wait for the person on the other end to speak first. After a short silence, I heard the voice I'd waited for for so long that I no longer expected to hear it.

As if he had recognized me from my breathing, he asked me, 'How are you?'

I could hardly believe what was happening to me.

'Is that you?' I said.

Then, in the same tone of amazement, I asked, 'How did you recognize me?'

'From your silence,' he said with that endearing sarcasm of his. 'Silence is our password.'

The only reply I could make was a stream of feverish words that I blurted out however they happened to come: 'I've missed you! How could you have abandoned me and given me over to this crazy city? I want to see you. How can I see you? Answer me. Don't you know that my life is worth nothing without you? What have you done to me to make me love you this way?'

He made no reply, as though my words hadn't reached him. He only asked me, 'Where are you calling from?'

'From Constantine.'

'Where exactly in Constantine?'

'From home.'

'Call me from somewhere else,' he told me.

'Why?' I asked.

He didn't answer.

'When?'

'Whenever you'd like. I'll be home all morning.'

Then he hung up. All of this had happened within minutes, and all it had taken was those few minutes for me to go back to being the woman I had been several months before.

I'd been drawn back into the same vortex of joy, fear, trepidation, hope, and uncertainty.

Why did this man always have to come back just when I'd stopped waiting for him? And why did his arrival always coincide with major political events? Why hadn't he given me some forewarning if he had been planning to come back from France? Why did he want to know exactly where I was calling from? And why was it that I always seemed to be drawn towards him by a raging stream of desire that sent me down towering waterfalls of madness? Carrying me along from one gasp to another, his love drew me on to destinations unknown.

Something lovely was happening to me on this particular morning. It was like waking up after a winter sleep, lazily pulling back the curtains with the curiosity of someone who wants to know what's happened in the world since the last time she was awake, only to find love reading a newspaper on a chair in her back yard and waiting for her!

There was nothing between us but a wet windowpane and a season. But wherever you are, you're bound to wake up to a love that has nothing to do with the seasons.

The rain wasn't going to keep me from leaving the house, since on this particular morning I had my own private weather forecast to respond to. Within half an hour I had put on my clothes and was ready to go out.

My mother was surprised to see me at an hour when I would usually still be in bed. However, she proceeded to make the most of my visit – which she could find no explanation for other than the fact that I was bored and that I missed her – by sitting me down with a cup of coffee and treating me to a litany of her health problems and other woes.

I listened to her with all the patience I could muster. As she spoke, I came up with a quick fix for her problems that was tailor-made for me: for the two of us to go to the capital for a little holiday!

Of course my mother took to the idea right away. In addition to the fact that there were all sorts of friends and relations she could visit while she was there, it would give her the chance to have me all to herself under one roof for several days. This was what my mother referred to as 'a change of atmosphere'.

The adventure I had just proposed had an energizing effect on my mother, who went to the kitchen and made me lunch in honour of my surprise visit and our impromptu journey.

As for me, I headed nervously for the telephone with a joyful anticipation to dial the same number I had dialled from home.

As calmly as it had before, the voice came, 'How are you?'

'Only now can I say that I'm all right,' I said dreamily.

'So how were you before?'

'I felt as though my whole life was a vacuum.'

'Beware of vacuums. They make people wicked. Like they say, "The empty mind is Satan's workshop."'

'Well, the times we're living in are wicked anyway.'

'Things might get better. We just have to trust.'

'You yourself once said that you didn't trust anything any more. Do you remember? You said that the day we met at the newspaper stand.'

'Yes, I remember. But there's a certain man I trust, and because he's come back, my confidence in Fate has been restored.'

'Did you come back on his account, or . . . ?'

I fell silent, wanting to give him the chance to make some sort of romantic confession.

Ignoring my hint, he said, 'Yes, I did.'

'So, what about me?'

He sank into another silence.

'The day we met at the newsstand, you advised me not to read any newspapers, and I haven't read one since. If I hadn't happened to leaf through a newspaper this morning, I wouldn't have known you were here. How could you have come back without telling me?'

'But I did tell you. Do you really think you came across that newspaper by accident? Nothing ever happens by accident. There are things that we want so badly that they actually happen, and when we look back on them, it seems as though we had planned them out in one way or another.'

'But you seem so cold towards me, as though you haven't missed me!'

'Actually,' he replied sardonically, 'I've missed you with a passion, but . . .'

'But what?'

'But your home phone is under surveillance. In fact, this one might be under surveillance also. Avoid calling me from home. I would prefer you to come to the capital. That would be better.'

'I will,' I said confidently.

Then, before hanging up the receiver, I added, 'Of course.'

* * *

If women, like the peoples of the world, truly desire life for them-selves, then Fate is bound to let them have their way even if the one who appears to be controlling their destinies is a high-ranking officer or a petty dictator in the form of a husband.

Speaking of husbands, I still don't know how I managed to persuade mine to let me travel to the capital for a holiday on the beach in the dead of winter.

How could he have failed to be suspicious of such a request?

It makes me think of a sarcastic quip I once heard to the effect that, 'There are two types of idiots: the ones who suspect everything, and the ones who don't suspect anything.'

My husband, a good military man who has enough professional savvy always to be on guard, started out his married life with me by spying, making inquiries, and being suspicious of everything.

When he came up with a lack of evidence, he gave me a surprising amount of freedom. At the very least, it gave him enough time to do the things he needed to do, confident that the stars on his uniform would keep me under his thumb.

In this particular case he was probably too busy with political developments to go spying on my womanly preoccupations, which had thus far given him no reason for concern, and in relation to which I had nothing to hide. My problem now was with other people who, instead of eavesdropping on terrorists, spent their time eavesdropping on lovers' phone conversations.

A mere hour on an aeroplane, and I was hundreds of kilometres away from my shackles, back in the same house I'd come to four months earlier with Farida. I called it the 'dream house', because it was a place where everything became possible, just as in one's dreams.

As soon as I arrived and put things around me in some semblance of order, I rushed to the telephone. The voice was warm this time, assuring me that I wasn't dreaming.

'You finally got here! If you only knew how much I've missed you! I'll be seeing you tomorrow, right?'

Just a few words and a question, and the whole world seemed brighter. There were bigger questions as well, of course, but I had no time to answer them. I was too busy being infatuated to distraction. The infatuation also robbed me of sleep.

A certain saying of Baudelaire kept me awake: 'Everyone worthy of the name human has a yellow adder crouching on his chest that says, "No," whenever he says, "I want."'

I spent the entire night trying to kill that adder. As dawn drew near, I realized that this adder's 'No' has seven heads, and that whenever you kill one of them, another one appears, thrusting this or that warning or negative imperative in your face. Nevertheless, I dozed off munching on the apple of forbidden desire while those seven heads looked on.

I had a date with 'Yes', and everything inside me was in agreement on that fact. Good morning to 'Yes'! Good morning to love! Contrary to custom, the entire universe had woken up beautiful, and I couldn't help but wonder who had told it my news.

It was as if all the songs being played on the radio that morning knew what had happened to me, and in my mind I saw visions of tree-lined streets that led into my heart, pavement cafés on a winter's day awaiting their lovers' arrival, and unmade beds awaiting their consummation in the cities of 'yes'.

The previous evening's 'maybe' had been followed the next morning with a resounding 'yes', and all of its 'nos' had been swallowed up in the morning light.

Given the battle I'd fought with my yellow adder, I felt as though I'd spent the night sailing a stormy winter sea. Then my morning was booby-trapped by my mother's questions and projects. However, I managed to foil all her plans for joint outings and embarked instead on a private, and much preferred, venture of my own.

The car set off with me at noon down the same road it had travelled on the way to my first love tryst. It seemed longer this time despite the driver's speed, the light traffic, and the absence of checkpoints.

Reassured to see that the streets had gone back to normal, being empty now of demonstrators and bearded men, placards and shouted slogans, I got out at Emir Abdelkader Square and went the rest of the way on foot.

One number, two numbers, one building, two buildings, and I had arrived. Propelled forward by longing and a racing heart, I ascended the four flights of stairs with a burglar's haste and a lover's breathless enthusiasm.

A door opened at the first knock and closed behind me. It was a door that separated me from the city of 'no' and ushered me into the world of 'yes'.

There I was awaited by a nameless man who, his eyes fixed upon me, folded me in his arms, and a kiss behind the door that had been closed upon my joyous exhilaration pinned me between two worlds.

As I caught my breath he asked me, 'Did you have trouble getting here this time?'

I said, 'The hardest thing every time is getting through that door!'

After a pause, I continued, 'Both on the way in and on the way out!'

'So,' he quipped, 'just stay here!'

I flung myself, exhausted, on to the sofa and said, 'Take me hostage. Would that be possible?'

'All of us are hostages,' he returned sardonically.

'Whose hostages?' I wanted to know.

I had expected him to say, 'Hostages of love.' Instead he said, 'Hostages of the homeland.'

'Please,' I said a bit irritably, 'spare me the politics! I didn't come here to talk about the homeland. You have no idea what a risk I take to come here, just to experience a moment of love.'

'But there isn't any love outside of politics. Haven't you figured that out yet?'

I didn't reply because I didn't understand, nor did I want to understand, why politics had to be a third party to every human relationship. Whatever the reason, the fact was that politics slept in the same bed with both spouses and lovers. It ate breakfast with us in the morning, and all of our other meals, too, for that matter. It accompanied us on our visits to our relatives, both the living and the dead.

It would reach the cities of our dreams before we got there ourselves, and when we finally arrived, it would share a seat with us. On one occasion it would send someone near and dear to us into exile, and on another, bring back to us someone we loved.

'Maybe you're right,' I said. 'In the end it was politics that brought you back.

'Fortunately for love,' I continued.

'And what if that weren't the case?'

'I don't believe you came back on my account.'

'I didn't say I'd come back on your account. Let's just say that I came back so that we could go on writing the novel together. Isn't that what you care about?'

'I guess so. But I don't see why it would matter so much to you.'

'Of course it matters to me!' He laughed. 'I don't want to miss my own ending. And I want it to be a nice one.'

'Really?'

'Of course. Endings are important in books, just as they are in life.'

'Do you know what matters to me the most right now? What matters to me is to know who you are. That's all I care about. Ever since the day I saw your picture in the newspaper, I've been buying one every day. I look at all the pictures, and I read all the interviews with members of the National Council. I know everything about everybody. I read their statements on every topic under the sun. But I haven't read anything relating to you. Why is that?'

'Well,' he said cynically, 'they shine on account of the things they say, whereas I shine on account of my silence!'

'But whose side are you on? What party do you belong to?'

'The real question isn't: What party do you belong to? but rather, which one have you defected from?'

Seeing that I had no choice but to turn questions on their heads the way he always did, I asked, 'So which ones have you defected from?'

After a pause, as though the question had taken him by surprise, he said, 'I have more than one answer to a question like that. Let's say I've defected from my dreams. I, Madame, am the final witness to the Arab decline. I've spent my whole life observing disappointment and failure. I've sat and watched my dreams sink over the horizon, one homeland after another. I've seen it happen in my own homeland as well. So do you understand now why it matters so much to me not to miss my own ending in the story? You want to know the secret behind my silence. Before Boudiaf came back, I was empty. I had no dreams left. All my dreams were behind me.'

'And what about me?'

'You?'

'Where do I fit in?'

'You fit in exactly where you are right now.'

'Meaning . . . ?'

'Meaning, on paper. My dreams with you, just like your projects with me, take up no more than a single page, although that page might be the size of a bed. That's our destiny.'

This man was so skilled with words that he could bypass all your questions without giving you a single answer. Or he could give you the answer to a question you hadn't expected him to answer on that particular day, since it wasn't the one you had asked him.

Here he was answering a question that had preoccupied me in the beginning. In fact, it was the question that had led to this story's being written. The question had to do with why this man had retreated into silence and reduced language to nothing but the words 'inevitably', 'definitely', 'of course', and 'always', as though all of life could be reduced to these.

Why had he turned the world into a crossword puzzle or a game of Scrabble in which no woman could keep up with him, still less defeat him?

As a writer who made words her profession and who refused to be defeated by a protagonist of her own making, on her own turf, in her own book, I had joined him in a linguistic fencing match in which I found myself being defeated in round after round. I was also becoming more involved with him with every question I asked, since every question led me to still more questions.

From the beginning I had known full well that questions would only increase my romantic involvement. What I hadn't known was that, with this man in particular, answers also would lead to an infatuation no less overwhelming.

I loved his answers although, I have to admit, I often didn't know exactly what he meant by them. There were times when he seemed to be speaking to some other woman about some other man. Even so, I loved everything he said, maybe because I was so taken by how mysterious he was.

Fiddling with his hand, I said, 'I love you. I need you to free me a little from my slavery to you.'

He put his arms around me and drew me towards him, saying, 'Love means letting the person you love take you by storm and defeat you. It means letting him take over everything that's you. It's all right to be defeated now and then. Love is a state of weakness, not strength.'

'But . . .'

'But because you haven't understood this, you're repeating a mistake you made in a previous book.'

I wanted to ask him when this had happened, in what book. But before I knew it, his lips were stealing my questions and sweeping me away in an unexpected kiss. I surrendered to his lips' assault, as though I wanted to prove to him, with every region that fell under his manly sway, how much I loved him.

Actually, I would have had neither the strength nor the will to resist him. I took pleasure in being overwhelmed by him as he placed his keys in my body's secret locks.

In pleasure there is a bodily code that renders one person another's slave without his realizing it. This man who had used nothing to arouse me but his lips, who had told him how to give me such pleasure? Who had told him how to traverse the secret passageways of desire that no other man's lips had ever probed?

Suddenly he planted two staccato kisses on my mouth as though he were placing ellipses after an unfinished sentence. Then he got up to look for a pack of cigarettes.

While he was busy with his search, I went to the bathroom to spruce myself up. I cast a casual glance at the toiletries on the shelf above the sink. My attention was drawn to two bottles of the same type of cologne, one of them opened, and the other still wrapped in transparent plastic.

I picked up the open bottle and began examining it with the curiosity of someone who's happened upon a clue. I thought back on all the times when I had been about to ask him what kind of cologne he used. I also remembered how my story with this man had come into being thanks to a word and a whiff of cologne. In fact, it might have been this very cologne, without which I may never have found my way to him.

I was still holding the bottle in my hand when he came down the hallway towards the kitchen.

As I sprayed some of the cologne on my hand, I asked him jokingly, 'Is it because I told you I liked your cologne that you've started buying two bottles of it at a time?'

'No!' he said with a laugh. 'Whenever I go to France, I bring one bottle for myself and one bottle for my friend Abdelhaq. Actually, he's the one that got me using it. He never uses anything else.'

I was about to come out of the bathroom when he came back as though he'd remembered something. Then, as he handed me the unopened bottle of perfume, he said, 'I apologize for not having brought one for you too. I was in such a hurry, I didn't think of it. So how about if I give you this one? They say women like their sweethearts' cologne. So you can put some on whenever you miss me.'

As I took the bottle from him I said, 'I had never heard that, but it sounds like a good idea. It's just that I might need a whole bottle a week!'

Then I added, 'And your friend?'

'Don't worry,' he said. 'I'll get another one for him.'

Delighted with this gift, I felt as though I was drawing him closer every time we met. I was infiltrating his private world in ways he would never have expected, and taking hold of everything that might bring me nearer to him.

When I went back to the living room, he was sitting quietly on the sofa across from me smoking a cigarette. It was as though he had decided to meditate on me, or what he had done to me in the course of that long kiss.

I stowed the bottle of cologne in my bag with the same exultation I had felt on the day when I borrowed Henri Michaux's book from him, hoping against hope that at long last I could figure this man out.

As I put my bag back down, I found myself saying unthinkingly, 'Guess what kind of present I'd like to have from you?'

'What's that?' he asked, still smoking his cigarette with his feet propped on the table.

'The truth!' I said. 'Could you give me the truth? I have the right to know who you are!'

'Better to postpone your disappointment a little longer!'

'What's your name?' I insisted. 'Is that such a difficult question to answer?'

'No!' he replied, laughing. 'So which name do you want to know?'

'And do you have two names? Why is that?'

'Because we're living in a time when even states, organizations and political parties change their names with the stroke of a pen. In Russia alone there are twenty-eight cities that have changed their names, including Leningrad. So why can't people do the same when they change their beliefs, or when something happens to change the course of their lives?

'The Chinese have a lovely custom of choosing a new name for themselves at the end of their lives. It's as if, now that they've experienced life, they're ready to choose a name that would fit them in another realm. After all, the names that suit us best are given to us by our lives. As for the names that we bring into life, they often tyrannize us and do us wrong. So let's just say I like this idea, and I decided to be a man with two names.'

As usual, his answer was no answer at all. Instead, it simply manifested his ability to avoid people's questions.

But I didn't give up. I kept after him.

'Give me any name you like. I just want something to call you by.'

'My name is Khaled Ben Tubal,' he replied evenly.

'Khaled Ben Tubal?' I repeated, aghast. 'But . . .'

'I know,' he interrupted me. 'I know it's the name of a character in your novel. But it's my name, too.'

I sat on the edge of the sofa looking at a man that I was just getting acquainted with, and recalling another man that I had known in a previous book who was also a painter from Constantine. He was a man I knew everything about. I knew him as well as I knew myself. The only thing that set him apart from me was the fact that he was a man, and that his left arm had been disfigured by war.

Could he possibly be the same person? I gazed at him in disbelief. I expected him to say something, but he didn't. He just went on smoking his cigarette as calmly as before.

For a moment I felt I was getting close to the truth, that I was just a question away from it. 'Is Khaled Ben Tubal his first name, or his second?'

The answer to this question was going to be frightening and decisive. It was bound to turn our relationship upside down and, with it, the story. However, given his evasiveness, I didn't expect him to answer it easily.

I asked him, 'Is this the name your friends and colleagues call you by?'

'Of course,' he said. 'It's also the name I sign my articles with.'

Then, to my amazement, he handed me a newspaper that lay nearby and showed me a political article written by one Khaled Ben Tubal.

I took the newspaper from him, not believing my eyes.

From my reading of Henri Michaux's book, I had suspected he might be a journalist, and I clearly remembered the verse in which Michaux had written, 'In the absence of the sun, learn to grow ripe in the cold,' below which he had added in blue ink, '. . . or in a newspaper!'

However, I hadn't given much thought to the verse that followed it: 'I have no name. Rather, my name is a squandering of names.' The reader had underlined this verse twice, as though it was the one that described him the best.

I held on to the newspaper as he went on smoking his cigarette and avoiding my glances. Then, as if to drive home the point that he was ignoring me, he turned on the television and absorbed himself in watching a news report. He almost seemed to have forgotten I was there.

The report included a live broadcast of the national tour Boudiaf was making to explain the principles of the National Assembly. Gesticulating to the crowd, he said, 'There's a mafia in this country, and certain government officials have pocketed funds that don't belong to them. Rest assured that I will declare war on such individuals. The Ministry of Justice will investigate all relevant files and take whatever steps are necessary. In this context, I ask citizens to help the Ministry by writing in and providing it with any information they may have. From now on no one will be above the law. Everyone will be held accountable. The people have the right to know the truth. They have the right to know where public funds have gone.'

The crowd responded to Boudiaf's extemporaneous speech with loud shouts and ululations, which changed the mood of our time together somewhat. Breaking the silence between us again, the man turned to me and commented, 'They aren't going to let him accomplish what he came to do. I'm sure of it.'

I didn't know exactly what he meant, as my thoughts were still scattered. However, in hopes of keeping the conversation going, I said, 'Why?'

'Why?' he retorted. 'Because they didn't bring him back to open those booby-trapped files. They brought him back to be a front behind which they can go on plundering the country just the way they have been. The people closest to him say he shuts himself up for long hours day and night. He's looking for the facts that he intends to present to the people in three months' time on the occasion of Algeria's Independence Day celebration.'

After a short pause he continued, 'Are you looking for the truth? Everybody's looking for the truth, but everybody's afraid of it. You know why?'

'Why?' I murmured.

He put out his cigarette in the ashtray, crushing it slowly. Then suddenly he got up and began unbuttoning his shirt with one hand.

I realized then that never once had I seen him use anything but his right hand. I was startled by this belated discovery, which took me back again to the character in my novel. But before I could think any further, I saw him fling his shirt on to the sofa and turn to me bare-chested. Then, as though he were continuing a conversation about another subject, he said, 'Because the truth expresses itself badly.' After a pause he went on, 'In fact, sometimes it's downright murderous, even if its only crime is to murder our illusions.'

Suddenly my attention was drawn to his left arm, which appeared to be paralysed. His upper left arm was disfigured in several places, as though it had been operated on without any aesthetic considerations. A terrified shudder went through me, not because of what I saw, but because of my fear that I might have gone insane, and lost the ability to distinguish between fiction and fact.

It was as though I'd dreamed about the events now taking place, and was being confronted by a man I had created and maimed with my own hands.

I knew he was testing me, and taking careful note of the surprise's effect on me. Doing my best to conceal my embarrassment, I told him honestly, 'I don't care what you believe now, but trust me when I say that I love you the way you are. Otherwise I wouldn't have created a man just like you so that I could live years with him in a book.'

'Well,' he replied sarcastically, 'you've certainly exercised love's destructive powers to good effect.'

'All I've done is to exercise a writer's power of imagination,' I said.

'Stop it, then. Everyone you've worked so hard to create has been snatched up by life. A writer's only real accomplishment consists in the blank spaces he leaves. Every blank page in a book is a space stolen from life, since it can serve as the beginning of another story or another book. It's out of that kind of blank space that I came to you, not out of what you would think of as literature.'

Wanting to avoid an argument, I said, 'It doesn't matter to me where you came from. All I know is that I want you.'

'Is that so?' he replied sceptically. 'I thought you wanted the truth!'

'What kind of confession do you want exactly?' I asked irritably.

'I don't want any confession from you,' he said. 'All that matters to me is for you to admit to yourself that what is happening between us as man and woman is your first concern, and that if it weren't for that, this story wouldn't even be worth writing.'

'Then?'

'Then nothing, apart from the fact you're bypassing this major fact by distracting yourself looking for another, less important fact having to do with the question of who I am.'

He had me cornered, and all I could say was, 'I'm here because it's my duty as a writer to look for the truth. And as a woman, it's only natural that I'd be looking for love. However, I agree with you that I'm not good at distinguishing between the two.'

In a professorial tone he replied, 'I'll show you a sure way to tell them apart: the truth always expresses itself in an ugly sort of way, while love always seems more wonderful than it is.'

As he spoke he was putting his shirt back on, his right hand fumbling clumsily with the buttons.

Instead of reaching out to help him, I took his shirt off again, and my lips began descending over his chest. Then they slid in the direction of his motionless arm and covered it with kisses with the ferocity of passion, which alone is capable of turning any reality, however unsightly, into a thing of beauty.

* * *

When I left him, I was beset by conflicting emotions – from satisfaction, to disappointment, to an astonishment that was as painful as it was pleasant.

To go to a love tryst and find yourself with a person who has just emerged from a book you wrote, who has the same name and even the same disfigurement as one of the characters in that book, and to find that in spite of it all, you still feel the same overpowering desire for him – an experience like that is bound to leave you in a huge muddle of feelings and questions. The resulting inward chaos will be all the worse when you see that the very name you invented yourself, and worked so hard to come up with, has left your book and placed itself at the end of a newspaper article as the name of a man who has nothing to do with you, or, at the very least, would have had nothing to do with you if it weren't for a particular astonishing detail: namely the fact that he, like the character in your book, has a disfigured arm.

It blew my mind to think that this man was continuing a story that had begun in a previous novel of mine. It was as though he were planning to publish a single-copy, reality-based edition of the book.

The day when he kissed me for the first time in front of his bookshelves, he had said, 'We're continuing a kiss that we began on page 172 of that book, and in the very same place.'

Afterwards I went looking for page 172 in every book I had ever written, and I found that kiss: prolonged, detailed, unplanned, just the way it had happened one day between that artist and that writer.

Then, when I borrowed the book by Henri Michaux, he had told me he was afraid he might be repeating a stupid mistake he had made in a previous book. He was alluding to the fact that the heroine in that earlier story had fallen in love with the main character's friend . . . on account of a book.

As for me, I noticed that I was doing some of the same things that that heroine had done after the aforementioned kiss. For example, I had borrowed a book.

From the start everything had taken us back to that story, including the city that had brought us together. In his talk about Constantine and bridges, there was both a return to, and a seemingly deliberate retreat from, the things that artist had said in the novel. It was as though the temporal and emotional distance he had traversed had caused him to rethink and correct his views.

Yet in spite of everything, it was still confusing. I didn't want to believe that this man, who had been turning my life upside down for the past six months, was himself Khaled Ben Tubal, the creature of ink that I'd brought into being several years earlier, then forgotten inside of a book. I had cast him into the bowels of a printing press the way one casts a body into the sea after weighing it down with heavy rocks lest it resurface. But he'd resurfaced anyway.

Here was someone I knew inside and out. I had lived with him for four hundred pages and nearly four years. Then we'd gone our separate ways. His life had come to an end on the last line of the book, and my life without him had begun.

But in the time that had passed since then, which of us had been looking for the other? And which of us had needed the other more?

A novelist was once asked, 'Why do you write?' to which he replied in jest, 'Because my characters need me. I'm all they have in this world!' This writer had been dodging the question, of course, and was tacitly admitting to the fact that he felt like an orphan. In the end, every novelist is an orphan at heart, a peculiar creature who abandons his family in order to create an imaginary set of family members, friends and other loved ones made of nothing but ink. He then proceeds to live among them, so preoccupied with their concerns and so ruled by their moods that it can be truly said that they're all he has in this world!

This being the case, what was so amazing about the fact that this man had become my entire family, occupying the place previously held by my husband, my brother, my mother, and everyone else around me?

Actually, the only thing that really amazed me was the fact that, of all the characters I had created, I'd grown attached to this one in particular. It might make perfect sense for Pygmalion to fall in love with a statue he had made with his own hands and which was a paragon of perfection. But what sense would it make for a sculptor to fall in love with a statue he had failed to create, or for a novelist to fall in love with a character she herself had disfigured?

That evening, I'd hoped that sitting with my mother would help me get away from myself. I had been neglecting her somewhat after having persuaded her to contact some acquaintances of hers in the capital, and I had planned a schedule for her that would give me the freedom I wanted.

She was happy, or at least she seemed to be, as she talked about a distant relative of hers whose son was getting married at the weekend. She had invited us to the wedding, and it wasn't difficult to imagine how my mother would be spending the next few days.

My mother's whole life was spent between one wedding and the next, one pilgrimage and the next. Wherever she went she ran into someone who was about to marry off a son or a daughter, someone who had a relative who had just come back from a pilgrimage to Mecca, or some sheikh who would invite her to a celebration of a local saint.

Yet even with all of this she wasn't completely happy. Her happiness was missing something, something called Nasser. Before he went away she'd been hoping to marry him off, to have a daughter-in-law she could boss around, and grandchildren she could raise and enjoy.

Now that Nasser was gone, every wedding reminded her of him, and all she wanted was for him to come back and share with her what remained of her life. What hurt her most about his leaving was the fact that she hadn't been prepared for it. Nothing in Nasser's personality or lifestyle suggested that he might make such an unexpected decision.

Ever since Nasser had left three months earlier, I'd been trying to give my mother an answer to her questions while at the same time hiding half of the facts from her. She would ask, 'Why did your brother go away? He tells you everything.'

'He was uncomfortable here,' I would say. 'He wanted to try his luck overseas the way everybody else is doing, but he'll be back. He promised me he would.'

'But when? In a few weeks? A few months? A few years?'

I didn't have any answer to give her. 'When things settle down a little,' I said. 'When conditions improve.'

'What conditions?' she wanted to know. 'What is it that he expects to improve? Didn't you hear about what happened two days ago in Blida? I heard from a woman today that they . . .'

'I don't want to know about it,' I interrupted. 'Don't tell me anything please.'

I didn't want my mother to ruin my night with news about death. From time to time she would call me in the evenings, whether out of boredom or fear, and all she could think of to tell me were stories more hair-raising than any horror film I had ever seen.

There had been a sudden increase in the perverse practice of mutilating corpses lest the departed rest in peace or find their way to heaven. Or maybe it was to teach a lesson to the 'infidels' or people who worked in the service of the 'infidel' state.

This sort of epithet was applied most frequently to security personnel or certain unfortunate traffic policemen, whose breed had nearly gone extinct over the past few months. Most of them had either been shot to death or had their throats slit, while many had been assassinated while escorting a relative to his final resting place.

As for the 'smart ones' who came to visit their dead two or three days later, their assassins would lie in wait for them in the cemeteries night and day, and before they knew it they were sharing a grave with their dead loved one, since graves in this country lay open, waiting for the slightest excuse to close in on an unsuspecting visitor.

So what could my mother have possibly added to the macabre soap opera I was already watching with horror every day along with everyone else in the country?

Harping again on her most gnawing preoccupation, my mother suddenly asked me, 'Did Nasser leave an address in the letter he sent with that friend of his?'

'Yes,' I told her.

'Write to him, then.'

223

'I will as soon as I get back to Constantine. He asked me about some things that I need to check on there.'

As a matter of fact, all he had asked me was how my mother and I were, but I wanted to put off dealing with his letter for a while. All I could think about was one thing: Khaled, just as all my mother could think about was Nasser. Now that he was gone, he reminded my mother of my father, who had disappeared just like that more than thirty years earlier. He had disappeared with a handful of other men in order to plan out what later came to be known as the November Revolution.

Since that time, my mother had developed a fear of men who go away all of a sudden without leaving an address. They may never come back at all and if they do come back, it may be after such a long time that we've stopped waiting for them. There are times when a little voice near us keeps insisting – They're coming today, maybe even right now! Then suddenly the miracle happens – there's a hurried knock on the door, and it opens to reveal a weary man, his clothing covered with dust. He picks us up like a doll, wraps our little body in his arms and bathes us in kisses, but we're too young to know whether he's laughing or crying.

There is a remarkable incident that my mother relates from the time I was five years old. It was Ramadan, and my mother was making a special Algerian pastry for our evening fast-breaking meal. I kept asking her to make some for my father, since it was one of his favourite dishes. She replied that he was gone, and that he wouldn't be able to eat any of it. 'But he *is* coming!' I insisted with childish stubbornness. 'So make some for him!'

No sooner had we sat down to eat than a knock came at the door. It was my father, who had come back from the front after an absence of exactly one year. His last visit had been during the previous Ramadan. When she saw him, my grandmother burst into tears, saying, 'Hayat told us you were coming, but we didn't believe it!'

In light of this memory, I expected my mother to pester me with the question, 'When will Nasser be back?' in the belief that I still had that sixth sense that gives children access to things adults can't perceive. Of course, I had lost that kind of intuition long ago, along with a number of other lovely things that I had left behind as I got older.

If I had still had it, I would have found the answers to many other questions. In the past one of these had been, 'When will that man come back?' Other questions were, 'Who is he?', 'When will I see him?' and 'Where is this strange story taking me?'

The minute I thought of him, I had an overpowering desire to talk to him and hear his voice. So I waited until my mother had gone to bed, and then I went to call him.

His line was busy for the first fifteen minutes, which surprised and irritated me. I didn't expect him to have anyone else in his life that he might talk to at night.

Finally the telephone rang, and his voice came, saying, 'How are you?'

'I miss you. The line has been busy for a long time.'

'I was talking to someone in Constantine.'

'Is your family still there?'

'No, I was talking to my friend Abdelhaq.'

'You were talking to a friend at this hour of the night?'

'He's a man of the night,' he replied somewhat defensively.

'What do you mean?'

'He's a journalist and works nights at a newspaper.'

'Is there any news?'

He seemed about to say something, but paused. Then, as though he were hiding something, he said, 'No.

'And you?' he asked absently.

'I just wanted to hear your voice.'

He was quiet for a while. Then he said, 'And I want you.'

His directness took me by surprise. Amazed, I said, 'Really? So why did you wax eloquent yesterday in defence of the beauty of abstinence?'

'Last night . . . I don't know. I was just drunk on opposites. At times like that you can't expect me to say anything logical.'

'As for me, I have lots of things to say to you, but I've started to avoid being too candid. Based on things you've said, I'm afraid somebody might be eavesdropping on us.'

'Don't worry,' he quipped. 'What's the use of having a secret if nobody ever hears about it?'

'Are you out of your mind?' I shouted.

'No,' he insisted, 'but don't you think there's something nice about love scandals?'

I was appalled at his nonchalance.

'But I'm married!'

'I know. That's why I'm constantly marrying you and murdering you.'

'Why is that?'

'To legitimize loving you. I want to make you mine so that I can do all sorts of forbidden things with you.'

'Do you need all of that in order to love a woman?'

'Of course. I was once a man of principles. At that time you were the most delectable woman I could imagine refusing.'

'Then what happened?'

'Nothing. Now I want you without questions. There isn't much time left.'

After a pause he continued, 'Come tomorrow. I want to infect you with my madness.'

'Do you promise me if I come that you'll tell me who you are?'

'All I can promise you is pleasure. And you will come.'

'How can you be so sure of that?'

'Because there's someone hovering around me who might steal me from you. Don't you feel jealous of some being that might take possession of me for ever?'

Incredulous, I asked, 'Are you getting married?'

With a kind of muffled sadness he said, 'You might call it a marriage of sorts. It's the only permanent bond that we don't choose, and from which we can't escape.'

I didn't understand what he was saying, but I concluded he was joking with me as a way of getting me to come.

'All right then, I'll be there. But beware of my jealousy. I'm a Sagittarius, and people with that sign of the zodiac make up the largest percentage of those who commit crimes of passion. I'll bring you a report to document it.'

'Come then,' he said with a laugh. 'Maybe I'll be the one to kill you!'

Why did this man insist on setting fire to my body and my notebooks? He who had always stood on the edge of the forbidden, contenting himself with a kiss, what had led him to change his convictions? Was there really another woman hovering around him? Who might she be? And how could such a thing have happened when I was talking to him every day?

I tried to sleep, looking for answers to these questions. Then I remembered him saying, 'The time for questions is over.' So I hid my question marks under the pillow and began dreaming about our next tryst.

* * *

227

My mother's preoccupation with that wedding was an absolute godsend. Knowing of my dislike for such occasions, and having despaired of my going with her, she attended it by herself and left me to get ready for my secret celebration.

It was noon when I arrived at the house. He opened the door for me in what might best be described as a 'seaish' mood, in that he seemed as mysterious and unpredictable as the high seas.

He kissed me without saying a thing.

I sat gazing at him on the sofa opposite his. I said, 'You have something of the sea in you.'

'Was my kiss salty?'

'No, but there was something deceptively calm about it.'

He made no reply.

Silence made us more eloquent. The vibrations that passed through us in the stillness placed us on a faultline where an earthquake might strike at any moment. And since passion is a state of silent anticipation, we both loved and feared the silences that would suddenly come over us.

The call to the noon prayer rang out from a distant minaret. He seemed to be listening to it intently, so I didn't dare speak to him.

When it was over I got up. He was busy smoking a cigarette. As I headed towards the kitchen, I said, 'May I bring some water? I'm thirsty.'

He didn't answer.

After reaching out to stop me, he pulled me towards him. Then suddenly he asked me, 'Do you still like Zorba?'

His question surprised me. It made me feel as though I was being accused of loving another man.

'Maybe,' I said.

'But you do. You still have a fascination with everything dazzling and deadly. You love the type of painful losses that turn logic on its head.'

'That's right,' I said.

'Come, then. I've got the kind of enjoyment that will suit your mood.'

His tone revealed a trace of derisive melancholy that I didn't understand. I was going to ask him what he meant, but before I could speak, he had taken me by the hand and drawn me onward towards other questions.

In an adjoining room furnished with a huge bed, one corner of whose modest carpet was covered with an assortment of newspapers and books scattered here and there, he left me standing for a few moments. He went over to a tape recorder next to the bed and spent a few minutes looking for a certain cassette tape. He placed a tape by Demis Roussos in the machine, then came back.

Flustered at finding myself in his bedroom, I said, 'It seems you like music.'

As he carefully drew the curtain over the room's sole window, he said, 'Music makes us miserable in a better way. Have you heard that saying?'

'No,' I said.

'It's a saying of Roland Barthes's. Are you familiar with this tape?'

'I'm familiar with most of Demis Roussos's work, and I like everything he sings, but I don't know this tape in particular.'

'I don't either,' he said. 'I found it here among a number of other tapes, and it includes a song you're sure to like.'

I didn't ask him which song he meant, but I had a sudden feeling that we were appealing to music in an attempt to rescue ourselves from the destruction that was bound to follow an experience of pleasure which, for more than one reason, would cause us sorrow.

However, a frightening unspoken desire, and senses in a state of high alert, left us devoid of emotional resistance in the face of that throaty, sorrowful Greek voice singing about its romantic disillusionments.

We were on the verge of a kiss when the music came on. Taking us by surprise, it advanced upon us slowly, even lazily at first, before picking up speed in keeping with the mood of our wildly contradictory desires. It communicated its passionate rhythm like the steps of a dancer twirling in the pouring rain, his feet clad in nothing but the buoyancy of our ardent craving.

In the presence of Zorba, the sea took off its dark glasses and black shirt and sat gazing at me.

A man who was half ink, half sea denuded me of my questions between high and low tide, and drew me towards my destiny.

A man who was half timidity, half seduction inundated me with a feverish torrent of kisses.

Holding me with one arm, he cancelled out my hands and began writing me, pondering me in the midst of my perplexity. He said, 'This is the first time I've looked off the page at your body. Let me see you at last.'

I tried to seek refuge behind a blanket of words. He said reassuringly, 'Don't hide behind anything. I'm looking at you in the darkness of the sea and nothing but the lamp of craving is lighting your body now. So far our love has lived its entire life in the darkness of the senses.'

I wanted to ask him, 'Why are you so sad?'

But a storm at sea swept my questions away, scattering me like foam.

The sea advanced, inundating everything in its path and staking the banners of its manliness on every spot it passed.

With every region that he declared occupied territory, and which I declared liberated, I discovered the greatness of the losses I had suffered before him.

Like someone fidgeting restlessly inside the body's cage, he got to his feet. He wanted to take leave of himself and be united with me.

I asked him, 'What are you doing to me?'

'Trees have no choice but to make love standing up. Come stand with me. In you I want to escort my friend to his final resting place.'

'What are you saying?' I asked, taken aback.

Trying to hold on to me, he said, 'I have a poem for you.'

Suddenly his words, like his fingertips, turned into matchsticks that set fire to everything they touched. I didn't know what he meant, nor why he wanted us to be consumed in such a huge, frightful conflagration.

Overwhelmed by his manhood, I floundered in his arms like a fish out of water before entering little by little into a state of surrender.

'Do you love me?' he asked me all of a sudden.

His single arm was infecting me with his passionate ferocity.

'Of course I do,' I said, terrified. 'This is the first time love has led me to sin.'

In a cynical show of distress, he began to recite,

> How long will I go on being your first sin?
> You have room for more than one beginning.

231

All endings are short,
and I now come to an end in you.
But those who give life an entire lifetime
deserve more than one beginning.

His voice had the belated taste of tears.

I nearly asked him, 'Can the sea cry?' But he had disappeared.

When the storm subsided, the sea left me a corpse on the shore of bewilderment, and cast me a fleeting glance.

One kiss, two kisses, one wave, two waves, and the sea had withdrawn furtively in anticipation of an approaching tear.

After rolling in with a swift, tumultuous fury, it had departed on tiptoe. So is it possible that the sea makes love out of pain?

The sea had receded, leaving my body between two poems and two tears, and nothing but salt remained.

As for me, I stayed where I was, a sea sponge.

At that moment, with the awareness of one who has been prematurely betrayed, Zorba danced barefoot on the shore of grief, spreading his arms wide like a crucified prophet. He pranced about next to me to the rhythm of successive thrusts, with the ferocity of the masochist working himself into a state of pained ecstasy. So I danced with him, trembling like a fish that's just been released from the sea's power.

When the storm had come to an end, he lit a cigarette and sat smoking, leaning against a cushion of questions. But by the time he found the answers, he had turned back into a man.

After lovemaking there are certain eternal questions that always come back, questions men always pose as a way of reassuring themselves of their ongoing virility.

'I've always worried about how you would handle a situation like this,' he said. 'On the bed of reality, romantic feelings lose some of their beauty.'

'What happened between us was beautiful,' I reassured him. 'I don't want to know whether it was beautiful in fact, or whether love just made it seem that way.'

I tried to avoid looking at his arm as I spoke, but I continued to be uncomfortably aware of it. The problem novelists face is that they can't help but observe everything and everyone, including the people with whom they share a bed.

Adjusting his sitting position, he asked, 'What is it that you want to see?'

His sarcastic tone took me by surprise. Like someone trying to justify a crime, I replied, 'I want to read the secret history of your body so that I can know whether you really are Khaled Ben Tubal. You act like him in every way. It's amazing how much you resemble him! So tell me please, who are you?'

'All your men are alike,' he rejoined with a touch of sarcasm.

After a pause he added, 'But I'm not him.'

He uttered these last words calmly as though they were nothing out of the ordinary, as though he hadn't said something that would change the entire course of our story.

I said, 'So why did you hide the truth from me all that time?'

'There isn't just one single truth,' he said. 'The truth isn't a stationary point. It changes in us, it changes with us. So I couldn't tell you or show you anything that would be the perfect truth.'

Then he added, 'You used to say you loved my body, and I would tell you that one body might conceal another, but you didn't believe me. You used to say you liked forty-year-old men, and I would correct you by telling you that I wasn't the man

233

you thought I was, but you wouldn't believe me. As if that weren't enough, you fell in love with my hands, and you would ask me all sorts of questions about them. You told me you loved my hands and you asked me how old they were. In reply, I told you that you had always loved my complexes, but you didn't understand. And now this body is all I have to answer your questions with.'

'But there was no need to be so evasive about it,' I said. 'I like your body the way it is.'

He smiled and said, 'You're mistaken. The fact of the matter is that you were ready to fall in love. I might have come to you disguised as anyone, in any form. I might have said what you were expecting me to say, or I might have said nothing at all, but you still would have loved me.'

Then he added, 'That's because love adapts itself to all sorts of situations. It has the ability to see beauty in even the most ordinary people. So when you discover who I really am, you'll see amazing new details in our story, and you'll find that you love me, not who you expected me to be.'

'But you showed me a newspaper article you had written under the name of Khaled Ben Tubal.'

'That's another reality. And it really is my name. Or, if you will, it's the name you chose because it fits me. When I started getting death threats, I had to choose a new name to sign my articles with. I don't feel as though I stole it from anyone, since I'm sure that every word I've ever written in a newspaper is something that the man in your book would have said if he'd been able to speak.'

I was astounded by what he was saying. It was as though, because we lived our lives as storytellers, everything that grew out of our lives became a narrative.

'Other than that, who are you?' I asked him.

He replied with a laugh, 'I'm a good reader.'

'I don't understand.'

'Let's just say that I've read you well. I've always read you. In fact, I'm your alternate memory. I know things about you that you've forgotten.'

'But what do you do in life?'

'I work as a journalist. You probably wouldn't believe me if I told you that three years ago I was obsessed with the idea of meeting you on the pretext of interviewing you for the newspaper.'

After a pause he added, 'As a matter of fact, I wanted to ask you questions that concerned no one but me. The publication of your book happened to coincide with the accident that paralysed my arm. So I spent my convalescence reading your works. My friend Abdelhaq gave me your book when I was in the hospital, and as he handed it to me, he said, "I've brought you a book I think you'll like." Imagine: I was afraid of it before I read it. Then I was afraid of it because I read it so much! I was amazed to have found a character in a book that was so much like me. We had a city in common, interests and disappointments in common, and we even shared a physical impairment and similar tastes. You're the only thing that we didn't share, since you were his sweetheart, and his alone.'

He continued, 'The day I met you, I was sure that in one way or another, my life would parallel your story with that character in your book. I was even afraid of you, and I would often feel that I didn't want to call you. If you only knew how I've loved you, and how angry I've been with you on account of a book!'

'So?'

'I think that when you write, you go to the heart of things, for example, when you choose a main character who's missing an arm. But life is still stranger than fiction. What a big trap it is! Imagine: all I wanted from you was answers, but life was preparing me for a counter role of sorts. I came to you at a time of questioning. Now the book has run its course, and I'm answering your questions rather than you answering mine. I have to admit, it's a nicer role than I had expected. But it isn't one that I sought out. Rather, I would have been content simply to go along with my fate, and with the various coincidences that went to make it up.'

'In the meantime, you were leading me into a text whose emotional labyrinths I could easily get lost in, and into encounters whose outcomes no one could have predicted.'

'Rather, I was leading you into love, and no love is more wonderful than the kind we find when we're looking for something else. I know you were looking for a man who had come out of something you'd written, someone you had created yourself and who was tailor-made for you. But isn't it nicer for me to be a man who enters into your writing rather than one who comes out of it?'

'Is that why you wanted me to come today? So that you could claim later that you had shattered my pleasant illusion, and that you now had a woman of whom the only part you could hold on to is books, and questions that have no answers?'

'Of course not. You know very well that that isn't true. There are things I could say to convince you of anything I like. But I've taken care not to break anything in you or in the bond between us. I've always believed that desire alone is a state of possession, whereas enjoyment is the beginning of loss.'

'So what brought us to this bed, then?'

'Death.'

'Don't you think you're insulting love by saying that?'

'On the contrary, I think I'm restoring it to the position it deserves. Don't think that it's easy to approach pleasure through pain, or to have sex because one of your comrades has died. We need a lot of love to take revenge on death.'

'So whose death is it that's making you so sad?'

'The person who died was Sa'id Muqbil. Didn't you hear about his dying yesterday?'

Apologetically I replied, 'I haven't watched television or read a newspaper for days. Was he a close friend of yours?'

'No,' he said. 'I've never met him in person. He became my friend just yesterday. With a couple of bullets, his murderers raised him to the status of "friend".

'Imagine – I have twenty-nine friends most of whom I've never met anywhere but on the obituary pages of the newspaper. However, he was a close friend of Abdelhaq's. The two of them worked together at the same newspaper before Abdelhaq left it to go to Constantine. I contacted him some time ago to offer him a job writing for the newspaper, and we were supposed to meet up sometime soon.'

'How did they kill him?'

'He was having lunch with a colleague at a small restaurant near the newspaper when someone came up to him. He thought at first that this person just wanted to talk to him. But then he pulled out a pistol, shot him, and calmly walked away. Imagine: the name of the restaurant was al-Rahmah – Mercy!'

'But why hadn't he taken precautions?'

'He was being careful, of course, since an assassination attempt had been made on him two months earlier. He'd begun sleeping in different places and coming to work at different times of day. He'd also started varying the routes he took home from the office, and the places he frequented. Yet none of this had done anything to alter his fate. Two weeks before his death, he'd written a moving piece describing the terror journalists in Algeria have to live through every day, and the newspapers reran it today on their front pages as part of his obituary. Haven't you seen it? It was carried by most news agencies.'

'No,' I said softly.

He left the room and came back with a newspaper. He handed it to me, saying, 'You can read it here, and weep over a lost friend.'

I'd hardly reached the title of the piece – 'The Thief Who . . .' – when he took the newspaper from me and began reading aloud:

> 'The thief who steals home by night along the
> walls . . .
> The father who instructs his children not to speak of
> his profession in public . . .
> The "bad" citizen who paces courtrooms, waiting for
> his turn to appear before the judge . . .
> The individual who is led away during a neighbour-
> hood raid, then thrust by a rifle butt on to a truck
> bed . . .
> The one who leaves home every morning uncertain
> whether he will reach his place of work . . .
> The one who leaves work in the evening not knowing
> whether he will reach home . . .
> The homeless person who no longer knows under
> whose roof he will spend the night . . .
> The one who comes under threat in clandestine
> detention facilities . . .

The witness who is obliged to swallow everything he
knows . . .
The unarmed citizen whose wish is simply not to die
of a slit throat . . .
The corpse on to which they sew a severed
head . . .
The one who doesn't know what to do with his hands
but to go on with his petty writings . . .
The one who clings to hope against hope that roses
will spring up on the refuse heaps . . .
The one of whom I speak is a journalist.'

He flung the newspaper on the table and said, 'It's a bitch to
have to mourn a fifty-seven-year-old man who faced death with
such stubborn defiance, and who published one outspoken newspaper article after another at a time when no one was willing any
more to risk even putting his signature on a single one. He called
his column "The Gadfly", to make it clear that he intended to
make himself obnoxious to everyone without exception, since he
poked fun equally at the government and the terrorists.'

He took a drag on his cigarette and, his tone frustrated,
continued, 'I don't understand how a country can assassinate
one of its own citizens, especially one as brave as he was. Most
governments at least show a kind of motherliness towards their
subjects so that, although they might be opposed to one of them,
they don't declare outright enmity against him. Around here,
though, the government might assassinate somebody without
even having been opposed to him. Abdelhaq once commented
that we do everything in our daily lives as though we were doing
it for the last time, since nobody knows when, or on what charge,
the government's wrath might descend on him.'

Suddenly he asked me, 'Do you know why I asked you to come today?'

Before I had a chance to reply, he said, 'Because I was afraid I might die before I experienced this moment.'

'What are you saying?' I interrupted reproachfully. 'We aren't here to talk about death.'

'Of course we aren't,' he retorted. 'We're here to play with it, to outsmart it. But it's there on our subconscious agenda. Pleasure also, which we experienced a little while ago with such ferocity that we nearly consumed each other, is nothing but a state of normalized relations with death in a time of unexpected endings, premature demises, and nameless, ugly, petty wars in which you might die without being a party to them. Sex is the only way we have to forget ourselves.'

'And what about writing?'

'Writing? It's our big illusion that others won't forget us!'

'Are you saying that to get me to stop doing it?'

'Rather, I'm saying it to make you stop indulging in such big illusions. My friend who died, who's being buried and surrendered to the maggots at this very moment, also believed that writing was a worthwhile undertaking. He believed that his daily newspaper column was necessary to change society, and that his readers couldn't start their day without his wisecracks and caustic jokes. But now he can't amuse or challenge anybody any more. Now it's death that's challenged him and amused itself at his expense. He had mistakenly imagined that he was changing the world every day with a few lines in a newspaper. But life is going on without him, and so is the newspaper. The people he died for will forget all about the place he occupied for a few years on that page of the newspaper. There's plenty of ingratitude in the world of journalism.'

What he had said plunged me into a state of sudden frustration. It robbed me of my desire to argue, or even to love.

I felt cheated: Had I taken all these risks, suffered all this trepidation, and made up a million artful excuses just so that I could be alone with a man who wanted to talk to me about death?

'It would have been better if you'd stayed a creature of ink, a fictitious character. They don't get assassinated, at least. They don't die at all, in fact, and we never have to worry about anything bad happening to them. So why did you come if you were going to insist on being a real man?'

Drawing me towards him, he said, 'I came to share desire with you. I came to give you pleasure, and to give myself pleasure through you. Storybook characters can't do that, can they?'

Then he began kissing me all over again with the same ardent desire as before. It was as though we had just met, or as though he had just noticed my presence with him despite the corpse that lay between us.

I enjoyed observing his romantic mood shifts.

I tried to understand what had suddenly aroused him all over again, causing him to storm me with such insatiable appetite.

I gazed at him as he busied himself with me. It wasn't his body that I loved as much as it was his generous masculinity, his body's noble ethic.

His body had a bountiful presence about it that gave and gave, the way love does. It was as though he was compensating for what he lacked by giving, although he also received with the same eagerness. He was possessed of the kind of masculinity that knows how to be humble in the presence of the woman, as though it sees itself as indebted to her for everything it has.

Suddenly he put his arm around me and said, 'I'm going to confess something to you. But don't laugh!'

Before I could answer, he continued, 'I've felt jealous of Ziyad. Imagine – I've never once felt jealous of your husband, but here I am jealous of a creature of ink who was a character with me in that book of yours. I still feel as though he really exists in your life, and that he enjoyed your body before I did.'

'Silly!' I said. 'That man has never existed in real life. I brought him into being because I like love triangles. I find love duos too simple and naïve for a novel, so I needed a man who would live alongside the story before becoming part of it. After all, that's the logic of love in life – we're always off by one digit.'

'But I still envy him. I wanted a destiny like his, so much so that I've memorized his poems. I keep dreaming of some big love, some big cause, some heroic death.'

'But the days of heroic deaths are over. Nobody can die in a big battle any more, not even in a novel. All our causes have gone bankrupt. That's why I wanted Ziyad to die in the Israeli invasion of Beirut. Imagine – he had been dreaming of going back to Gaza. If he had lived, though, he would have gone straight to prison. Either that, or he would have ended up a policeman who imprisons and tortures other Palestinians on charges of threatening Israel's security. Think of all the illusions that died with him. There's no such thing as Palestine any more. So I'm happy for those who will come after us, since we've spared them having to spend their lives in illusion the way we have.'

He adjusted his sitting position, leaving my head on his shoulder. He lit a cigarette and began smoking it unhurriedly.

'Let's not talk about Palestine. Tell me now: Are you happy with me?'

His question took me by surprise, and I didn't know how to reply.

'When we're miserable, we know it. But when we're happy, we only realize it later. Happiness seems to be a belated discovery.'

'So,' he asked, 'will I have to wait until your next book comes out to know whether you were happy with me or not?'

'Of course not!' I laughed. 'I can answer you right now. But I think I've learned to be afraid of happiness, since whenever I find it, I lose it.'

'That's why you have to experience it as a moment under threat. You need to realize that, like joy and love, pleasure is a form of robbery. Pleasant experiences, whatever they happen to be, have to be stolen from life, or from others. The only way a person can experience pleasure is by stealing it in anticipation of death, which will strip him of all his booty.'

'You remind me of *Dead Poets Society*. Do you remember the first scene, where the students gather around the teacher to look at pictures of students who had graduated from the Academy in earlier generations? The teacher tells them to seize the day, to make their lives extraordinary, since one of these days they'll stop being anything. They'll be gone as though they'd never come.'

'I haven't seen the film,' he said somewhat indifferently, 'but it sounds as though it was a nice scene.'

'You really haven't seen it?' I asked in amazement.

Taken aback by my tone of voice, he said, 'Should I have?'

Realizing that I had no good reason to be amazed at this discovery, I said feebly, 'I just thought you might have seen it. It's won several awards.'

I retreated into my silence, reviewing our story from the beginning. I thought, if we didn't meet at the cinema, then who was the man who, wearing the same perfume and exhibiting the same taciturn manner, sat beside me that day?

Questions were taking me in all directions when he interrupted my train of thought, saying apologetically, 'Abdelhaq told me about that film. During my last visit to Constantine, he suggested that I go to see it with him. He wanted to write an article about it for the newspaper. But I was busy that day, so he went by himself. It must still be showing in the capital, so I'll try to go see it. Then I can discuss it with the two of you instead of listening to one or the other of you tell me about this or that scene.'

Caressing my hair, he went on, 'Would it make you happy for me to see it?'

'Of course it would,' I said, planting a kiss on his cheek.

It seemed to me as though I were using Abdelhaq's style with him, since I said nothing else.

As I left soon thereafter, he was retreating into his state of mourning, and I was retreating – of course – into my questions.

*　*　*

When I was alone that evening, I opened the black notebook and began leafing through my story with this man, which I'd written in a series of daily entries.

244

I recalled its beginnings, pausing at its various twists and turns in an attempt to understand how the story had come into being, and where this man had come from.

How, over the course of the past eight months, had he managed to evade all my questions and wriggle out of all the traps I'd set for him? How had he managed to live inside my notebook disguised as another man, only to spring the truth on me when he himself was good and ready?

But what truth? The truth that he'd divulged to me? Or the other truth that even he didn't know, but had led me to without realizing it? As he himself had once said to me, 'There isn't just one single truth. The truth isn't a stationary point. It changes in us, it changes with us. So I couldn't tell you or show you anything that would be the perfect truth.'

His love also had become subject to question, like a moving target that kept eluding me. Yet the fact remained that there was a secret time that had been ours alone, a shared memory of something in the order of love that we'd experienced together even before we met.

He had said, 'No love is more wonderful than the kind we find when we're looking for something else,' and I had believed him. I had been so infatuated with him that I'd forgotten exactly what it was I'd been looking for on the day I first met him.

And now, in his most recent incarnation, he'd become my reader. But how could a reader do all this to an author?

It boggles my mind to think of the way the irrational dimension enters into people's behaviours and decisions. The secret life of emotions is a strange thing indeed. I once read a psychological study which said that when we fall in love, it has nothing to do with the person we fall in love with. Rather, he or she happens to come into our life at a time when our emotional resistance is low because, for example, we're on the rebound from a failed romance, so we 'catch' love the way we catch a cold when the seasons are changing. So I concluded that being in love is a pathological condition.

After that I read an article entitled 'The Chemistry of Love' which argued that we make our stupidest mistakes in the summer because of the sun's effects on our mood and behaviour. Its rays penetrate our skin and our blood cells, which causes an imbalance in the nervous system and turns us into weird creatures that are liable to do anything.

So, I said, falling in love must be a seasonal phenomenon.

Something else I read was that writing changes our relationships with things. It causes us to commit sins without feeling guilty, because the overlap between life and literature gives you the illusion that you're continuing in real life a text that you began writing in a book. Not only that, but the urge to write tempts you to experience things not for themselves, but for the pleasure of writing about them. So the writer's problem is that sometimes he can't resist the temptation to leave the text and let literature get mixed up with life, even in a bed.

After giving it some thought, I saw that what had happened to me had nothing to do with logic but was, rather, due to the confluence of a number of random conditions. This man had come into my life one summer at a time when I had no emotional resistance and was busying myself writing a love story. So falling in love with him had been the coincidental outcome of several exceptional circumstances.

I also discovered that my problem lies in the fact that I'm not illiterate. Just think about all the things that might happen to us on account of what we read! In fact, some of the things we read have the same effect on us as writing, taking us to places we would never have expected to go.

Argentinean writer Luis Borges was once asked in an interview, 'Once, when asked about your life, you said that few things had happened to you, but that you had read a great deal. What did you mean by that?' He replied, 'What I meant was that because I read a lot, many things have happened to me.'

As for me, I'd been dreaming of writing a single book, after which I could die 'an author'. The book I'd dreamed of writing would have such an impact on readers that they wouldn't be able to sleep at night, and it would make them rethink their entire lives. With one reader, at least, I'd managed to have such an impact, the resemblance between him and my main character being so extraordinary that the book had turned both his life and mine upside down.

What I'd concluded in the end was that an author had better think a hundred times before writing a story. At any moment life might decide to take her story seriously and punish her with it. Or it might punish some unsuspecting reader who falls so completely under its spell that he loses the ability to distinguish between fact and fiction.

When Goethe wrote his tragic love story, *The Sorrows of Young Werther*, thousands of European youths began dressing and behaving like its main character in public places. They would carry copies of Homer's poetry under their arms, and several of them committed suicide just as Werther had. Consequently, Goethe was accused by critics of having fomented these young people's self-destruction by painting an idealized picture of death for them. In reality, however, Goethe hadn't idealized death for these youths; rather, he had idealized life as depicted on the pages of a book: in that space reserved for dreams of distinction most commonly referred to as 'literature'.

And if it's conceivable that you might love an author so much that you imagine yourself to be a character in one of her books, then what's so strange about the idea of an author loving one of her characters so much that she imagines him really to exist, and that some day they'll meet in a coffee shop and start reminiscing together?

My mother's return restored a semblance of normality to my life, and brought me for a while out of my constant questioning. She came bearing news of another wedding, and I expected her to bend my ear about it in the days that followed, since she was sure there was a confrontation brewing between the first and second wives.

I amused myself by listening to her, knowing ahead of time where the conversation would lead, since she was convinced that my co-wife was the cause of my infertility as well as some other things that had happened to me, though I myself didn't believe it.

It hadn't been easy, of course, to accept the idea of sharing a man with another woman. I could have stipulated that he divorce her before marrying me, since he had wanted me so much at the time that he would have been willing to do anything I asked. But I felt sorry for this woman who was fifteen years my senior, and who had shared twenty years of my husband's life with him. Not only this, but she had borne him three children before he became a high-ranking officer and inevitably, like other high-ranking officials around him, began rethinking his marital situation.

She resigned herself to the new arrangement from the very beginning, which I think disarmed me. I don't think she was so kindhearted as to be excited about the new marriage, but she wasn't wicked either, and she never plotted against me. As time went on, a kind of unspoken womanly collusion grew up between us; each of us realized that she could neither cancel the other one out, nor have this man all to herself.

I'd often wondered if I was jealous of this woman. My husband was most likely at her house now, sharing with her a bed that he rarely occupied unless I was away. Amazingly, the answer to this question was always no. Even so, my body had never completely accepted the idea of her existence. She was on my mind my entire wedding night, and I couldn't stop thinking back to her silent presence at the wedding party out of consideration for my husband, who had wanted to prove to everyone that he was marrying me with her blessing. And maybe this is why my body created a barrier that my husband couldn't penetrate despite his virility.

Despite my desire for him, something in me beyond my control refused to surrender to him, while Nasser's decision to boycott all wedding celebrations had put me in a negative frame of mind.

All these thoughts were going through my mind as my mother gave me a blow-by-blow account of the aforementioned nuptials. It appeared that the couple's wedding night hadn't been to the macho groom's satisfaction, which set the women to speculating about what might have gone wrong.

The development of greatest relevance to me personally was the fact that my mother suddenly felt bored and wanted to go back to Constantine as soon as possible. When I heard her say this, I got a taste in my mouth that seemed like a foreboding of sadness, a sadness I made a point of concealing from her. I've learned over the years to hide both my sadness and my happiness from my mother, lest I find myself obliged to explain the

249

former or justify the latter, since she and I have never shared the same criteria for what constitutes a happy or sad event.

Happiness is like a sparrow perched eternally on either the tree of anticipation or the tree of memories, and now it was about to escape from me again. Because I realized this, I began living my love for Khaled with the ferocious intensity of someone who knows the object of her passion will soon be gone.

Like those who live their lives under threat, the death all around me had taught me to live in the shadow of evanescence. It had taught me to love this man as though I'd lose him the very next moment, to desire him as though he belonged to someone else, to wait for him without believing he would come, and when he came, to receive him as though he'd never come again. It taught me to search for a joy too vast to be contained by a lovers' tryst, and for a parting too poignant to be a mere farewell.

Yet suddenly he seemed indifferent to the fact that life was about to run out on us. In fact, he placed so little value on the time we had left that he insisted our last meeting be not in his house, but at a seaside café half an hour's walk from there.

In vain I tried to convince him that we might not see each other again for a long time, and that this kind of place wasn't suited for a farewell meeting. But he said, 'On the contrary, our time will be even nicer in a place like this.'

So we met, at a café where love had arranged, impromptu, a place just for us. There he was, he and the sea, at a table drenched in summer evening light.

There we were, he and I, between us the sighs of the waves.

'We could have met at your place,' I said reproachfully. 'Why do you insist on squandering our dream this way?'

Still smoking, he replied, 'Squandering life is also a part of life.'

'But I want you, and we might not see each other again for a long time.'

As usual, he placed between us the ashtray of silence, filled with the butts of unfinished sentences. Then he said, 'I've wanted you so much myself, I understand what it means for you to want me. But we have to get used to deprivation, even when we're together.'

'Why?'

'Because we're destined not always to be together.'

'So why did you give me all that pleasure if you were just preparing me for pain?'

'Actually, I'm preparing you for an even better pleasure. Before I knew you, I didn't see deprivation as beautiful. But in order for it to be that way, we have to want it. It has to be a kind of secret collusion between two people, and when that happens, it takes on a new name.'

After a pause, he asked me, 'Do you know what its new name is?'

'No.'

'Fidelity!'

The words were followed by a trail of smoke as he exhaled indolently in my direction.

'I understand what you're saying, but don't you think you're trying to get ahead of destiny, and punishing us even more than life has already?'

'What I think is that you've always been love's pampered child. I imagine it's always given you what you wanted without your having to exert any effort to speak of. There are people who have an extraordinary ability to trample on other people's hearts without feeling guilty.'

251

I murmured, 'So is that why . . . ?'

'No,' he interrupted me. 'That isn't why I'm punishing you with deprivation. In that case I'd be punishing myself as well. But it's a good thing for you to be broken in by a man who's never known anything about horses.'

Before I could reply, he said, 'You know, the hardest part of breaking in a wild horse is approaching it for the first time. Once you've done that, taming it is just a matter of time. That's why cowboys invented the rodeo, where they compete to see how many minutes a rider can stay on a horse's back before it throws him. Within those few minutes, a rider might win a horse over, or he might get all his bones broken or even lose his life!'

Flicking his ashes leisurely into the ashtray without taking his eyes off me, he said, 'So, contrary to what you may believe, I didn't win you over the last time we were together. Rather, I won you over the first time we saw each other. It happened in the café when I asked you whether I could sit down at your table with you. You were about to say no, but instead you said, "Of course." After that, all I had to rope you in with was a string of words. That was the first time I experienced the terror of approaching a wild mare.'

'What else?'

'Well, here we are together facing our most difficult test so far. We aren't the ones testing each other today. We aren't the ones measuring our willingness to persevere in the face of love or our ability to bring others down. Rather, it's life that's testing us, and testing love through us. In order to pass tests like this, sometimes we have to put ourselves on the level of bankrupt lovers and dispense with the luxury of owning keys to a flat. By doing that we restore to love its pristine beauty and impossibility.'

'What you're saying sounds nice enough, but all you're doing is spouting theories of love that don't apply to our situation. Don't forget that I'm married. Don't forget that I'm here with you by stealth, and at great risk to myself.'

'I haven't forgotten. But you yourself have said that you aren't ashamed of our love, and that you hate clandestine relationships that live their lives lurking on back streets. So give our love the legitimacy of living in the light. Give it a bit of dignity so that we don't have to be classified as thieves.'

'What if someone saw us together? How would I defend myself against their accusations? How would I justify my being with you here?'

'Defend yourself against their accusations? What accusations? And before whom? Before your husband? He's one of the prime suspects in this country! How amazing, that of all the actions people commit, loving is the one they're most anxious to hide, as though it were an accusation they have to clear themselves of. You can be a criminal: a thief, a liar, a traitor, someone who fleeces the entire country. Then you can flaunt all your booty without the slightest compunction and carry on with your life as a respected member of society. Now, isn't that outrageous?'

Continuing his tirade, he said, 'Compared to the people who've destroyed our past and insist on destroying our futures, who've emptied out our bank accounts and hijacked our dreams, those of us who've got rich on love are downright honourable.'

Flicking the ashes irritably off his cigarette, he went on, 'Since my arm was paralysed, I've learned something – that it's better to define a person by what he's lost than by what he still has. We're always the product of what we've lost. But nobody ever asks you about that. They only ask you about what you have.

You yourself have never asked me how or when I lost the use of my arm. Wouldn't you like to know?'

Taken by surprise at a question I hadn't dared ask myself, I said apologetically, 'I thought it might bother you to be asked.'

'And why should I be ashamed of something I didn't do?' he rejoined bitterly. 'After Picasso had finished his famous painting, *Guernica* – in which he depicts the ruin the city became at the hands of the Fascists – someone asked him, "Are you the one who did this?" To which he replied, "No, you are." If you asked me a similar question, I would answer, "I didn't do it. They did."'

Not knowing who he was referring to exactly, I asked, 'When did it happen?'

He slowly pulled out a new cigarette like someone defusing a memory. Then he said, 'It happened in 1988. I was a photo-journalist at the time, and I'd gone to photograph the demonstrations that had flooded the streets without warning. I could hardly believe what I saw: cars whizzing by, faces every-where – some terrifying, and others terror-stricken – stray bullets, and people being shot point blank. It was a city ruled by tanks, where everything standing, even telephone poles, had been levelled to the ground.

'Military personnel had lined up in a kind of human barrier in front of the thousands of young demonstrators, who had begun shattering everything in their path that symbolized the state. Sometimes the soldiers would fire into the air, and sometimes into the crowds in a vain attempt to frighten them. Meanwhile, soldiers had occupied the roofs of government buildings. I remember trying to take a picture of a soldier standing on top of the party headquarters building with an Algerian flag behind him. He was firing a machine gun into the street. Suddenly a shot was fired from the building, and it penetrated my left arm. I didn't know whether the soldier had become suspicious of me when I raised my camera to shoot the picture, thinking that my camera was a weapon, or whether I was hit by a stray bullet that was meant for somebody else.'

As if he were talking to himself, he continued, 'Imagine: the moment I took that picture, it was stored not only by my camera, but by my body as well. It's become an indelible memory in the flesh, a memory I share with the hundreds of wounded and dead who fell during those events.'

Once again this man had surprised me with a story he hadn't been intending to tell on this particular day, in this particular place, or in this particular circumstance. And as usual, he'd answered a question that I'd refrained from asking, so beleaguered had I been by all my question marks.

I sat pondering him as he undid the last button on that many-buttoned overcoat, and as he solved the last of the riddles that had so preoccupied me over the previous months. It was as though he'd grown weary of evasion and had decided at last to give me . . . the truth.

In his glowing youth he was even more beautiful than the illusion I had formed of him.

I said, 'You know, the truth makes you even more alluring!'

'I would have liked for it to make me more respectable. I don't think we can love or desire someone who's lost our respect, so it means a lot for me not to have grown smaller in your eyes because of my disability, but more worthy on account of it.'

I said, 'I've never met a man so drunk on pride!'

'Shall I take that to mean that you love me?'

'Absolutely.'

He continued, 'Would you mind me asking you if you love your husband?'

'I did once,' I replied.

'And are you happy with him?'

'I don't know. Sometimes I discover how miserable I am, and then I forget again.'

'So why have you stayed with him?'

'Because he's my husband, because I'm alone, and because I don't know how to make any decisions.'

'But you're free to change the course of your life and separate from him if you want to.'

'I think it was André Gide who once said, "It's easy to know how to be free, but it's difficult to be free." I might succeed in freeing myself from this man, though I wouldn't expect it to be easy. But the hardest part would be handling my freedom after that. The life of a divorced woman in a country like this is a slavery worse than marriage, since everybody else makes themselves your guardians.'

Suddenly I fell silent. Then I asked him, 'If I separated from him, would you marry me?'

'Marry you?' he asked, surprised. 'Are you kidding?'

'Wouldn't it make you happy for me to be your wife?'

'Of course it would, but . . .'

'But what?'

'Madame, I own nothing of the things that you've grown accustomed to. My whole fortune might be summed up in the words of Imam al-Shafi'i, who wrote, "Rich without money, in need of no one, the wealthy are wealthy not by virtue of what they own, but what they can do without."'

'None of that matters to me. I love the flat you live in, and it would be enough for us. We could be happy there.'

'But even that flat isn't mine. I'm only living there temporarily.'

'Whose is it, then?'

'It belongs to Abdelhaq, the friend I've told you about. He left it after receiving death threats and went to live for a while with his family in Constantine. He might move back when conditions improve.'

'Does everything in the house belong to him?'

'Of course.'

'Including the library?'

'That too.'

'And the book by Henri Michaux that I borrowed from you – is that his too?'

He was surprised by my questions. As for me, I was flummoxed, and I fell into a silence for which he could find no explanation.

He asked me jokingly, 'So which bothers you more – for the house to be his, or the book by Henri Michaux?'

Smiling at him wanly, I replied, 'Neither. You just surprised me, that's all.'

'You surprised me too. This is the first time a woman has ever asked for my hand. Of course, the military took my left hand, along with my camera, during the events of 1988. And as soon as I switched to written journalism, the Islamists demanded the right one! Imagine: I'm so obnoxious that both sides have agreed to cut my hands off. So you'll have to decide quickly whether you really want me or not, since the time may come when nobody in this country can ask for a journalist's hand in marriage any more!'

I laughed at his 'joke', and at the irony with which he always kept his sorrow out of view. But he didn't laugh with me.

I asked him, 'You rarely laugh. Why is that?'

'Life has taught me to smile ten times before I laugh, and to rephrase what I want to say ten times before opening my mouth. This is why I decided to become a photographer. The photograph is an extended moment of silence. Like drawing or painting, it's an experiment in wordlessness.'

'What else has life taught you?'

'It's taught me patience. Patience is my sign of the zodiac, but it's the last thing I would want to teach you!'

He slipped his hand in his pocket and drew out a leather keychain which he set on the table. Then he continued, 'All that lies between us and pleasure is a key. But I refuse to let that key control us. That would be an insult to love. I feel just as much desire as you do right now. In fact, I need this love and the pleasure that goes with it even more than you do. But when we reach a certain level of pleasure, every pleasure that follows it only makes us that much hungrier. What we need to do now is to experience the pleasure of abstinence, to be reconciled with our bodies and learn how to live inside them when we aren't together. That way we can discover the beauty of fidelity born of deprivation.'

'I don't understand,' I broke in. 'Why did you tempt me to infidelity if you were going to demand that I be faithful to you?'

'You're misunderstanding me again. I haven't demanded anything of you. I've prepared you for faithfulness, but without demanding that you be faithful to me.'

'I was hoping you'd say something else. It would have made me happy for you to ask that of me.'

'But faithfulness can't be asked for. Asking for it is like begging, which is an insult to love. If it doesn't come spontaneously, it's no more than an attempt to avoid or suppress the temptation to infidelity. In other words, it's infidelity in another form. So, calling infidelity an adventure is a misnomer. It turns the facts on their heads. The real adventure is fidelity, since it's inevitably a lot harder.'

'Why are things always so complicated with you? All I want is simple words, like the ones lovers say to each other when they're about to be separated. Words that are short and sweet, unsettling, joyful and painful at the same time, words that go to the heart and never leave us. But you haven't said anything like that.'

'I don't want a love that feeds on words, one that will be killed by our silence when we're apart. You want words like the ones you've read in books or heard in movies. But our story is better than anything you've ever read or heard.'

He paused briefly. Then he added, 'When I read your book three years ago, I wondered how my story could start where Khaled's left off – in the same year, and with the same events. I wondered: Did I lose my arm just so that I could give life the luxury of conforming to a novel, or so that I could give literature the proud distinction of carrying on in real life? When we met, I knew the answer. Literature and life have colluded to give us a love story more beautiful than any reader or author has ever dreamed of. You yourself, novelist that you are, were outdone by our story, since it's been more bizarre than anything you could have thought up and put down in a book.'

'I've got to admit,' I replied, 'I never expected anything like this, though I've always dreamed of a reader who would take revenge on me through my writings. It's amazing the things that can happen to us on account of a book. We might be honoured, we might be thrown in jail, we might be assassinated. We might be loved, we might be hated, we might be revered, we might be exiled. We can't squeeze a verdict of not guilty out of a book, since it would amount to nothing more than the suspicion that we aren't really writers. The weird thing about our story is that life punished me by turning what I had written into reality. Maybe it happened because I'm a writer with criminal impulses, who sits down at her desk every evening and, without the slightest compunction, kills off some men whose love she doesn't have time for and others that she's loved by mistake, whereupon she proceeds to build them fancy tombs in a book, and then goes to bed.'

After a pause, I said absently, 'How was I supposed to know that in everything we write, we're writing our destiny? Life comes disguised in the simplicity of a book, and at any moment someone may discover that a page out of his writings has fallen into the clutches of reality and become his life.'

He suddenly stopped puffing on his cigarette and, in a mix of sadness and sarcasm, asked, 'Might I have the honour of knowing whether you intend to kill me off?'

'Of course you may,' I replied jokingly. 'You in particular, I'll fight to the death to keep alive!'

Then, as though to confirm what I had said, I went on, 'Besides, Khaled didn't die in that novel.'

'I know,' he interrupted. 'It was Ziyad who died. But I don't see anybody left standing around me. All my friends have been killed off, and now it's my turn, isn't it! Where do you think I am on the hit list?'

I didn't know whether he was talking to me about the writing game or about real life – that is, real death. In other words, I wondered if he was concerned about being assassinated the way all his friends had been.

260

Before I had a chance to reply, he added, 'Hayat, put off my death for a little while, but love me as if I'm going to die. I've made a frightening discovery about love: that you can't really love somebody until you know that death is going to take you by surprise and take him or her away from you. You'll forgive the people you see every day for a lot more things if you remember that they aren't always going to be around, even to do those little things that irritate you and make you angry. If, every time you see people, you think about the fact that you may never see them again, you'll appreciate them more. If everybody thought this way, they'd love each other better.'

'So,' I asked, 'is that the way you think?'

Amused at the note of alarm in my voice, he said with a chuckle, 'Since I met you, I've adopted a new philosophy of life: to strive in this world as though I'll be seeing you tomorrow, and to strive for the next world as though we're going to die together! So every day I prepare to meet you, whether here or there, with the same yearning.'

'That scares me,' I murmured. 'From the way you're talking, it sounds as though love is just a way of bypassing life, and that all we have time left for is a hug and a couple of kisses.'

'On the contrary,' he reassured me. 'We've still got plenty of time. I'll wait for you in life and in books, too. A moment of love is enough to justify a lifetime of waiting. Can you see that?'

'I'm trying. But everything is against us.'

'Like all great causes in life, love is something you have to believe in deeply, sincerely, and doggedly. Only then will the miracle happen. Take Boudiaf, for example: a seventy-eight-year-old man who spent half his life struggling against imperialism, and the other in exile. He was exiled even from the national memory, his name blotted out of our textbooks. Then, after twenty-eight years of exile, history brought him back to his country as its president. Now, isn't that amazing? Isn't it marvellous? Believe me, it's just a matter of time before . . .'

'But I'm afraid of time. Time is the enemy of lovers.'

'Rather, it's the enemy of revolutions, both the big ones and the little, fly-by-night ones. They all get knocked off by time. And sooner or later, I expect to see the death of revolutionary illusions.'

* * *

Of course, time is the enemy of lovers.

It brings us a few steps closer together, only to disappear through a man who retreats into his initial darkness clad in black.

When that happens, I go back to walking along the seashore. I walk, and the questions walk with me as though my feet were shod in question marks.

Nietzsche used to say that the greatest ideas are the ones that come to us while we're walking. So I walk. But every idea the sea brings in goes out with the next wave.

I used to believe that the novel was the art of cunning deception, the way poetry is the art of amazement. So I couldn't figure out how this man, who hadn't seemed prepared for the role of either poet or novelist, had managed so thoroughly to dupe my senses that I felt like an illiterate in the face of his manhood.

How was it that, without knowing it, he had written the story in such a way that it was tailor-made for me in a book in which we had switched roles in so many places? And how had that absent friend suddenly become the main character?

It seemed clear by now that this was the man who had sat beside me during that film and in whose presence I had been living ever since – breathing in his cologne, reading his books, listening to his music, sitting on his sofa, talking on his phone, and falling in love with his home!

Somehow I had managed, with perfect stupidity, to fall for all the false signals love had placed in my path, and lo and behold, as I imagined myself discovering one man, I'd been discovering another.

At some station or another I had missed the train to my 'first' love, and had taken one that led me to another.

Like a wandering tourist taking the metro for the first time, like an adventurer accidentally discovering a continent, I had missed my way in a moment of sentimental distraction. After discovering America, Columbus died thinking he had discovered India. And like explorers, novelists always die ignorant!

You definitely haven't arrived.

You're a traveller on a train headed towards questions, but who said you'd arrived? Who said you knew where the answers were leading you? After all, answers are blind. Only questions can see.

Time is a journey . . .

Ships laden with illusions have come into port, while others laden with dreams are on their way out.

The sea laughed when it saw me launching out on a boat of paper, hoisting words as sails in the face of logic, in the hope of discovering how all this had happened.

Time is rain . . .

A cloud wafting out of the telephone and coming to live in my suitcase. Outside autumn's window, a light drizzle knocks gently on my heart.

Time is destiny . . .

The sea rolls up its collar by night and buttons up memory all the way to the top lest the salt seep out into the words.

Then it puts on its best voice and dials a number.

'Yes?' a woman answers.

Time is pain . . .

Why do we always say 'Yes' when we answer the telephone, even when it's time to say 'No'?

Time is 'no'.

In sorrow's sumptuous entryway, learn to celebrate pain as an unexpected guest. It's only pain, so there's no need to prepare yourself for it.

Tears come belatedly over a sorrow which, like a dreaded farewell, has come too soon.

Time is a farewell . . .

Love says, 'Hello? Yes?'

And life replies, 'Hello? No,' as salt seeps across the telephone line, gradually inundating us. Meanwhile, between the tyranny of memory and the timidity of promises, things carry on their journey . . . without us.

* * *

I left Sidi Fredj at dawn, before the sea had awoken and begged me with a tear to stay.

He had the waves and I had the salt, as well as an aeroplane waiting for me.

When I had arrived at this place two weeks earlier, I'd been escorted by the lovely saying that used to precede Baudelaire whenever he went on a journey: 'I'm summoned by desire, crowned by love.'

And now I left love's throne behind. The life of legitimacy summoned me, Constantine awaited me, and the life whose rules I had broken was bringing me back to the 'house of obedience' crowned with the glitter of memories.

As I came back to Constantine, I avoided looking at it. I wished I could see it the way Borges saw Buenos Aires through his sightless eyes. I wanted to look at it without any visual memory.

Sometimes we have to lose our sight in order to recognize places we've seen so many times before that we have ceased truly to see them. Here in this city there were streets where we would have been afraid to look into other people's eyes, restaurants we wouldn't have dared frequent, houses we couldn't have entered together.

Here was a city that recognized love nowhere but in the songs of Farqani, that only left home to go to the mosque or a coffee shop, and that never opened a window to look at anything but a minaret.

I had arrived in the city lovesick, my head ringing with the words of Achilles when he beheld Athens: 'Abandon the gods for a time, Madame, and give me a bit of your magnificent misery.'

Is there anyone more miserable than a lover in Constantine?

My husband welcomed me home so kindly, it made me suspicious. Of course, maybe I was blowing up his mistakes in my mind. Maybe I was even on the lookout for them as a way of countering the guilt I felt towards him.

He seemed happy to have me home again. Or maybe he was happy for other reasons. Since Boudiaf's return, everybody had started feeling safer, and life in the city had returned to normal. Together with the feeling of normality came the pre-summer fever that sent families out in droves to Muruj `Ayn al-Bay and Djebel El Wahch.

People had begun daring at last to go on excursions here and there, trusting that the country had emerged from its long dark tunnel. This sudden tranquillity taught me to give myself over to time and place, confident that this man's words were something I could rely on.

But had he taught me optimism, or just how to bide my time? I often had to resist the temptation to make inquiries to find out who Abdelhaq was.

It unsettled me to see that even where I was, I continued living alongside him, sharing with him the same city.

Sometimes I would fantasize about bumping into him somewhere. I realized that he might not recognize me, even though he had read me and had even written me throughout this entire saga. After all, he was the one who had given that novel of mine to his friend, which had led him unwittingly to me.

The only thing that might place him in my path was the book by Henri Michaux. If only I'd brought it with me. I might find him through his silence, or through that taciturn manner that was his distinguishing mark and which, like his cologne, he had passed on to his friend.

I would ask him, 'Do you recognize me?'

And the reply would come, 'Of course,' two of the five words he had spoken on the day he sat beside me in the cinema.

Then I would confess to him, 'I miss you. Do you realize how wonderful it is to miss someone you've never met before?'

I started imagining all sorts of beginnings for us, and more than one way to find him. But then I thought better of it, since I realized that I was repeating, down to the last detail, my romantic adventure with his friend.

This time also I was dealing with a man whose name I didn't know. After all, Abdelhaq wasn't a family name, and it wouldn't be enough to lead me to a journalist when I didn't know what newspaper he worked for, which language he wrote in, or what name he used to sign his articles at a time when virtually all journalists had two names.

As a matter of fact, I was glad for this man to be 'no one' – a man without any name in particular, with no particular description, no identifying features, no credentials.

I'd learned from my previous experience that in what we don't know there is a beauty that surpasses the satisfaction we take in what we do know.

So I decided to leave my encounter with Abdelhaq to chance. I'd let life arrange things however it chose. This way I wouldn't miss out on the element of surprise or try to make the finale come before its time.

When we find the thing we've been looking for so long, it's the beginning of the end.

More importantly, I decided not to look for him because my constant preoccupation with him involved a kind of hidden betrayal of the man who had spent our last time together persuading me to be faithful to him. It was as though he could see what was coming, or as if he knew enough about me through what I had written to be wary of my capacity to be in love with two people at the same time.

Was this why he had loved me with such an erratic ferocity that he seemed to be more than one man? As he was bidding me farewell over the telephone, he made a confession that pained me: 'All I have to defend you from love's perils is love itself.' When I remembered him this way, a wave of desire for him came over me. I tried to escape from it by immersing myself in writing. But . . .

The hand has a memory of its own, a memory that haunts you with questions about what you've lost. I still couldn't understand how it was that this body of his, though it wasn't the most beautiful, had become so wildly alluring to me that it had disturbed my tranquillity and robbed me of the ability to write for days on end.

* * *

Two months went by, during which time I fed on dreams and quenched my thirst with quick sips of ink, leaving others to their banquets of tedium followed by slander-sweetened coffee.

From time immemorial, fire has puzzled over how to be united with water. I've never mastered the art of sitting around and gossiping with other women. I'm the mistress of sorrow, and they the maidens of frivolity. I've always enjoyed men's company more than women's, since when I'm with women, all I end up with is frayed nerves!

Nevertheless, I accepted an invitation from a relative of mine to attend the celebration of her daughter's passing some test or other. It was the end of June, and the women around me were chatting over coffee and sweets. Wanting to avoid their chatter, I stole periodic glances at the television, which had been left on to add to the racket.

From time to time I would listen to a speech by Boudiaf being broadcast live from the House of Culture in Anaba, but

268

I wasn't getting much of it, so I contented myself with just looking at him. Little did I know that I was witnessing this man's final appearance.

Even when he had no voice, Boudiaf would penetrate you with his eyes, which reflected a hard-to-define sadness that left you no choice but to believe what he said.

They were eyes that could see how the country had practised itself in treachery from time immemorial. They were eyes that forgave and forgot. Yet, given the suffering of exile and betrayal by those who had once been his comrades, sorrow had taken up permanent residence in them, and they'd lost their ability to laugh.

As he stood there before us for the last time, Boudiaf had his back turned to a curtain behind him – the curtain of Fate (and treachery).

He seemed so confident, so trusting, so brave, so innocent.

So how could what happened to him not have happened?

I don't know exactly what he'd been talking about at that moment, but I remember that the last word he said was 'Islam'.

Before he had finished the sentence, one of his security men emerged on to the platform from behind the curtain. When he was a step away from his target, he threw a fake bomb, and at the sound of the blast, everyone there threw themselves to the ground. He then proceeded to empty his weapon into Boudiaf's body. Just like that, right in front of all those looking on. Then he disappeared again behind the curtain.

It was 29 June, 11.27 a.m.

Algeria was looking on as its dreams were assassinated. Everyone expected an ambulance to come, but none came, at least not for a long while.

The Algerian flag over the podium now fluttered over a man lying prostrate on the ground. He had come to raise our heads, to make us proud, but we had left his dreams wallowing in a pool of blood.

Forty years earlier, in the very same month, his comrades had led him away to desert prisons. Then the country had brought him back as president for 166 days, only to reward him five months later with a spray of bullets, and a shroud.

In a mere seven days, on 5 July – Algeria's Independence Day – he had been planning to deliver a long-awaited speech to the Algerian people.

Like a car spinning its wheels in the mud on its way to some happy outing, Fate suddenly brought us to a halt.

Everything – including the ambulance that lost its way to the hospital, causing him to be the last of the wounded to arrive – colluded to prevent Boudiaf from missing his appointment with death this time.

On the day Boumédienne died, Boudiaf had said, 'I disagreed with Boumédienne on a lot of issues. But when I saw his funeral procession, I felt I'd been unfair to him. After all, anyone whose loss causes people this much grief has to have done something right for the country.'

At the same time, of course, there were people who cheered from their balconies when they heard the news of his death, venting their malicious glee at his demise in front of the television cameras without the least embarrassment. People like these flocked to the mosques, donating feasts of couscous in celebration of his shed blood.

The forty thieves who were secretly delighted at the sight of his corpse rubbed their hands with glee over the spoils they were sure to divide among themselves for years to come.

People like this supposed that Boudiaf wouldn't be missed, that his death would be a mere blip on the screen of Algeria's history.

So I wonder if they expected his funeral to be as it was?

Things had undergone a shocking collapse. An entire nation went into hysterics, crying like babies in the streets for the men it had lost and shouting, 'Here we are!' Women came out wrapped in Algerian flags, in their hands the picture of a man who hadn't governed in order to have his image plastered all over the streets but, rather, in order for the image of Algeria to cover the pictures of the slain that filled the newspapers.

Though he had never been able to tread on his homeland's soil with a sense of real safety, he was now being carried by waves of grief-stricken humanity towards the soil where he would rest.

He had departed and left us orphans once again, and as we escorted him to his grave we cried, 'Go in peace – we are here!' And history chimed in after us, 'Sleep well, Abu Nasser. Sleep in peace. They are here!'

I didn't leave home to attend the funeral. My grief was too overwhelming to share it with anyone else.

But somewhere deep inside, I was happy for him.

This country that hadn't given him a life commensurate with his dreams had given him a funeral commensurate with his life.

It was the funeral of a man who had governed the land for a mere 166 days with his feet on the ground. However, he had been vulnerable to the wiles of those who had ruled for a quarter of a century with an army of informers, and who had held sway over peoples crushed by a never-ending degradation.

Those who are so confident of their tanks' loyalty to them should try dying some time, and when they see what kind of a funeral they're given, they'll be in for a big surprise!

Week after week, death after death, I came to realize I was living a life in the making, a life created sometimes by major events, and at other times by peripheral happenings.

At every moment, for whatever reason, my fate might take a different course.

I was a woman living among three men whose lives hung from the bullet of Fate! Their lives and destinies were controlled by those who engineered such daily death and terror in this country that I didn't know when one of them might be brought down by an accusation, or when another of them might be brought down by its opposite.

I'd become possessed by a fear of some shock lurking in the shadows, obsessed with an unexpected death that I saw hovering over everyone around me.

Between my fundamentalist brother being trailed by the authorities, my military husband under the fundamentalists' watchful eye, and the journalist I loved and whose blood was the stuff with which the other two men settle their scores, how could I possibly live outside the realm of terror?

After Boudiaf's assassination on national television in front of millions of viewers, it was obvious that it was now open season, and after every new death the question was: Whose turn is next?

I used to try to ward off fear by writing or by loving. I thought back on everything Khaled had told me in an attempt to prepare me for a time like this. However, since Boudiaf's death he hadn't been here to reassure me, and all my attempts to communicate with him were in vain.

Since my home phone, being owned by the military, was tapped, even calling him from Constantine was a risky undertaking. So I would try to call whenever I found myself at a relative's house. My mother's telephone was tapped so that the government could spy on Nasser's comings and goings. This man's telephone was bound to be tapped, too, since he was both a journalist and a member of the Consultative Council. This made me lonelier than ever, and intensified the feeling that I was suffering a fate set against love.

One morning I woke up in the mood to harass memory, so to speak. After four months of anxious waiting and anticipation, I was tired of having time's corpse lying between us, and I could think of only one place that might lead me either to the man in black or to Abdelhaq.

Consequently, I made the craziest decision of my life. I put on the most modest clothes I could find and left the house without makeup or accessories of any kind. I also left without the driver. All I had in my bag was the book by Henri Michaux, which I'd brought with me so that I could use it to ward off curious glances, and the ennui that would ensue from what might be a long wait. I'd also brought it, I suspect, so that if Abdelhaq came to the café and saw me reading his own book, he would recognize me, and I would be spared having to initiate the conversation myself.

After walking a short distance, I nearly stopped to buy a newspaper. Reading newspapers had become one of my bad habits, in which respect I was like everybody else in Algeria, who would mob the newsstands every morning, whether out of boredom or fright, as though something important had happened or was going to happen. This time, though, I thought better of it, since I knew that if I took it and read it in a café, some people might suspect me of being a journalist.

Happily, I managed to find a taxi a block from my house. As warmly as I knew how, I asked the driver to take me to 'The Date' café. I felt somehow as though I had to prove my innocence to everybody I met, including taxi drivers, since I knew what a crazy thing I was doing.

Actually, I had a lot more craziness in store than I had good sense, and my patience level was nil. I was happy for my worldly fortune to consist in no more than a few novels I'd written for my own satisfaction and which brought me no income, but whose characters intervened in my life to the point where they might lead me to my death!

On the upper floor of the café, I sat down across from love's vacant places, expecting the appearance of a man for whom I'd grown accustomed to waiting in silence. I sat looking at a table in the right corner, remembering how lovely it is to have desire's mines explode at the moment of a first encounter.

But was I really waiting for him? Or was I, as was more likely, only waiting for someone who could lead me to Abdelhaq?

I was there for Abdelhaq. That was a certainty. So I set Henri Michaux's book on the table in hopes that he would notice it if he came.

Downstairs I could hear raucous laughter that concealed people's grief, and it struck terror in my heart. Why hadn't I had enough sense to resist a cold morning's whim? Why was I so infatuated with men with a penchant for insubordination, and with fates so impossible to get hold of?

I set about trying to diagnose a case of love, which is always preceded by symptoms of an urge to write, and followed by some calamity.

What had brought me here? What sort of intuition had brought me out on this particular morning looking like someone who hadn't been planning on meeting anyone, then sat me down across from a desireless table?

It must have been my writer's sixth sense, which never misses the mark, and which had promised me some surprise today.

The male voices, whose numbers increased the later it got, intensified my terror, and the only thing that protected me from them was the presence of a couple talking in a nearby corner. Yet even they weren't entirely comfortable. On the contrary, they seemed flustered and nervous.

The terror had suddenly become a group contagion that could easily pass from one person to another, and was likely to become all the more potent with the passing of the days. In the face of it I found myself growing smaller and smaller until I was the size of an insect that didn't know whose stomach it was going to end up in or in which meal it would be served, just as I wondered on what charge I would end up being killed. This is the absurd, haphazard logic of death in the time of undeclared wars, the painful absurdity that Khalil Hawi summed up in the words, 'All I know is that I'm going to die, a tiny morsel in the belly of a whale.'

There being little in the café to arouse my curiosity, I took to studying an unpretentious-looking young man reading a newspaper at the table next to mine. He looked too young to be Abdelhaq. Even so, I began sneaking glances at him out of boredom, periodically raising Henri Michaux's book in the air, either by way of camouflage, or as a signal to some stranger who might appear. Then – out of despair, or rather, out of fear – I got up to leave. I was being assailed by scenarios from detective novels, especially now that I'd noticed I was in a café frequented by journalists.

What if the man sitting just steps away from me was concealing a pistol, hiding behind a newspaper as he lay in wait for someone or other? Most assassinations were committed by men in their twenties who were regular café-goers, or who would lean against some wall reading a newspaper while they waited for their victim.

As I gathered my things in a panic and left the price of my coffee on the table, I saw the young man open the newspaper and begin reading something with rapt attention. Then suddenly, on the front page I glimpsed a large photograph of someone whose features I knew unmistakably. Above the photo were two words in French in large bold print – two words that made me freeze in place, dumbfounded.

I would have expected anything from death – almost any, at least, of the despicable surprises that it's so inimitably good at. But that morning, a newspaper I hadn't bought brought me news of the one death I would never have expected.

The day before, the whale had opened its jaws and, for its evening meal, swallowed – among others – Abdelhaq.

A sadistic sniper par excellence, Fate takes up some forgotten corner of our lives. Then it opens fire randomly on people we love without a pang of remorse.

I'd been confronted with two surprises relating to Abdelhaq – the first being his death, and the second his picture. It was as though he had had to die in order to become, at last, a real live man: with a full name, features, a life story, and a death story.

For me, the story had begun with his picture. I hadn't forgotten that face, which I'd contemplated at length with secret admiration one day in this very place.

So, had I come here this morning because Fate was preparing me for one of its cruel surprises, and in the very place where I'd seen him for the first time?

Had I come to witness his absence, to contemplate his unoccupied table in order to complete the cycle of leave-taking in a story in which there had been nothing but a single encounter, and the abundant stillness of absence?

As I sat there thinking, someone walked up and asked the young man to come with him because he was needed at the printer's.

So the poor guy was a journalist, after all, or, at least, he worked for a newspaper. I nearly threw my arms around him and burst into tears, and if no one else had been around, I would have. But all I could muster the courage to do was to ask him for the newspaper he'd been reading. So he handed it to me and left.

Feeling my legs giving out on me, I sat back down. This time I wasn't sitting with a figment of my imagination. I was sitting with pain.

Sorrow sat neglected in a corner of that café. The table in that corner concealed a secret, like a piano waiting for someone who was accustomed to playing it, and which remained silent without him. That table was the only thing around me that shared in my grief for him, and it seemed to wonder why he had chosen to sit there, and not elsewhere.

I turned to the page that held his picture. The caption, for all its simplicity, pained me: 'Adieu, Abdelhaq.'

Why did the addition of the word 'Adieu' before a name make it so painful?

So this was Abdelhaq, then.

He was the one who, dressed in a white shirt and white trousers, had occupied this very table on the day when . . .

I remembered how he'd kept writing and smoking nonstop, and how, for the nearly half hour he sat there alone, all he exchanged with me was silence and a few moments of distraction.

Then his friend had arrived, clad in black, and greeted me from afar as if he knew me. The two of them talked for quite a while, and the whole time I kept wondering if he was the man who . . .

Then all of a sudden the man in black had got up and brought me a bowl of sugar when I was about to ask the waiter for one.

I remember being surprised by his cologne, which reminded me of the cologne that . . .

So I'd tested him with an apology, only to have him reply with those terse words that . . .

That was when my senses escaped from me, and seemed to turn him into what I'd imagined him to be.

Little did I know that love was making fun of me, and leaking the same password to more than one man.

Now I realized that, by virtue of a word and a colour, I'd missed the love train that I would have taken otherwise.

In a moment of sensory chaos, I had followed the man in black, and lost my way.

He'd told me once that 'no love is more wonderful than the kind we find when we're looking for something else'.

How was I to know now whether what I'd experienced with him was really more wonderful than what I would have experienced if I'd followed the other colour?

On the other hand, had there really been another colour?

Love had struck me with colour-blindness that day. It had even impaired my vision.

I remember telling the man in black on the day we first met, 'I've never seen a man wear black in this city, even if he was in mourning.'

'So what colour did you expect me to wear?' he asked in reply.

'I don't know, but people around here tend to wear clothes that don't have any colour.'

Then, after a bit of thought, I went on, 'Your friend doesn't seem to be from around here either.'

'Why?' he asked, laughing. 'Because he wears a white shirt and white trousers?'

'No, because he wears white with a kind of happy flamboyance, whereas everybody else in this city wears it to show how pious they are.'

He smiled and said, 'My friend isn't really happy. He just has an extravagant way of showing his sadness, that's all. White, for him, is actually the equivalent of black.'

In the end, I realized that I was dealing with two men who, each in his own way, wore the same colour. It seemed clear now that love wouldn't have made fun of a woman with so much self-confidence.

Of course not.

Love is nothing but a state of suspicion.

How can you be sure of a feeling that's based on the chaos of the senses, on a mutual lack of understanding, on a situation in which each person thinks he or she knows enough to love the other? In reality, neither of them knows more than what love wants him or her to know. Nor does either of them see more than what he or she has already loved in some previous relationship. Hence, when each love comes to an end, we discover that in the beginning we were loving someone else!

Of all the deaths I'd heard of, Abdelhaq's came as the greatest shock to me. Is there anything more painful than to enter someone's life just when he's about to leave it?

This was a man I hadn't known, yet about whom I'd known everything. So what could newspapers add to my knowledge of him apart from the details of his death, which I didn't want to know about anyway? All the national newspapers carried his obituary on their front page, together with a large photo of him with a caption that read, in one language or another, 'Farewell, Abdelhaq.'

Journalists in this country have a custom of publishing pictures of their deceased colleagues along with elegies they had written for themselves. And Abdelhaq was no exception. Hence, the newspaper he'd written for published a large photo of him on its front page alongside a poem he had composed after the assassination of his journalist and poet friend Tahar Djaout, and which read like an elegy for himself. The deaths of these two men had differed in nothing but a few minor details.

Tahar Djaout had been taking his last article to the newspaper when his assassins came up from behind and pumped two bullets into his head. As for Abdelhaq, he had been kidnapped in front of his mother's house in Sidi al-Mabrouk after coming in secret two days earlier to say goodbye to her before she left for the minor pilgrimage to Mecca. His body had been found with one bullet in the chest, and another in the forehead.

In other words, he had been looking defencelessly at his slayers as they shot him, because one of his hands had been bound with his own belt, and the other with a metal wire attached to the belt. When his body was found, he was lying face down on the side of the road.

At the time of his death, he may have recalled Che Guevara's last words as he saw his executioner aiming a gun at him, incredulous that this great leader was now within range of his pistol. Guevara shouted at him, 'Shoot, you coward! You're killing a human being!' Two months before his death, Abdelhaq had begun using these words as the title for his daily news column. This had coincided with his elegy for his journalist friend Sa'id Muqbil, whose killer had shot him point blank as he was eating his lunch.

Abdelhaq spent the last three months of his life thinking up thirty-six ways to eulogize himself, thirty-six being the number of his friends and colleagues in the profession of troubles, tragedies and death who had already met their end. Death couldn't surprise him any more, so whichever way it came, he already had a description for it, and whichever direction his killers came from, he had already gone there to vilify and defy them. In this way he had hastened his death, and he became number thirty-seven on the hit list whose end no one could predict.

I came home with several newspapers in both Arabic and French. So this was Abdelhaq, then. Now I could read the newspapers and discover who he was:

281

The thief who steals home by night along the
walls . . .
The citizen whose wish is simply not to die of a slit
throat . . .
The corpse on to which they sew a severed
head . . .
The one who doesn't know what to do with his hands
but to go on with his petty writings . . .
The one who clings to hope against hope that roses
will spring up on the refuse heaps . . .
The one of whom I speak is a journalist.

Like someone who's fallen in love with a man through correspondence, having learned everything about him but never
having had the chance to get to know him up close, I was explor-
ing his life with a belated fascination, reading the newspaper like
thousands of unnamed readers who had learned this morning of
the death of a man they had never met.

But he would never know me: the clandestine, unnamed
female presence in his life. How could he have known what his
death would do to me? I had lived in his house, slept in his bed
with his friend, talked with another man on his telephone, and
without this knowledge, read a book that revealed his thoughts
and preoccupations. I'd used his cologne and, in the darkness of
a cinema, shared with him in a sudden conflagration of desire
and a moment of weeping. And, sitting a table away from him at
a café, I had conducted with him a conversation that could only
be carried on in silence.

Yet he hadn't expected my presence in his intimate world at
the far end of his life. Do we need to die in order to love, and to
know that there were those who loved us?

As I looked at his picture that evening, I tried not to dwell on it, lest I see on his lips the vestiges of the last kiss he had shared with a woman, and grieve for her, or of some woman he might have kissed if he hadn't died, and grieve for him.

I avoided his eyes, which were fixed on a place that only he could see, and his moustache, which, like his dreams, refused to humble itself even after his death.

Before I knew it, I found myself cutting the picture out and hiding it among my papers.

At first I had wanted to cut out the poem and keep it in my black notebook. Then some old, unsettling feeling came over me. It took me back to my childhood, to the day, thirty years earlier, when I'd cut my father's picture out of the newspaper. The same size as Abdelhaq's photo, it had been on the front page of all the newspapers. However, that was during a war in which the murderers were foreigners, and death was seen as noble, not as a tragedy.

Indeed, every war changes the definition of death for a time, and in this way it draws a fine, unseen distinction among the generations.

The yellowed picture, in which my father's gaze was frozen for ever, had hung on the wall ever since I'd found it several months earlier. I was separated from that gaze by the glass of time, while it was separated from time by a new name for death.

Beside my father's picture hung a picture of Abdel Nasser. However, Abdel Nasser's picture was bigger. It was as though, in the broken youth of which it was a reminder, the picture epitomized a death more painful than all others – death by defeat.

In their silent presence, these two pictures embodied all the martyrs and great causes I'd believed in since I was a child. It was a faith I hadn't questioned any more than the other beliefs I had been raised on.

It didn't matter to me that Nasserism existed nowhere but in the realm of feeling, or in a generation which by a historical coincidence bore the name of the last Arab warrior-poet.

What could be lovelier than for my father to have given his only son the name Nasser before he was martyred? Mohamed Boudiaf's oldest son was also named Nasser and he had books in his library about Abdel Nasser, while everyone who had died in a national tragedy had left us something of the illusion of pan-Arabism.

These thoughts came to me as I worked to remove a picture from its frame so that I could stealthily place another one behind it. I'd discovered that this was the best way to keep it, like the person it depicted, present and absent at the same time. It was also a way to avoid the questions it might arouse if people saw it in my office.

Behind my father I was hiding a man I had loved, since I knew he would understand, as men had often approached me disguised as him.

I was hiding one death behind another, one country behind another. I was also hiding one suspect love behind another.

As I looked at my father's picture nearby, I could see that one man might conceal a second, and possibly even a third, and that this was something only I knew.

The next morning I woke up unusually early. I probably hadn't slept at all. I was looking for a way to live the day that would fit the bitter sweetness of life.

I tried to write, but I couldn't.

The man who had disappeared two months earlier had laid mines on all the roads leading to the act of writing. He had succeeded in convincing me that empty space is the endpoint to every narrative, the only thing any book really accomplishes, and that every novel has to end with a possibility-laden blank page.

So what was I supposed to do? How was I supposed to cope with all this 'sweet ruin' without a pen? I remembered him saying on the day his friend died, 'In a time of unexpected endings, premature demises, and nameless, ugly, petty wars in which you might die without being a party to them, sex is the only way we have to forget ourselves.'

'And what about writing?' I had asked.

'Writing? It's our big illusion that others won't forget us!'

So what was I going to do with my sadness today?

Should I make love? To whom? How was I supposed to pursue pleasure on the pretext that a man I had hoped to belong to some day, but never would, had died?

The manliness that had sat in silent provocation across from my womanhood, the manliness I had wanted to experience if only just once, life had withheld from me and fed as a sumptuous repast to the maggots.

The body my lips had longed to cover with kisses would soon be covered with soil, and I would never have the chance to set it on fire even in my imagination. It had entered the world of frozen tundra. 'The grave is cold, Mama. Send me a wool sweater.'

I would have preferred that my encounter with this man had been on another day, alone, away from the weeping and the prayers. I would have liked it to be intimate and romantic in spite of the distance that now lay between us.

However, I would have to be at the funeral in order to carry on, as an anonymous woman, my secret presence in the final scene of a love story. I'd come to pay my respects to a man whom I knew but who didn't know me, and to search for another man who knew me, but whom I still didn't know.

So I timed my arrival at the cemetery such that the burial ceremony would be over but people would still not have left, hoping to see that man in the crowd.

It definitely wasn't on account of the funeral that I'd come.

There are people who only care about others' assassinations to the extent that they give them a platform for bashing the enemy, reminding people of the barbarity and sadism on the other side.

In the midst of this duel, pens fall dead one after another, victims of a well-publicized death.

I'd always imagined that creativity makes death different somehow, so I attended the funeral the way one goes to a lovers' tryst.

Once upon a time Cleopatra put on her jewellery, perfumed herself, and, in preparation for her death, put on a dress in which Antony would recognize her when they met among thousands of people. Like her, I put on makeup and some of the perfume with which this story had begun. I wore the black dress with the big gold buttons that go all the way down the front, leaving the last one open as usual. With it I wore a black belt that hugged my waist and showed off my curves. It made me look like an Italian actress. At least, that's what the man in black used to tell me. He loved this dress, and whenever he saw me in it, he would say, 'Black suits you.'

'That's nice of you to say,' I'd reply absently. 'It would make a good title for another novel!'

286

I most definitely wasn't wearing black in mourning. I was just being extravagantly sorrowful, extravagantly alluring, defiant in excess. I didn't go disguised in my chaste-looking cloak – it would have been foolish to face death in a get-up like that.

I had dressed this way with the intention of seducing two men I'd seen together for the first time in a certain café wearing this very same dress. If one of them came to pay his respects to the other, he would be bound to see me and recognize me. As for the other . . .

It didn't matter for me to see him so much as for him to see me, and I wanted to look as ravishing as I would have liked to be on a first date. I wanted to catch his eye and distract him from his death by the surprise of seeing me there. I expected him to notice me, since I was the only one carrying a notebook, whereas most women come to cemeteries laden with loaves of bread and dates to distribute as charity.

I was also the only one who had thought to bring him a pack of cigarettes for his first night. After that he would have to stop smoking, not because smoking is bad for your health, but because I wouldn't be able to bring him cigarettes all the time.

When I stopped on my way to buy the cigarettes, the vendor looked askance at me. I even thought he might throw me out of his shop. Any woman who has the audacity to buy cigarettes in Constantine has to be either immoral or crazy.

Even though I've never smoked a cigarette in my life, I thought it would be silly to exonerate myself by explaining to him that the cigarettes weren't for me, but for a man who was going to be buried that day. He would need them if he wanted to write something that evening, and I suspected that on this day in particular, he wouldn't be able to keep himself from putting pen to paper.

287

I've always loved writers who have the ability to say the most painful and serious things with levity and disdain. I've always wished I had their ability to treat everything as if it were its opposite. Like the characters in their books, they act in a way that goes against logic in relation to death, love, infidelity, success, failure, tragedies, victories and losses. That's why I love Zorba, who starts to dance when he ought to be crying.

I suppose I'd always been looking for an occasion like this, the chance to go with my madness, against logic, a once-in-a-lifetime opportunity to try out some of the scenes that I had hoped, in my wild writing fantasies, to experience myself just for the pleasure of writing about them later.

For some unknown reason, it wasn't sadness I was feeling that day, but rather, an overwhelming sense of defiance of which my jewellery and my fashionable appearance were simply the outer expressions.

I don't think I went there to defy death. Death is a decree from God before which all of us are equals. Nor do I think I went to be a heroine. All I wanted was to defy the killers, brandishing the two accusations that I knew might be levelled against me: being a woman, and being a writer (which was a silent tool of defiance in my hand), and with me I carried a notebook containing the story whose main character was the act of writing itself.

In the face of death, neither being a woman nor being a writer is any consolation. On the contrary, both of them are constant reminders of death's presence. But in the face of crime, what does a writer have but her words, and the life which, from the time she began writing, hasn't belonged to her?

If he came, I hoped to say all these things in silence to the man in black. Or maybe what I hoped was that if he came, we could go on writing our story.

During our last time together, he had wanted us to put ourselves on a level with bankrupt lovers, and had refused for us to meet in Abdelhaq's flat. So now we could meet at his funeral and be truly on a level with the lovers of this city, whose lives had become so desperate that they'd begun meeting in cemeteries, disguised in the garb of mourning, exchanging their intimate secrets on any grave they came to. Love alone has the ability to make everything beautiful, even trysts in a cemetery.

But even such a bittersweet rendezvous hadn't awaited me there. I stood at a distance among the graves, midway between pain and the temerity it required to scrutinize scores of men's faces, men being the only ones allowed to escort the dead to their final resting place. I was looking for a man who resembled no one, and nothing, and who couldn't possibly fail to keep an appointment such as this.

After depositing their burden underground, everyone withdrew, and I found myself in a peculiar position. It reminded me of a scene from some silent movie in black-and-white. There I stood in my black radiance, alone against the backdrop of a vast white marble decor with a black notebook in my hand in the hope that if he came, he would recognize me and approach me.

As I waited, my sense of defiance turned into an overwhelming sense of sadness and disappointment. I had wanted to show my defiance through him, for him. Had he stayed away in order to defy me through his absence? How could he stay away like this when Abdelhaq had been his closest friend? Was he out of the country? Had he decided to visit the grave later, on his own?

Or had he already said goodbye to his friend in his own way, by making love to a woman?

I don't know how, but grave after grave, the questions kept leading me onward towards the other man until at last I stood before him. A corpse of dreams, he lay beneath a flower-festooned mound of dirt.

Oddly, I didn't cry. I was writing in my head, looking for the words I needed to describe this extraordinary encounter and reviewing some of the passages from Henri Michaux's book that he had underlined or commented on.

I thought back on the poem he had written to eulogize Tahar Djaout and which had been published again the previous day next to his photo and obituary. I'd clipped it out of the newspaper and stuck it into my black notebook. To my surprise, I had a sudden urge to look at it again, so I got it out and began reading, noting its effect on me in this particular place.

Not knowing whether I was doing this for myself or for him, I read in a soft voice that he would be hearing for the first time since the day when I sat beside him in a cinema and we had shared just two brief exchanges. Still his silent self even in his final role, I carried on with my soliloquy.

> He went out one morning to buy a notebook,
> some pens and a newspaper.
> No one will ever know what he was going to write
> at the moment when ink spirited him away
> to his final resting place.
> He had an outline in his head, as well as a bullet,
> so instead of putting roses on his grave, they put the
> pens he'd bought.
> Nor did they write anything on his epitaph.
> Instead they left the white marble slate clean.

Consequently, you won't recognize him there,
where the headstones are nothing but pens,
and where every evening hands awaken to carry on
writing.

I think my voice died in the last verse, and when I closed the black notebook on that poem, I felt as though I'd been playing a part in a movie. I didn't try to look back at the scene, which I knew would never repeat itself. But I also knew I'd be able to describe its impact on me in future novels because it had actually happened.

For two years I had wanted, if only just once, to experience what it felt like to place a manuscript on a grave and walk away with no regrets. And now I'd done it, though I hadn't exactly planned on it. I had brought the notebook in order to give it to the other man, but when he didn't show up, I couldn't resist a certain crazy idea that came over me.

In response to the unexpected situations in which life places us, I think people should follow their inner voice and go with the first idea that comes to them, without weighing it or comparing it with any other. The first idea is always the right one no matter how perverse or strange it might seem, because that's the idea that best reflects who we are.

There was an idea that suited a certain writer I knew. It suited her so well that I felt I was avenging her on a time long past, when she used to amuse herself creating characters of paper and killing them off in books in keeping with the logic of life, where love and murder follow their own absurd reasoning.

Then life in turn began transforming everything she wrote into reality. As if she'd been trying to provoke a response from life, it brought her book out in a new, reality-based edition. She then found herself the sole reader of a forged copy, an ingenious plagiary in which Fate had changed a few names here and there and the order of events.

The strangest thing that can happen to an author is to discover that with every page she writes, she's writing her own future. Yet if this does happen, she can't accuse life of having conformed to her imagination or shamelessly imitated her work, since it usually happens the other way around!

A certain author, having written a novel with the intention of pre-empting pain, killed off the character dearest to her. She didn't realize, of course, that she was writing her own fate and that, like the character in her novel, she would rush back to Algeria on board an aeroplane of sorrow in the midst of a curfew with the manuscript of this very novel. When faced with an ill-tempered customs officer determined to rummage through her luggage, she told him the only thing she had to declare was her manuscript, the memory she had come to bury along with her father.

She didn't cry at his grave. She was too busy wondering: Why had he died now? Why had he died three months after Boudiaf?

Why had he died two weeks before the book's release when he had been waiting for it for several years? During those years he had been supplying her with information about a city she had never visited, a city named Constantine, and with a memory he'd grown weary of carrying alone.

Had he gone away in order to leave more room for that book, as though life wasn't big enough for the two of them? Had he left so that this text would become more beautiful by virtue of his death? Or was it simply that, because they were living in a time of contrived death and booby-trapped cars, they had booby-trapped his dreams and put a bullet through his memory before his very eyes? If so, he had descended into a stupor, not out of old age, but because the nation had entered the age of despair, and the age of the nation had always been inseparable from his own.

Indeed, being a man of history, he was bound to choose the right time to die. She remembered the morning of 1 November, and the national anthem whose strains could be heard throughout the military hospital as they brought his body out. It seemed as though they were playing it for him, or as though he had stopped the pallbearers so that he could hear it one last time:

> By the blows of Fate and blood shed pure
> By flags aflutter on mountains high
> That Algeria might live, we rose up to die
> Bear witness, bear witness, bear witness!

Military ambulances drowned out the strains of the national anthem, ploughing ahead with their sirens blasting. The bodies of Algerian soldiers who had fallen at the hands of other Algerians, some wounded, others dead, their corpses maimed, were loaded on to stretchers, and the dead were taken to a refrigerator to await their families.

So she forgot to weep for her father, and wept instead over the blank stares of soldiers who would never know why they had died.

When she visited his grave the following day, she tried to look her best. She dressed up, as she usually did, to set herself apart from the other women there and in order to give him, as she always had, a reason to be proud of her in his final resting place.

Knowing how dear she had been to him, she refused to be the equal of those who would come to mourn him for a day, then go their separate ways.

There is a kind of grief so profound that it renders weeping banal, even an insult to the one being mourned.

So why cry, when those who die take part of us with them without realizing that, as death follows upon death, we the living become more to be pitied than the dead themselves? Their departure has turned back the hands of the nation's clock by generations.

Quite inexplicably, she left everyone gathered around her father and, to their consternation, went looking for another grave.

In the courtyard reserved for Algeria's greatest martyrs, who lay beneath bouquets that had been laid upon their graves on the occasion of 1 November, she stopped in front of the grave designated as Boudiaf's. However, her attention was drawn to another grave nearby. Small and unpretentious, it seemed almost apologetic for being located to the right of the great leader's resting place.

Here lay Suleiman Umeirat, a man she had never heard of until the day when his bizarre, painful death made the front pages. He had fallen dead of a heart attack at Boudiaf's grave. A small burial place had been set aside for him next to that of Boudiaf, and the two of them hadn't parted since.

This was where his journey had ended.

From the tender age of seventeen to the ripe old age of seventy, he had devoted himself to the love of Algeria. He had known the inside of both French prisons and 'revolutionary' Algerian prisons, where he had spent a number of years on charges of fomenting democracy.

In his last television interview, by which time he was aware of the danger that the weapon of democracy might fall into the hands of those who, rather than believing in it, merely exploited it for their own ends, he declared, 'If I were forced to choose between Algeria and democracy, I would choose Algeria.' And indeed, he had chosen – he had chosen death at the feet of the homeland.

Homeland? How could we have called it a homeland when its every grave harboured a crime, and every piece of news involved tragedy and loss?

Homeland? Was this the homeland we had dreamed of dying for, only to find that we had died at its hands?

Was this a homeland, this country that whenever we knelt to kiss its soil, stabbed us in the back, slaughtered us like sheep? One corpse at a time, we had blanketed its surface with men who had the stature of our dreams, and the youthful bloom of our proud aspirations.

Between two graves, the only difference between which was that one of them had a fancy marble headstone, I saw a woman sobbing and who, by virtue of her sobbing, had become like all the other women gathered there.

There was nothing I could do for her. In a brief moment, she had become a woman I didn't recognize. With its primitive rites of sorrow, tragedy had turned her into an illiterate woman, and her sudden cry of pain rent the silence around her.

It was as though she wanted to imitate that man in his death, to experience a state in which, through her weeping, she could die in defeat at the foot of the grave.

Was this how al-Khansa' had died as she mourned her brother? Had she wept over every grave she came to, as though any one of them might hold her dear Sakhr?

I couldn't ask: Why now? Why here? Why these two?

This eccentric woman had no answers to obvious questions, since otherwise she wouldn't have left the crowd weeping for her father to go and weep for someone else. Something about her suddenly started to frighten me, terrify me. So I left her sobbing at Boudiaf's grave and hurriedly left the place.

These memories, which had suddenly come upon me because I'd placed that notebook on a grave and left, did nothing to change my mood. At least, they didn't change it enough to make me cry.

As a matter of fact, I wasn't feeling anything. I wasn't feeling anything at all.

Suddenly, as though my brain had short-circuited, all sensations came to a halt, and things around me began happening to another woman.

At the same time, I was experiencing a kind of lightness, something bordering on happiness that I couldn't find any explanation for. Then I remembered that the reason for it was the notebook I'd left behind, indifferent to the literary gains I might have made by publishing it even though I'd spent an entire year writing it. As a matter of fact, I'd been afraid that if I kept it, I might meet the same fate as that writer, who never forgave herself for hesitating to leave the manuscript of her novel on her father's grave and return to exile.

She had taken it to him on the day of his death, excusing her absence for those many years by telling him that she had been busy writing to him, and for him. She'd been lying, of course. The fact was that she'd been writing for herself. Otherwise, she would have left the manuscript on his grave and gone her way.

But because she hadn't dared part with it, she hadn't been able to write a word since the day of her father's death.

Through years of silence, she punished herself for the crime of preferring thousands of readers over one particular reader who would never see what she had written, and who alone had reason to do so. It may be on account of that writer's cowardice that my own view of writing, and the prestige that attaches to it, underwent a change. The fame that descends without warning on a writer on account of a single book is, in reality, merely a reminder of the betrayal of a single reader somewhere, a reader from whom we have stolen, on one pretext or another, the manuscript that was written for him, so that we can produce thousands of copies for readers who care nothing about us.

Every successful publishing venture means that someone, somewhere, has been betrayed.

* * *

So then, this is life . . .

What happens to people isn't what they deserve but, rather, what fits them best.

So why does there have to be pain? Why should there be pain if the endings to our stories fit us so well, as though death made us more beautiful?

One womb casts us forth into another, and all of us arrive here in the same way. Yet we never ask why there's only one form of birth, but so many forms of death.

With sorrow's nightly raids, I'd been assassinated by the perfume of a man who'd just died, leaving me nothing but the odour of time, and a mountainous city with a penchant for scaring you with the bridges of unknowing and bottomless valleys of misfortune.

Through the ambushes life sets for us, Fate had proceeded, slowly and deliberately, to blast my illusions.

This was what had happened. So had it been nothing but a hypothetical love?

He had known enough about her to love her.

She had known enough about him to love him.

Even so, neither of them had known the other well enough.

Despite my sadness, I left the cemetery feeling more or less content.

If every joy entails some degree of sadness, then it should come as no surprise to find that every sadness entails some degree of joy. It's a joy we feel ashamed to recognize, but those gifted with the creative spirit know it well.

I have to admit, it made me happy to be rid of that notebook. For an entire year I'd gone on writing on the pretext that it was my only way of staying alive. This wasn't true at all, of course, not only because writing is the ideal prescription for spending your life isolated from life itself, but because in this country in particular, it's the charge on which you're most likely to lose your life.

So, after getting rid of it, I decided to explore the virtues of ignorance, the blessings of being illiterate in the face of love, death, and the world. I didn't know how easy it would be to descend into ignorance. Even so, I'd always believed Jabra Ibrahim Jabra's observation that, 'The writer . . . is someone who knows how to go up and down the ladder of life with perfect ease.' I may have spent my life going up and down that ladder without letting on that I'm out of breath. Actually, it's the words inside me that are out of breath. And that's why I am a writer.

I came home a woman stripped of all desire, a woman who had nothing of that story left but a perfume stored inside her body, the perfume she still dabbed on occasionally as a way of getting a rise out of memory.

A scent is the last thing left to us by those who depart, and the first thing asked of us by those who return.

It's also the only thing we can offer to assure them that we've been waiting for them.

This is why, when a certain great lover by the name of Napoleon sent news of his victory to his wife, he asked her to keep her scent for him, saying, 'Don't take a bath, Josephine! I'm coming home in three days!'

Alone among military commanders, Napoleon had mastered the art of conversing with women and allowing himself to be defeated before their femininity with the same passion with which he defeated his enemies.

As for me, I had decided to take a bath that evening and go to bed!

Before that, I would sit with my mother after having neglected her for so long. I had also been neglecting my brother. My mother had been pestering me to write to him, but I hadn't done it since I was so distracted with that notebook and the life of fiction I'd so immersed myself in.

No sooner had I freed myself from my slavery to writing than I was overcome by longing for Nasser. The longing came on so suddenly, it frightened me, and filled me with pangs of remorse.

How could I have abandoned him all that time? Why hadn't I thought about all the tricks life might play on him in his place of exile?

How could I have lived all that time without him, without his grumbling and complaining, his sarcastic remarks, and the quarrelsome affection that meant more to me than all the romantic sweet talk in the world?

I decided to write him a long letter. It would be as beautiful, as poignant, as unsettling as a love letter. I wanted to show him my mischievous side. I wanted to make him laugh, to make him cry in the hope of winning him back. I even told him I'd be willing to ask my husband for a divorce if that would make him happy, although I also made it clear that things were improving between the two of us.

I wanted to celebrate my return to life, and to serve notice of this to everyone around me. I wanted to share in their ordinary existence, with its mundane preoccupations and trivialities, with its chitchat and its boredom, with its joys, sorrows, its dangers. I wanted at last to become an ordinary woman again, with a family and a home.

My husband was the beneficiary of my suddenly renewed interest in him, which rescued a relationship that had been stricken with a tepidity for which he could see no reason, and he worked to win me back with small gestures.

As usual, my mother understood nothing of what had happened to me, and contented herself with taking over my entire schedule.

For example, she spent the entire first day dictating a letter to Nasser, and the first thing she did the next morning was to remind me to send it.

I was about to give it to my husband so that he could send it for me, but then I remembered that I needed to keep Nasser's address a secret from him.

Consequently, I had no choice but to get dressed and go to buy an envelope and some postage stamps from the stationery shop.

I was leaving the house for the first time in two weeks when I was accosted by unexpected autumn winds. An approaching grief suddenly came over me, taking me by surprise like a rain storm that comes one season too early.

Shop windows were displaying warm winter coats for the coming season, while stationers' offered displays of books, notebooks, pencils and pens.

Life was preparing for the end of one season and the beginning of another – preparing to start all over again.

As I saw children running to school with their book bags, I remembered that the last time I had come to this shop was exactly one year before, and that I had come there to buy exactly the same items.

As on this occasion, the weather had been autumnal and enticing, though what it was enticing one *to* wasn't exactly clear.

For the last two weeks I had been an illiterate woman who avoided questions for fear that she might get an irresistible urge to write.

It was the beginning of the school year, as I recall . . .

The sky was putting on a new face between one season and the next, while a writer was renewing her ink supply between one book and the next.

The shopkeeper was engrossed in arranging his new shipment of school supplies, spreading an array of notebooks, pens and pencils before me.

And on this day, as the year before, he stopped and came over to me, set his load of new notebooks on the table that stood between us, and asked me hurriedly what I wanted.

I was about to ask him for envelopes and postage stamps when . . .

Glossary

'All the Arabs' lands are my lands': a pan-Arab anthem entitled *Bilad al-`Arab Awtani*, composed by Syrian politician, military leader and poet Fakhri al-Barudi (1887–1966) and set to music by Lebanese composer Mohamed Flayfil (1899–1985).

André Gide: winner of the Nobel Prize for Literature in 1947, French writer André Gide (1869–1951) was known for his fiction as well as his autobiographical works.

Bendjedid: a reference to Chadli Bendjedid (1929–2012), who was president of Algeria from 9 February 1979 to 11 January 1992.

Ben-idir: a kind of hand-held drum, often made of wood and goatskin, which is traditional to Morocco, Algeria and Tunisia.

Basisa: a dish made from roasted wheat, chickpeas, fenugreek and lentils with turmeric and cumin, served variously with butter, honey, ground almonds or peanuts, figs or dates.

Borges: born in Buenos Aires, Jorge Luis Borges (1899–1986) was a novelist and poet who also worked as a librarian and public lecturer. He went blind in his fifties due to a hereditary condition. He came to international attention in 1961 when he received the first International Publishers' Prix Formentor.

Eid al-Adha: the Muslim Feast of Sacrifice, the most important holiday of the Islamic year, commemorating Abraham's willingness to sacrifice his eldest son in God's honour, and God's provision of a ram to replace Abraham's son.

Eid al-Fitr: the holiday that marks the end of Ramadan, the Muslim month of fasting.

Fatihah: the first chapter of the Qur'an.

Jubba: a long outer garment, open in front, with broad sleeves.

Little mama: when an Arab mother addresses one of her children, male or female, she calls him or her 'Mama', as though the child were a reflection of herself. Similarly, an Arab father addresses his child, be it a girl or a boy, as 'Baba' ('Daddy').

Rodin: known for his realism and his celebration of individual character and physicality, Auguste Rodin (1840–1917) has been viewed as the progenitor of modern sculpture.

Tammina: a dish made from a mixture of honey, clarified butter and chickpea flour. The name of the dish is derived from the same root as the Arabic verb *tam'ana*, which means to check on someone or reassure oneself that someone is healthy and safe.

Yukio Mishima: the penname of playwright, poet, novelist and film director Kimitake Hiraoka (1925–70). Viewed as one of the most important Japanese authors of the twentieth century, he was nominated three times for the Nobel Prize in Literature.

A NOTE ON THE AUTHOR

Algerian novelist and poet Ahlem Mosteghanemi is the bestselling
female author in the Arab world. She has more than 6 million
followers on Facebook and was ranked among the top ten most
influential women in the Middle East by Forbes in 2006. The
previous book in her trilogy of bestselling novels, *The Bridges of
Constantine*, was published by Bloomsbury, and has been translated
into several languages and adapted into a television series.

A NOTE ON THE TRANSLATOR

Nancy Roberts is a prize-winning translator with experience
in the areas of modern Arabic literature,
current events, Christian–Muslim relations and
Islamic thought, history and law.

A NOTE ON THE TYPE

The text of this book is set in Bembo. This type was first used in
1495 by the Venetian printer Aldus Manutius for Cardinal Bembo's
De Aetna, and was cut for Manutius by Francesco Griffo. It was one
of the types used by Claude Garamond (1480–1561) as a model for
his Romain de L'Université, and so it was the forerunner of what
became standard European type for the following two centuries.
Its modern form follows the original types and was designed
for Monotype in 1929.